BEACON STREET GIRLS

This book belongs to:

VERITAS AMICITIA GAUDIUM
truth friendship fun!

™

BEACON STREET GIRLS

Be sure to read all of our books:

BSG Special Adventure Books:

Coming soon:

BEACON STREET GIRLS

Ready! Set!
Hawaii!

BY
ANNIE BRYANT

ALADDIN MIX
NEW YORK   LONDON   TORONTO   SYDNEY

ALADDIN M!X
Simon & Schuster Children's Publishing Division
1230 Avenue of the Americas, New York, NY 10020
First Aladdin M!X edition August 2009
Text and illustrations copyright © 2009 by B*tween Productions, Inc.,
Home of the Beacon Street Girls.

For information about special discounts for bulk purchases, please contact Simon & Schuster
Special Sales at 1-866-506-1949 or business@simonandschuster.com.
The Simon & Schuster Speakers Bureau can bring authors to your live event. For more information
or to book an event contact the Simon & Schuster Speakers Bureau at 1-866-248-3049 or
visit our website at www.simonspeakers.com.
Designed by Dina Barsky
The text of this book was set in Palatino Linotype.
Manufactured in the United States of America
2 4 6 8 10 9 7 5 3
Library of Congress Control Number 2008939757
ISBN 978-1-4169-6436-0
ISBN 978-1-4169-9626-2 (eBook)

Who's Who

BSG

Katani Summers
a.k.a. Kgirl . . . Katani has a strong fashion sense and business savvy. She is stylish, loyal & cool.

Avery Madden
Avery is passionate about all sports and animal rights. She is energetic, optimistic & outspoken.

Charlotte Ramsey
A self-acknowledged "klutz" and an aspiring writer, Charlotte is all too familiar with being the new kid in town. She is intelligent, worldly & curious.

Isabel Martinez
Her ambition is to be an artist. She was the last to join the Beacon Street Girls. She is artistic, sensitive & kind.

Maeve Kaplan-Taylor
Maeve wants to be a movie star. Bubbly and upbeat, she wears her heart on her sleeve. She is entertaining, friendly & fun.

Ms. Razzberry Pink
The stylishly pink proprietor of the Think Pink boutique is chic, gracious & charming.

Marty
The adopted best dog friend of the Beacon Street Girls is feisty, cuddly & suave.

Happy Lucky Thingy and alter ego Mad Nasty Thingy
Marty's favorite chew toy, it is known to reveal its alter ego when shaken too roughly. He is most often happy.

more on beaconstreetgirls.com

Part One
Surprise!

CHAPTER

1

Not the Titanic!

W hoa!" exclaimed Avery.

"Isn't it grand?" gushed Maeve.

"Fabuloso," agreed Isabel.

"Sweet, very sweet," added Katani, nodding.

Docked in the Honolulu harbor was the biggest ship any of the Beacon Street Girls had ever seen. It gleamed white against the bright blue sky, almost as big as an island, with a large yellow and red flower and the word *Aloha*! in flowing red script painted on the bow.

"Did you know *Aloha* is Hawaiian for 'hello' *and* 'good-bye'?" Charlotte asked her four best friends.

"Aloha!" Avery shouted, walking backwards and waving. "Am I coming or going?"

Maeve playfully shoved her friend. Avery was so eager to get going she started jumping up and down, trying to see over all the people.

"Patience, BSG. We're almost ready to board." Mr. Ramsey, Charlotte's dad, pointed toward two men in official uniforms who were walking toward the gate.

Charlotte gave her father a quick smile. Her dad, a travel writer, was working on an article about Aloha Cruise Lines for *Family Travel* magazine. When he proposed a "special angle" of traveling with tweens, the magazine *and* the cruise line loved it. All the girls had the opportunity to tag along on their spring vacation. So here they were— ready for the best spring break ever!

Charlotte could almost feel the electricity running through the whole crowd. A few weeks ago she never would have imagined that one day she'd be boarding a ship in Hawaii with her four best friends in the whole world!

"A real *cruise!*" Maeve exclaimed. "Just the sound of the word is so *romantic.*"

"Romantic?" Avery stopped jumping for a second to adjust her backpack. "How about thrilling, exhilarating, and totally sweet! Surfing, more surfing . . ."

Charlotte shook her head at Avery's surfing obsession. She was the only Beacon Street Girl who had been to Hawaii before. But Charlotte, who had read her father's Hawaii travel guide before they left, knew there was more to the islands than just surfing. Hawaii had history, exotic forests, birds, beaches . . . and so much to explore that Charlotte couldn't wait for the adventure to begin!

Katani took out a list she had made of all the different activities and which decks they were on. "It always calms me down when I know what to expect," she explained to her friends.

"I'm a *little* nervous!" Isabel admitted, turning slightly pink. "I've just never been on a boat this big."

Maeve squinted at the ship, sizing it up. "It's at least as big as a shopping mall."

Isabel shook her head. "Try three shopping malls!"

Charlotte squeezed her friend's arm. "It's really no big deal. Izzy, you'll be so busy drawing all the amazing things we're going to see that you'll forget you haven't done this a million times."

Isabel took a deep breath and hugged her sketchpad close. She knew she was incredibly lucky just being able to go with her friends on an all-expenses-paid cruise! She even had a little bit of babysitting money saved up for some Hawaiian souvenirs. Charlotte was probably right. *Going on a huge ship is* no problema.

"Let's just hope it's not the *Titanic*," Avery joked, and started belting out in an off-key voice the theme song to the popular movie.

Maeve quickly joined in, and when Isabel started humming along in her pretty voice, Charlotte knew Izzy would be just fine.

"Come on, Katani!" Maeve urged. "You know you *love* this song!"

"I do not!" Katani fixed her friends with a serious look that soon melted into a smile. "Besides, no one," she pointed out, "wants to hear the Kgirl sing."

"Good point," Charlotte teased.

As the crowd started to inch forward, Katani gathered her luggage around her. Navigating through the throng with her three matching bags—which had been three mismatched suitcases until she gave them the special Kgirl treatment the week before— was proving to be difficult.

At least her bags were light and compact, unlike Maeve's two gigantic, unwieldy suitcases. "What do you have in here, Maeve, rocks?" Mr. Ramsey grinned as he dragged the larger one along the wharf.

"Just everything a girl on the move absolutely needs!" Maeve stopped and hugged her suitcase dramatically. "Katani, your bags are absolutely *gorgeous*," Maeve remarked suddenly.

"I bet you did that yourself?" Charlotte guessed.

Katani nodded and smiled, admiring her handiwork. She had covered each bag in orange canvas fabric printed with flowers; gold-thread stitching rounded out the look. "Thanks! I thought the floral print was spot-on for Hawaii. You never know—Kgirl may just rock out a luggage line."

"You have to!" Maeve squealed. "Then, when I'm famous, I'll carry them with me wherever I travel. They always like to take pictures of stars at airports." Maeve posed as if her own personal paparazzi were following her.

"It feels like we're doing less traveling and more standing," Avery complained. She climbed on top of her backpack to see how close they were to the boarding area. She could barely make out the gangway, which led into the belly of the ship. "Man, we're miles away," she said dejectedly.

"They deal with this many people for every cruise," Mr. Ramsey told her. "We'll be inside before you know it."

"But we're VIPs!" Maeve exclaimed. "Very Important Passengers."

"My article covers family cruising with *tweens*, not VIPs," Mr. Ramsey reminded them, jotting down some notes in a little pad. "And remember—you girls are my assistant reporters. I'm going to need your input every step of the way."

"I'm ready, Dad," said Charlotte as she rummaged through her book bag for her brand-new journal. Isabel had made one for her especially for the trip. It had a brown leather cover with an old-fashioned-looking print of a world map, and leather ties to hold it shut. Although she and her father had been all over the world, she had never been on a cruise. She wanted to make sure she got every last detail down on paper. *And maybe, just maybe, an original Charlotte tidbit will make it into Dad's article!*

The line started moving again, and Mr. Ramsey turned to the girls. "While I've got everyone's attention, I want to hear you list the two most important rules one more time." The girls huddled around.

"Charlotte, you first," he directed.

"Use the buddy system—no going off alone," she said firmly.

"Avery." Mr. Ramsey nodded at a fidgety Avery, who was jumping up and down again to see how soon they would reach the gate.

"Umm." She fumbled for a minute, then blurted out, "Let you or one of the BSG know where you and your buddy are going."

"Okay!" cheered Mr. Ramsey.

"OKAY!" the girls yelled, laughing.

When the line stopped *again*, Charlotte opened her new journal and started to jot down her first impressions of the ship and Hawaii itself. *Gulls' cries like music while palm trees sway to the beat—*

"Hello, you must be the travel writer!"

Charlotte looked up to discover a large man with a bushy red beard smiling down at her. He was dressed in a freshly pressed white uniform that she recognized from her reading as captain's whites.

"Captain Bob Frawley," the man said, saluting the girls. "I'm the commander of this vessel."

"I'm Richard Ramsey." Charlotte's dad shook Captain Bob's hand and explained that he was the one writing about the cruise for *Family Travel* magazine.

"Well, you'd better come on up to the front of the line, then, sir!" Captain Bob remarked, and ushered the group past the masses of people who were dressed mostly in brightly colored Hawaiian shirts and either chatting loudly or checking their watches.

"Excuse me! Coming through!" Maeve sang as she maneuvered her giant bags one at a time up to the front of the line.

Captain Bob was asking Mr. Ramsey if he'd include pictures of the crew in the magazine—maybe he could get in a head shot with his pirate eye-patch?—when some-one's cell phone started to make a sound.

"Someone's beeping," Isabel said.

"I didn't bring my phone," Charlotte replied. "Besides, all the people who would call me are right here!"

Maeve riffled through her pink and silver purse for her phone while Katani checked the cell phone compartment of her carry-on bag. Each of the girls shook her head. The beep-ing stopped, but Avery was still rummaging through her enormous backpack, clothes and shoes spilling everywhere.

"Avery, that backpack is a mess," Katani said. She had offered to make Avery a proper carry-on bag, but Avery said she didn't care about her luggage, adding, "It's not what you wear, it's how you tear." Avery's lack of interest in fashion made no sense to Katani at all.

"Are you sure you don't have Marty in there?" Maeve asked.

Avery hated being away from their dog, Marty, who lived at Charlotte's house. But pets weren't allowed on the cruise.

"He's at Charlotte's, promise," Avery assured her. "He's got Happy Lucky Thingy and Ms. Pierce to keep him company. Aha!" she exclaimed. "Here it is!" Avery pulled her cell phone out from a tangle of clothes and flipped it open. Her mother's number was on the display. "It's my mom."

"Shouldn't you call her back?" asked Isabel.

"I bet she's just wishing us *bon voyage*," Avery replied. "I'll call her back later."

A short woman with chin-length blond hair stood at the entrance to the ship, which was blocked off by a maroon velvet rope.

"*Aloha!* I'm Carla," she announced in a bright voice. "I'd like to welcome you to Aloha's seven-day deluxe cruise around the Hawaiian Islands. Now, if I could please see your tickets."

"These are my first mates, Carla!" Captain Bob turned to the girls. "I run a tight ship, so no shenanigans or I'll have you walkin' the plank, arrrg!"

"Where are the hair-and-makeup trailers?" Maeve whispered to Isabel. On a scavenger hunt to Cape Cod, Maeve and Isabel's team had stumbled onto the set of a real movie—all about pirates. Maeve had been cast as an extra!

Katani looked at Captain Bob skeptically. "They let pirates captain cruise ships now?"

He winked at her and leaned in closer to the group. "Can you all keep a secret?"

The BSG looked at one another and nodded.

"I just play a pirate on board for special occasions." He chuckled and disappeared into the ship.

"That was weird," Katani remarked at the same time as Maeve applauded. "Bravo! What a performance!"

Mr. Ramsey handed Carla a yellow envelope. She checked their tickets and then handed them each a folder and a brochure. "Inside you'll find a map of the ship as well as a schedule of the activities, our safety instructions, and your room keys."

"So what kind of shopping is on board?" Katani wanted to know.

Carla smiled. "We have some of the most exclusive boutiques in Hawaii, but looking at you, I'd guess you're into more cutting-edge fashion."

"You'd guess right!" Katani replied.

"Then you definitely want to check out Bananas, which is on the Celebration Deck." Carla opened one of the brochures, circled the location of the shop with her pen, and handed the brochure back to Katani.

Katani thanked her and studied the brochure. It was a lot more detailed than the maps she'd found online. Once she got into the room and got settled, she was going to make a list to make sure she covered all of the stores. She wasn't as much interested in buying things as she was in seeing the world and developing her eye and skill at fashion design. If she wanted her Kgirl line to totally take off someday, she was going to have to take advantage of every opportunity that came her way!

"I wouldn't mind finding a bookstore," mentioned Charlotte.

Maeve looked through her brochure. "There's a movie theater on board? Fantabulous!"

"We're in Hawaii and you two want to spend your time in the dark or reading?" Avery scoffed happily. "Forget that! I am all over the swimming pool. It has three water-slides and a swim-up juice bar!"

"We've got a little bit of everything," Carla assured

them. She slid their tickets back into the yellow envelope and handed it to Mr. Ramsey. "I've checked you in, so you're all set to go. You've got adjoining rooms on the Verandah Deck, which is level three. Just follow the platform to the Atrium, take the elevator up—"

"An elevator on a ship?" Isabel blurted out loud.

Carla laughed. "It's a pretty big ship." She helped them find their maps inside the folders and circled their staterooms. "Once you get to the Verandah, take a right out of the elevator and go down the hall. You're in cabins 6180 and 6182. You can't miss it!"

With a flourish, she unhooked the velvet rope to let everyone on board. "*Aloha!*"

"*Aloha!*" Avery yelled back. "Hello, Hawaii, and goodbye, land!" She slung her backpack over her shoulder and scampered up the gangway. There was one thing she was certain of: She wasn't going to miss a thing!

Stateroom of the Union

Maeve shook her head in disbelief. "I think this is the movie set level."

The Atrium was an enormous, sprawling space decorated in shades of gold and green. Floral print couches surrounded small tables carved out of wood, and people were everywhere, checking in with cruise ship staff, wheeling their luggage, or relaxing on one of the sofas listening to Hawaiian music piped in over the ship's PA system. Elevators with gold doors emblazoned with the ship's logo were tucked away in back, ready to take the passengers to the different decks.

The BSG squeezed into the elevator with their luggage. "She said we were on the Verandah," Isabel reminded Charlotte. Charlotte pressed the button for their deck, and everyone watched the elevator doors slide shut.

"I hope this elevator doesn't break down with the weight of Maeve's luggage," Avery joked.

"Hey, Katani brought more bags than I did!" Maeve retorted.

"Yeah, but yours are a thousand times bigger and heavier," Isabel noted, trying to budge one of them to make more room for her shoulder bag.

The elevator chimed and the gold doors slid open. "Verandah Deck, Beacon Street Girls Level!" Mr. Ramsey announced.

Past the elevator doors was a long hallway carpeted in the same green-and-gold pattern of the Atrium.

Charlotte opened her map. "Carla said to take a right—"

Avery let out a whoop and threw her backpack to the floor, running off down the hallway. She stopped about twenty yards ahead. "I found it!"

Charlotte smiled at Maeve, Katani, and Isabel. "Or we can use the Avery method."

The girls dropped their bags and dashed to the room, leaving Mr. Ramsey behind. Avery waved at them from inside the cabin. "You guys aren't going to believe this!"

Their room was perfect! Life jackets and towels and extra linens were tucked neatly in their places. Two sets of bunk beds lined either wall, each made up with green blankets with gold stitching. There were two closets, two cube dressers, and a desk made out of dark wood. A small foldout couch covered in floral fabric rested against the far end of the room, right under a large porthole that looked out onto the water.

Mr. Ramsey poked his head through the open door. "I think you girls forgot something." He nodded, indicating their luggage.

"Sorry, Dad!" Charlotte apologized, and the girls helped Mr. Ramsey bring their bags into their room.

"You girls settle in and unpack. I'm just through that door."

He pointed to a door that was next to the closet near the entryway. He opened it to reveal a similarly appointed stateroom, although instead of bunk beds there was a queen-size bed with a green-and-gold comforter and a gold-foil-wrapped chocolate on the pillow.

"I call top bunk!" Avery shouted, tossing her backpack up onto one of the beds.

"I'll take the one under you, Avery," Maeve decided. "I'm afraid I'll wake up in the middle of the night, forget where I am, and fall off!"

"Does anyone mind if I take the couch?" Charlotte asked. "It reminds me of my writing nook in the tower."

"Then Isabel and I will take the other bunk," Katani said. "Top or bottom?"

"Top?" Isabel asked. She thought it would give her a better view out the porthole. She could already see gulls diving outside the window.

"Fine. I'll take the bottom." Katani began to unpack methodically, removing her clothes from her decorated bags, shaking out the wrinkles, and either folding them neatly and placing them in the oak dresser or hanging them on hangers. There was no point in packing nice things for a trip if you ended up looking like a human wrinkle when you got there!

The rest of the girls looked on, impressed. "I gotta look sharp. It's part of the job of a fashion designer," she reminded them.

"Katani, unpack for me, too?" Maeve begged. "I thought as a VIP I would have someone take care of that stuff for me." She batted her eyelashes at Katani, who laughed and swatted her with a red-and-gold scarf. "I'm not going near those suitcases! They'll probably explode when you unzip them!"

Katani and Maeve had gone to a fashion show in New York City together, so Katani knew all about Maeve's packing problems.

Maeve sighed, dumped a wadded-up ball of clothes out of her first suitcase, and set it on her bed. She tried to mimic Katani's folding technique and regarded her work. "Still looks like a wadded-up ball," she complained.

"*This* is how you pack, girls!" Charlotte, the global traveler, opened her one suitcase and took out a few books to reveal lined-up rolls of clothing. All her toiletries were in a special pouch, and other compartments held things like a compass, binoculars, and a camera. "Each roll is one day's outfit," Charlotte explained. "So I don't even need to unpack! This suitcase is all the dresser I need."

"Charlotte, you're totally amazing!" Isabel said, awed by her worldly friend's packing talent.

"You guys are all crazy! *This* is how to unpack!" Avery called out from her top bunk. She unzipped her backpack and dumped out her belongings on the floor. "An unpacking world record! The crowd goes wild!"

Isabel giggled. "Impressive. But I think I'm going to try the Katani method since it's too late to pack like Charlotte."

The doorknob on their cabin started to jiggle.

"Is it your dad?" Isabel asked.

"Wouldn't he come through *that* door?" Charlotte replied, pointing to the one next to the closet.

The doorknob stopped jiggling, and everyone breathed a sigh of relief—until the door began to shake like someone was pulling on it!

2

Knock, Knock

The girls looked at one another nervously as whoever it was out there in the hallway knocked again!

"Who is it?" Avery yelled.

"I'm sorry to bother y'all. It's just Kara-Lee!" a syrupy sweet voice answered back through the door. "I just forgot my lil' ol' key."

Everyone relaxed. It was just a girl at the wrong cabin! Katani peered through the peephole and then opened the door to reveal a tall girl who looked to be their age. She was wearing a bright blue sundress, giant sunglasses, and a straw sunhat over her white-blond hair. At the sight of Katani, she pulled off her sunglasses. Her eyes matched the color of her dress.

"Oh, my word. I don't know what happened. I thought I had the right . . . ?" She giggled nervously.

"Yeah, this cabin's full!" Avery declared.

"Please excuse Avery, that's just . . . well, that's Avery. I'm Katani."

The girl smiled and held out her hand. "I apologize for disturbing you. Pleased to make your acquaintance, Katani. "

Katani shook Kara-Lee's hand, and then introduced the other BSG. "That's Isabel, and Charlotte, and Maeve, and well, you've met Avery. Sorry the place is so messy. We're still unpacking." Each of the girls gave a little wave as Katani introduced them, except for Avery, who threw a sock at Katani and missed by only a few inches.

"Hi, y'all," said Kara-Lee.

"I love your accent!" Maeve gushed. "Where are you from?"

"I'm guessing the South?" asked Charlotte with a big smile.

"Why, yes. You are indeed correct," Kara-Lee told them. "I just turned fourteen, and I'm from Savannah, Georgia."

Katani had only known Kara-Lee for a couple of minutes but she was already impressed with how she carried herself. Even though she was only a little bit older than they were, she seemed like a real teenager.

"I have to say that I was dreading coming on this vacation, because all my parents do is play mini golf and sit by the pool. But now that I know there are other girls my age here who are just as fashionable as I am," she said, smiling at Katani, "I am totally looking forward to this week."

"We are too!" Katani blurted out. Her friends always complimented her taste in fashion. But for a perfect stranger to notice—Katani was thrilled! "Stop by anytime!" she said to Kara-Lee.

"I will. Now I'd better find my cabin before my momma sends the coast guard after me!" With a wave and a smile, Kara-Lee was gone.

A knock came at the adjoining door. "Now *that's* gotta be my dad!" Charlotte exclaimed. Sure enough, Mr. Ramsey stepped through the door.

"Sorry, girls. Seems I must have fallen asleep!" He rubbed his temples gingerly. "Were you talking to someone? I thought I heard a voice I didn't recognize." The girls told him about Kara-Lee and the cabin mix-up.

"We asked who it was and then Katani looked through the peephole before we opened the door," Charlotte promised her dad.

"Good," he said, "because I want to take a second to continue our talk about safety onboard. Although the ship is pretty safe, we're traveling with three thousand strangers, and there are some basic guidelines besides what we have already gone over."

Mr. Ramsey explained that they should always carry their identification, taught them how to call a member of the ship's security, and listed basic onboard conduct.

"Do you know where your life jackets are?" he concluded.

"Life jackets?" Isabel asked nervously.

"Before any ship sets sail, you should always know where your life jackets are. Big cruise ships will always have a safety demonstration before they leave the dock, so grab your life jackets and we'll head on out. You guys are going to learn about the ship's alarm, lifeboat procedures, and where to go in case of an emergency!" He showed them where the big orange vests were tucked away in panels next to the bunk beds.

"It's called a Muster Drill," Charlotte said.

The girls put on their life vests. "This totally does not go with my outfit," Katani mumbled.

"But you look great in orange!" Maeve told her.

Lu-WOW!

After the Muster Drill, a pale Mr. Ramsey, who said he had the beginnings of a headache, went back to his room to lie down while the girls explored the upper decks, locating the pool, shopping boutiques, gourmet snack deli, and even a mini golf course and karaoke stage! They returned to their room with only a few minutes left to get ready for dinner.

"Katani, what do you wear to a *luau*?" Isabel asked.

They had already studied weeks ago the different activities and theme dinners that the cruise ship offered, but Isabel still wasn't sure if she had the right clothes for this extra-fancy adventure. Thankfully, Katani could turn any outfit into a winner.

"Hang on, let me look at you." Katani turned a discerning eye toward Isabel, who was wearing a calf-length denim skirt, an orange top with a picture of a parrot, and sandals. "I know exactly what you need!"

Katani checked her packing list, and then opened the

top drawer of the cube dresser she had claimed, taking out a yellow fabric flower. She pinned it in Isabel's hair and brought her over to the mirror. "What do you think?"

"I love it!" Isabel hugged Katani and admired her reflection. "What would we do without you?"

"Be way less fashionable!" Katani smirked.

"Hey, I do okay on my own!" Avery insisted. She emerged from under Maeve's lower bunk. "Has anyone seen my other sneaker?"

"You're supposed to dress up for dinner, Ave," Charlotte reminded her.

"They're my dress sneakers!" Avery responded.

"Ugh, this humidity is just terrible on my hair," Maeve complained from the bathroom as she attempted to tame her wild mass of red curls. "I might as well order in."

A knock came at the adjoining door. "Come in!" said Katani.

Mr. Ramsey was looking even paler than when they had last seen him. "I'm going to have to agree with you, Maeve, about the terrible humidity. This headache's only gotten worse."

"But you can't miss tonight's dinner, Dad! It's the *luau*!" Charlotte exclaimed. She was beginning to worry. Her dad was the definition of a seasoned traveler. This was completely unlike him!

"I'm coming, I'm coming. We've traveled so far for this. And . . . I wouldn't want to waste this tie!" Mr. Ramsey modeled a tie with a palm tree silhouetted by the sunset. "What do you think, ladies?"

"Umm. Maybe you'd better stick to writing travel books and leave the fashion to me, Mr. Ramsey," Katani said with a giggle.

The celebratory kickoff *luau* dinner was served in the ship's main dining room, located on the Upper Promenade, just a couple of long hallways away from their rooms. The dining room was even bigger than the fancy green-and-gold Atrium. Round tables decked out with festive Hawaiian-print tablecloths filled the space like a field full of colorful wildflowers. As the group paused in the doorway to take it all in, a young woman wearing a grass skirt over her Aloha Cruise Lines uniform placed a *lei* around each girl's neck!

"Clear out those tables, and you could play some serious soccer in here," Avery imagined, twirling her *lei* around like a slingshot.

"How do we know where to sit?" Isabel asked.

"We're at table seventeen," Katani read from the folder Carla had given them. As they made their way through the maze of tables, Maeve checked out their fellow passengers. Most of them seemed to be pretty old . . . retired couples or grandmothers and grandfathers with time to travel. Maeve was glad she was wearing a flowery sun dress and not a Hawaiian shirt! They passed a family with two adorable little kids, and then a boy who sort of reminded her of her little brother, Sam, caught her eyes. Sitting next to him was a tall, brown-haired boy with a gorgeous smile. *Crush alert!* Maeve told herself, adjusting her *lei* and flashing a smile of her own. *Remember table number 55!*

Soon after, Mr. Ramsey spotted their number and the

girls all sat down. Katani admired the tall blue vases filled with orange and red tropical flowers.

"They're birds of paradise," Katani noted. She had already started imagining an entire line of Kgirl cruise wear inspired by tropical flowers.

"Did you say birds?" Isabel asked.

"It's the name of the flower," Charlotte explained. "They sort of look like a flying bird, don't they?" Isabel nodded and did a quick sketch of the brilliantly colored, spiky blooms.

"Where are the candles?" Maeve asked. "The scene is set for romance and they forget the candles?" She looked around for the brown-haired boy, but the room was already too crowded to see all the way to table 55.

"It's dangerous to have fire on a ship," Katani told her. "It's part of the coastal safety regulations. I read all about it in the manual in the room."

"Plus, we're not setting the scene for romance. We're setting the scene for eating!" Avery reminded her. "Now bring on the food!"

Servers in Hawaiian-print shirts that matched the table-cloths started bringing out platters and platters of food featuring traditional *luau* dishes like *Huli Huli* chicken and *Lomi Lomi* salmon. The dining room went quiet as the passengers all dug into the plentiful Hawaiian cuisine.

"Everything's so yummy," Isabel joked, "they named it twice."

"I'm so full," Maeve groaned, "but they keep bringing more food!"

Everyone's plate had been practically licked clean, except for Mr. Ramsey's. He had pushed his food around, but eaten little. *It's not like him not to eat,* Charlotte worried. One of his favorite parts of traveling was sampling the local cuisine. "Are you sure you're okay, Dad?"

"Maybe I'm getting seasick?" he responded weakly. "Although I've never been seasick before."

"You're looking a little more white than green," Maeve told him.

"When I'm sick to my stomach, Grandma Ruby always gives me sparkling water," Katani added.

"Good idea, Katani." Mr. Ramsey flagged down a waiter and ordered a bottle of seltzer. "Maybe I'm just dehydrated."

Someone at the center table started clinking a fork against a glass. Everyone turned to see the captain stand up and address the dining room.

"Welcome aboard everyone. My name is Captain Bob Frawley, and I'm going to be piloting this vessel around these tropical isles of old," he announced to the room. "Of course, right now my first mate is standing in my stead. A captain's gotta eat, y'know!"

The captain waited for a few bursts of laughter to die down before continuing, "I've been a captain since I was but a wee boy found floating on a bit o' flotsam and jetsam in the stormy seas. I was plucked out of the water by a man known only as Captain Jack, who was the bravest sailor a man has ever known."

"D'you think that's true?" Isabel asked, wide-eyed.

"I think he's got a flair for the dramatic," Charlotte whispered.

"It's perfect!" Maeve insisted. "Born of the sea and returning to it—"

"Shhh!" Katani silenced her. "Captain Bob's still speaking!"

"In all my years o' captaining, I've seen it all. I've fended off pirate attacks and giant sea monsters . . ." There were a few hoots around the room, but then the captain switched to a less pirate-y voice. "But never on an Aloha cruise, I can assure you all!"

The room erupted in laughter. *Captain Frawley is definitely an entertainer*, thought Isabel as she opened her sketchpad and started drawing Captain Bob in full pirate gear, complete with an eye-patch and a peg leg. A pretend parrot on his shoulder completed the look. Isabel loved parrots—she'd made a papier-mâché one at her old school in Detroit that hung on her side of the bedroom she shared with her sister, Elena Maria.

Captain Bob spoke in a booming voice over the laughter. "So let's keep it that way. Welcome, everyone. And have fun." He lifted his glass to toast everyone in the room just as a waiter brought Mr. Ramsey his sparkling water. Everyone lifted a glass to toast along with Captain Bob.

"To the Beacon Street Girls!" Maeve exclaimed.

"And to Mr. Ramsey!" Isabel added.

"Not me! Thank *Family Travel* magazine and the Aloha Cruise Lines for sponsoring this adventure!" Mr. Ramsey added with a cough.

Everyone clinked glasses. Charlotte pulled her journal out of her purse and started writing.

"What're you working on?" Isabel asked.

"I don't want to forget any of Captain Bob's speech," Charlotte responded, "so I'm just getting some of the details down in my travel journal."

"Oh, then you should see this!" Isabel slid her drawing of pirate Captain Bob over to Charlotte.

Avery spotted them from across the table. "Are you guys passing notes? Lemme see that!" Charlotte handed Isabel's picture over to Avery, who chuckled. "You guys, check out this picture Isabel drew of Captain Bob!" She passed the drawing around the table.

"Isabel, I was going to journal this whole trip," said Charlotte. "Maybe you could illustrate it?"

"That's a great idea!" Isabel exclaimed. "I can't wait to see all of the wild birds and parrots. I've seen them at the zoo, of course, but never in their natural habitat!"

"I don't think there are any wild parrots on Hawaii," Avery mentioned thoughtfully. "Parrots mostly come from the Pacific Islands, Africa, and South America, right?"

"That's right," Mr. Ramsey affirmed. "But they've had problems with feral parrots on one of these islands. I found an article all about it in my reading before we left. The authorities actually wanted to shoot the birds so they wouldn't disrupt the local ecosystem too much!"

"No!" Isabel looked horrified. "*Qué terrible!* What does a feral parrot look like?"

"'Feral' means tame pets that got let loose," Charlotte

explained. She was the resident Word Nerd of the BSG. She just loved collecting words and their meanings.

The picture had made it to Katani, who studied it carefully. "Isabel, I knew you could draw, but this is really good. I mean, *really* good."

Maeve agreed. "I bet you guys could do an entire book!"

Before they could discuss feral parrots or their book plans further, the lights in the dining room began to dim. A voice came over the PA system. "Ladies and gentlemen, we invite you to turn your eyes to the dance floor to witness a traditional Hawaiian dance, known more famously as the *hula*."

A quartet of waiters cleared away the captain's table to reveal a square parquet dance floor. A trio of barefoot young women dressed in long, white dresses with festive *leis* made of flowers and green leaves entered. They were accompanied by a small band of musicians. As the band started to play, the women started to dance, swaying their hips to the rhythm.

"Aren't they wonderful?" Maeve whispered. "I would like to try that sometime."

Isabel was also mesmerized by how the dancers moved. She had taken ballet for years, until a knee injury forced her to stop. But the *hula* was different. The way the women swayed their hips caused their white dresses to ripple like water. She flipped to a new page in her sketchpad and tried to capture it in her drawing . . . which was tough because sketches didn't move! Instead, she spent extra time on the rings of delicate flowers and leaves that were strung around the dancers' necks.

Meanwhile, Charlotte was busy capturing her impressions of the traditional Hawaiian dance in writing. She had traveled all around the world and had seen the dances from all sorts of cultures, but nothing as hypnotic as the *hula. Arms outstretched as if welcoming us to get up and join the dance,* she jotted down.

The music came to a halt, and the room erupted in applause. The dancers took their bows, but the lights stayed low. A voice came over the loudspeaker again. "The dancers now invite you to please take the stage and learn the hula!"

The young women beckoned the audience to come join them on the dance floor, but everyone just looked around nervously. No one wanted to be the first!

Maeve leaped to her feet. She was never one to turn down an opportunity to go up on stage. "C'mon, guys, don't you want to go?"

Katani refused. "I've got two left feet!"

Maeve looked at Charlotte and Isabel, who had their heads bent down over their work. "Avery? Mr. Ramsey?"

Mr. Ramsey shook his head, still looking pale. "I already feel like I'm swaying."

Avery shook her head. "I think I'm gonna stick to snorkeling and surfing this trip. Besides, you've seen me dance!" It was true. Avery's dance moves were legendary . . . and not in a good way! If she went up there, one of the dancers might end up with a black eye.

"Okay, I tried!" Maeve jumped up and strode confidently to the dance floor. The audience applauded, and Maeve bowed, flashing her signature smile.

The trio of dancers showed Maeve some basic moves, and with her dance training, Maeve caught on quickly. Soon the group of four was moving as one. It didn't take long for a couple other women to abandon their tables and join the dancers. One woman who looked like she had to be more than eighty even got up on stage and joined the fun!

"Our dancers will now go into the audience and select partners," announced the voice over the loudspeaker. The girls watched as Maeve made a beeline to a table across the room. She returned to the dance floor with the tall, brown-haired boy. He had a petrified expression on his face.

"Shocker!" Avery exclaimed. Charlotte and Isabel laughed, but Katani just looked nervous. "Katani, what's up?" asked Avery.

"The dancers! They're coming this way!" Katani whispered.

Avery turned to see two of the pro *hula* dancers approaching their table. She and Katani slid down in their seats, while Isabel and Charlotte bent over their respective notebooks.

"The coast is clear," Mr. Ramsey announced as the dancers passed them by.

"Ha!" said Avery. "I wonder what suckers they found."

Avery turned to see what poor audience member the

dancers had selected to come up on stage. She could see the tops of their heads all the way in the back of the room. They were coming back now, right toward their table, and had someone in tow.

As the dancers got closer, Avery jumped out of her seat, spilling her fruit smoothie all over the table! The pineapple garnish popped off the glass and landed on Katani's lap. Charlotte and Isabel gathered their papers up quickly, while Katani dabbed at her skirt with a napkin.

"Avery!" Katani exclaimed. "What the—?"

"NO WAY!" Avery yelled.

3

Shipwrecking a Cruise

*A*very! Are you okay?" Charlotte asked.

Avery was on top of her chair, frantically waving down a man who was walking behind the *hula* dancers. He wore a Hawaiian-print shirt with a black tie that had a picture of a surfer on it, but the thing that really stood out was his enormous straw hat adorned with a *lei*.

Avery jumped off her chair and ran toward him.

"DAD!"

Avery couldn't believe it! A million thoughts raced through her mind as she ran and leaped at her dad, attaching herself like a monkey to his tall frame. *What's Dad doing here? He lives in Colorado. How is this even possible? Did he bring his surfing gear? This is so totally coolio!*

"Ave! What's up, snurfette?" He laughed and gave her a huge hug. "Long time no see, huh?" His *hula* dancer looked shocked at the loss of her partner, but quickly picked someone else.

Avery didn't even notice the *hula* madness taking over

the room as the stage got more and more crowded. She jumped down and dragged her dad over to the table to meet her friends.

"I bet these are the Beacon Street Girls?" Avery's dad asked.

Avery nodded and pointed everyone out, talking a mile a minute. "That's Charlotte, Isabel, Katani, Charlotte's dad, Mr. Ramsey, and hey, here's Maeve."

Maeve had rushed back to the table when she saw Avery jumping like a lunatic on her chair. She knew something exciting was happening, and she didn't want to miss a single minute of it! "Nice to finally meet you, Mr. Madden," Maeve chirped.

"Likewise!" He turned back to Avery. "So I wanted to surprise you. Surprised?" he asked.

"Totally!" Avery gushed. "And that's pretty major. It's way difficult to keep a secret from me!"

"There was this time . . . ," Mr. Madden remembered, pulling up an empty seat from the next table over and sitting down backward with his arms crossed over the chair back. "Ave must've been about six and Christmas was right around the corner. She was always snooping out her presents, but Bif and I went all spy school and hid them where we knew she'd never find them."

"I spent all of December looking for them, anyway. And I always found them!" Avery exclaimed proudly.

"But they weren't your presents, they were decoy presents." Mr. Madden burst out laughing. "Every year, Bif and I would adopt a family from the homeless shelter.

But we knew little Miss Snoop was going to search for her presents, so we made sure she could totally find those."

"I spent all of December writing Santa a letter a day asking for a bike and a soccer ball 'cause I thought all I was getting from my parents were books, pajamas, and toothpaste!" Avery erupted in a fit of giggles.

"I see where Avery gets her wicked sense of humor from," Isabel said to Mr. Madden. Isabel may have only moved to Brookline at the beginning of the school year, but she'd already picked up on the East Coast slang.

Avery smiled. She just couldn't believe it! She was beyond psyched at the idea that she'd get to spend the next seven days with her best friends and her dad. Normally she only got to see her dad during the holidays and summer vacations since he ran a ski and snowboarding shop in Telluride, Colorado.

"Okay, Ave, I have one more surprise up my sleeve," her dad said.

Avery inspected his sleeves—it was part of their old joke together. "I don't see anything."

"This one is major. Shreddy?" That was secret snowboarder code for "ready."

"Way shreddy!" Avery shouted, wondering, *What could be more major than Dad showing up? Does he have a special surfboard for me?* Mr. Madden ran a ski and snowboard shop called ATS, which was named for Avery and her brothers, Tim and Scott. Avery didn't think he sold stuff for summer sports, but you never knew. An all-new ATS surfing line would be a majorly cool surprise!

Mr. Madden waved over at his table, motioning for someone to join them. Avery craned her neck to see who it was; she couldn't see over the crowd of people standing up to watch the dancers on stage.

Suddenly, a tall girl with blond hair tied in orange and pink ribbons was standing right in front of her.

Kazie! Crazie Kazie!

"Surprise!" Kazie screamed. "Like, it's me! Totally crazy, huh!"

"Yeah. Crazy," Avery mumbled, suddenly crestfallen. "Can't believe you're here." That meant the person standing behind Kazie was—

"Avery, it's so good to see you," Andie said, kissing Avery's cheek. "I wanted to tell you, but your dad thought it would be much more fun as a secret."

Avery couldn't believe it! It was like catching air on your snowboard, only to crash-land moments later. Andie, her dad's girlfriend, was okay, but her daughter Kazie? *There's a reason she's called Crazie Kazie!* Avery thought miserably. When she was around, Avery was always on high alert. Kazie turned everything into a competition, even when Avery just wanted to kick back and have fun.

There was an uncomfortable moment while everyone looked at one another, not sure of what to say. Avery turned and wiped Andie's kiss off her cheek, half hoping her dad's girlfriend would notice, half trying to look on the bright side.

Avery had been to Hawaii surfing with her dad and

brothers before, and those were some of the best memories of her life . . . but Andie and Kazie were never involved. *I barely know them!* Avery thought. *This trip was supposed to be for me and the BSG.* She'd even *told* her dad in a dozen excited e-mails about the trip that she was psyched to be heading out to Hawaii on her own! Now that was completely ruined.

Thankfully, Katani was her business-as-usual self and took complete control of the situation, introducing the rest of the girls and Mr. Ramsey to Kazie and Andie.

Maeve thought there wasn't anything more romantic than a surprise. While she could see that Mr. Madden's surprise made Avery uncomfortable, she thought it was incredibly cute the way he and Andie held hands and kept sneaking glances at each other!

"So what brings you to Hawaii, Mr. Madden?" Maeve asked.

"Yeah, who's watching the shop?" Avery asked.

"We had such a rockin' ski and snowboard season that I just closed up shop for the week. I thought I'd continue rockin' it out here with you, Ave! When you said you were off to Hawaii, I knew that's where Kazie, Andie and I should go. We can all just totally chill! Together!"

"Together. Great," Avery stated sarcastically. She wanted to sound enthusiastic, but she was just sooo not prepared for this sudden change of plans!

"Of course, only if Charlotte's dad gives the A-okay." Mr. Madden looked toward Mr. Ramsey. "Although you're lookin' a little less than a-okay, dude."

"I'm actually relieved that you're here," Mr. Ramsey said. "I haven't been feeling well."

Avery was still in shock. *I can't believe Mom didn't call to warn me! Unless* . . . Avery dug her cell phone out of her pants pocket and looked at it. The message waiting light winked red. While everyone was chatting politely, Avery called her voice mail.

"Avery, it's Mom. Listen, I just got a call from your dad, who wanted to surprise you . . ." Avery swallowed hard. She could only hear about every third word over the noise in the dining room. "Andie . . . Kazie . . . sorry . . ." She ended with "I love you" and suddenly Avery realized she was listening to static. Someone punched her in the arm.

It was Kazie. "Awesome surprise, huh?"

"Yeah. Awesome." Avery rubbed her arm where Kazie had punched her. If only she had taken the opportunity to check her messages before she had come to dinner! Then, she'd . . . well, then what?

Sometimes before a soccer game, Avery would get bad news. Like when she discovered the awesome power forward who everyone thought was sick suddenly got better, or that her mom wasn't going to make it in time from work to cheer her along on the sidelines. So when she was hit with some unexpected news, she just took a deep breath and headed out onto the field, giving it everything she had, and not letting anyone notice that she was operating at anything less than Avery Koh Madden's absolute best.

So that's the deal. She was stuck with Crazy Kazie for a seven-day cruise, and that wasn't going to change. She was just going to take a deep breath and give it everything she had, even if that meant being nice to Kazie. The same Kazie who was going on a mile a minute about ATS's new snowboard designs for next season. Did that girl ever stop talking?

"Kazie, Katani is a fashion designer," Avery blurted out. "She's the one with the Kgirl fashion line I told you about in Colorado."

"No way!" Kazie yelled. She ran over to Katani, made her stand up, and then stood back to back with her. "I bet you design your own clothes 'cause you're tall like me!"

While Katani didn't totally know what to make of Kazie, she couldn't help smiling at her enthusiasm. It cut right through Katani's cool demeanor.

"Actually, that's one of the reasons I got into fashion design. Since I'm taller than everyone else, sometimes I have to alter my clothes to make them fit right," she told Kazie.

Charlotte sized up the situation. Avery looked worse than before as she sat slumped in her chair with her arms folded tightly across her chest.

Maeve knew what *she* did to deal with difficult situations: dance. Maybe that would help.

"It's back to the dance floor. Ave, want to join me?" she asked.

Avery shook her head. Maeve shrugged. *I tried!* She headed back to the dance floor to see if she could find that cute boy again—and get his name this time.

Charlotte and Isabel huddled around Avery, who was looking more miserable by the minute.

"Are you okay?" whispered Charlotte as her dad chatted with Mr. Madden and Andie.

"Can you believe it? An entire week with Kazie!" Avery groaned.

"It'll be okay, really," Isabel promised. "There's so much to do on this boat, maybe you won't have to spend much time with her at all. Then you'll get used to her being here."

"Yeah, maybe. I mean, Kazie might not even like surfing." Avery brightened.

Across the table, Katani and Kazie were deep in conversation. *Do they really have that much to talk about?* Avery wondered.

"I don't know, though. Crazie Kazie needs way more than an hour to get used to! Remember what I told you about her monster cat Farkle? He totally terrorized Marty the whole time I was in Colorado. And Kazie thought it was *funny*."

Isabel and Charlotte shared a look. Avery was usually so happy-go-lucky. She didn't let anything get to her; she just laughed things off. They had never seen her like this!

"Okay, so Kazie may be here," Charlotte told her friend, "but we're still here too. And we're your best friends. We should be having the time of our lives on this cruise!"

Avery knew they were right, but there was still a little voice in the deep recesses of her brain that whispered, *Why does Kazie have to crash my vacation?*

"Oh hey, y'all!" A familiar Southern drawl rang out from the crowd. It was Kara-Lee. "I was wondering what all the commotion was, and here I find my almost-roommates having a little gathering."

Charlotte introduced Kara-Lee to her father, Mr. Madden, and Andie. "Dad, this is Kara-Lee. She's the one who came to our cabin by mistake. Kara-Lee, this is Avery's dad, Mr. Madden, and Andie, um . . . ?"

"I'm Ms. Walker." Andie shook hands with Kara-Lee. "How nice that there are so many kids my daughter's age on this cruise!"

"A pleasure to make your acquaintance," Kara-Lee said politely.

"You found your way back to your cabin?" Mr. Ramsey asked weakly.

"I did. Thank you for asking! There are parts of this ship that look entirely the same; it's easy for a gal to get turned around."

She went over to Kazie. "I don't believe we've met, but I know the beautiful Ms. Walker must be your mama! I can see the resemblance. I'm Kara-Lee." She shook Kazie's hand. "I just love the way you've matched your ribbons to your outfit. And, Katani, I do believe the fabric flowers your friend Isabel is wearing must be your signature touch!"

Katani felt herself blush. It was always a thrill to have someone recognize her handiwork. "You'd be right!"

"I do believe the three of us might make this cruise's best-dressed list," Kara-Lee declared.

"The three of them?" Isabel mouthed to Charlotte, noting that Kara-Lee had left out half the table!

Charlotte watched as Katani, Crazie Kazie, and Kara-Lee all chatted excitedly. "She's just being friendly," she whispered.

"Does Katani have to be *so* friendly back?" Avery muttered.

Sometimes Katani could give people the cold shoulder, like on Charlotte's first day at Abigail Adams Junior High, when she'd managed to zip a tablecloth into her pants.

It was hard for Charlotte to imagine a time when the BSG weren't best friends, even though it wasn't that long ago. They had been assigned lunchroom seats at the beginning of seventh grade and Charlotte remembered looking around at Katani, Maeve, and Avery and thinking that they were all so different that there was no way they were ever going to end up friends. It wasn't until a sleepover at Charlotte's that they realized that they had more in common than they thought.

"It's always good to try and make new friends," an optimistic Charlotte pointed out. "You know. Expand your *circle*."

"Okay," Avery admitted, "I guess you're right. But I bet Kazie will drive both of them crazy . . . and by tomorrow she'll have them convinced you can snowboard in Hawaii!"

Charlotte and Isabel shared a smile. That was the wisecracking Avery they knew! She must be coming out of her state of shock.

"Guys?" Katani stood in front of them while Kara-Lee and Kazie stood expectantly behind her. "Kara-Lee, Kazie, and I are going up to the Navigation Deck. Wanna come?"

Avery wanted to see the top deck again, but no way did she want to hang out with Kazie just yet.

"It's probably kinda chilly up there," Avery replied. Charlotte watched her friend's face, thinking the only thing that was chilly was Avery's smile.

"Oh, we'll be inside! Kazie and Andie's room is *on* the Navigation Deck," Katani responded.

"Wow!" said Charlotte. "Those are supposed to be some of the best views on the entire ship!" Avery shot her a look. "But, um, we'll probably catch up with you later."

"And Maeve's gonna be the last one on the dance floor," added Isabel, nodding toward their friend. "At the rate she's going, she'll be *teaching hula* dancing soon."

"You sure?" Katani asked uncertainly. She could tell that Avery definitely didn't want to go along. She felt really torn. She kind of liked Kazie but she didn't want to hurt Avery's feelings.

Crazie Kazie bounced over. She was one of those people who couldn't stand still for a second, and her constant motion was making Avery feel seasick. *Or maybe it's just Kazie who's making me sick*, Avery thought.

"There's a deck off our room. The view is mega-awesome," Kazie continued. "The horizon just goes on forever."

"Maybe later." Avery shrugged, trying not to sound

disappointed. It did sound mega-awesome. And she really wanted to check out the top deck at night with all of the stars—Charlotte had gotten her interested in stargazing lately—but she wanted to do that with her *friends*. Not Kazie and Kara-Lee. *Who are they, anyway, to just walk up and expect us to hang out with them all day?*

"It's room 7008, if you change your mind!" Kazie sang. "Catch you later, kids."

Avery watched as Katani left with her two new friends.

"Yeah," replied Avery. "Can't wait."

A New Kind of Kgirl

"I cannot believe how spectacular this view is!" Kara-Lee crooned from the deck. "It's too much!"

"Totally," said Katani. She inhaled the clean ocean air. The cabin that Kazie shared with her mom was smaller than the room that the BSG were in, but it did have a tiny deck with an expansive view of the ocean. Right now, with the sun going down, the sky was like an orange-and-pink painting right at your fingertips!

Katani went back into the room and fell back onto the queen-sized bed. "Mmm. These sheets are so soft. I think my Kgirl line's totally got to include home décor with sheets and pillows, and well, the whole thing!"

Kazie jumped on the bed and struck a surfing pose. "You know what would be crazy? A surfing line!"

"Tidal wave!" Katani joked, sitting up and bouncing.

Kazie fought to keep her balance. "Cowabunga!"

Kara-Lee came in from the deck. "My turn!"

Katani and Kazie moved aside as Kara-Lee executed a perfect back walkover onto the bed.

"A perfect ten!" Katani declared.

"That was killer! Are you a gymnast?" asked Kazie.

"I used to be, but now I do most of my stunts on the cheerleading squad," Kara-Lee replied.

"We don't have cheerleading at our school yet," Katani added. "My friend Maeve can't wait until she can join the squad in high school."

"It's really big where I come from," Kara-Lee confided in the girls. "Practically everyone's a cheerleader— or wants to be."

"I snowboard!" Kazie shouted, jumping up on the bed again and pretending it was a snow-covered slope. She zigged and zagged like she was boarding down a mountain. "I used to do it for fun, but now I compete. That's how Ave and I met. Her dad owns this rad snowboarding shop where my mom works, and now my mom and her dad are dating. I thought they'd be tired of each other by now, but oh well . . ." Kazie shifted her weight from foot to foot, and then dropped suddenly. "Wipeout!"

"You guys competed in that Snurfer snowboard competition, right?" Katani asked, trying to keep up with the conversation.

"Yup," said Kazie, "but I'm *shreddy* to learn how to surf!" She jumped back on the bed. "Hang ten!" she yelled, took a flying leap, and landed with a THUMP! on the floor. "I'm okay!" she announced.

Katani couldn't believe Kazie and Avery weren't friends! Both of them had enough energy for about a dozen kids put together. "Isn't it great to be on vacation in Hawaii? We're so lucky!" Katani gushed.

"It'd be better just me and my mom." Kazie rolled her eyes. "She's always with Jake now. Like *always*. I'm psyched you guys wanted to hang out!"

"I think tomorrow there's horseback riding when we dock in Kauai," Kara-Lee told them. "Do you want to ride together?"

Katani breathed a sigh of relief. She had started riding horses with her sister Kelley a few months back, and she was getting pretty good at it!

"Sure! I ride with my sister Kelley all of the time back in Boston. She's been riding longer than I have, though. She's autistic, so she does it as part of her therapy program," Katani confided. She waited to see what her new friends would think about that.

"That is totally awesome!" Kazie declared.

"And isn't that funny," Kara-Lee remarked in her Southern drawl, "your sister's name is Kelley?" Kara-Lee started to giggle uncontrollably.

"Yeah?" Katani said, not getting the joke. *If she's not down with Kelley . . .*

Kara-Lee started to laugh harder. "We're all 'K's!"

"Ks?" By this time, even Kazie was looking at their new friend, confused.

Kara-Lee pointed at Katani, then Kazie. "Katani. Kazie," she said, and then, pointing at herself, "Kara-Lee."

"We're all Kgirls," Katani said.

"Ooh, I like that! We're the Kgirls!" Kara-Lee declared.

"Actually, 'Kgirl' is the name of my clothing line—" Katani reminded them.

"I dig it!" Kazie said, and started surfing on the bed again. "Kgirls will rock Kauai! Join the club! The Kgirls club!"

"But it's my clothing line," Katani repeated. She didn't know how she felt about using the name she had been saving for ages for her clothing line as the name of a club. Besides, she was already a Beacon Street Girl!

Kara-Lee interrupted her thoughts. "Of course it's the name of your clothing line! It's a super-fashionable name for a super-fashionable girl."

Katani couldn't argue with that! "We're all pretty stylin'," she admitted. *What's the harm of being in another club?* she thought. *I can't believe how well the three of us click and we've only just met!* The BSG would understand that there was room for everybody. "Okay, the Kgirls it is."

Kazie pumped her fist in the air and let out a whoop. "The Kgirls!"

Kara-Lee followed suit. "The Kgirls!"

Katani took a deep breath and pumped her fist. "The Kgirls!"

As Kara-Lee and Kazie discussed their plans for the week's activities, Katani went out onto the deck. She stared out over the ocean, watching the moonlight twinkle off the waves and thinking about friends . . . new and old. *What* is it Maeve says sometimes? *The old Girl Scouts line?* Katani thought. *Oh, right, that's it: Make new friends, but keep the old, one is silver and the other gold.* Katani smiled to herself. *And if there's one thing* this *Kgirl knows, it's silver and gold! Necessary to spice up any glam or vintage ensemble.* Yes, this was shaping up to be a fashionable and friend-filled vacation!

4

Totally Sick!

N ow that was dinner and a show!" Maeve exclaimed, dabbing the sweat off her forehead with a napkin. "I'm positively melting."

"You look as beautiful as always," Isabel assured Maeve.

"Why, thank you, Isabel!" Maeve bowed dramatically. "Did you see that boy I was dancing with? He was such a smooth dancer! Like Fred Astaire . . ." Suddenly Maeve realized she had forgotten to ask his name! *Maybe it's actually Joe or Jim Astaire, and he's a long-lost relative of the greatest movie star dancer ever.*

"Maeve! That kid was wearing *Heelys*," Avery pointed out.

Charlotte looked up as Maeve defended the Heelys. Charlotte had been trying to keep Avery's mind off Crazy Kazie and Andie's surprise visit by telling stories about Marty, but it didn't really work. Maybe this was the kind of distraction Avery needed.

"Maeve, have you already forgotten about Riley?" Charlotte asked. After the Valentine's Day dance, the only boy Maeve ever seemed to talk about was Riley, lead singer and guitarist of AAJH's coolest student band, the Mustard Monkeys.

"Riley would understand," Maeve explained. "It's not like I'm going to marry this boy or anything. He's just so adorable! Tell me he wasn't totally dreamy!"

Charlotte shook her head. They had been on vacation for just a few hours and Maeve was already boy crazy! "He was kinda cute."

"I'd say more than kinda!" Maybe Mr. Madden and Andie weren't going to be the only ones with a chance for romance on this trip! Maeve took a huge gulp of pineapple juice and dabbed at her mouth with a napkin. *Hula*-ing sure made a girl thirsty! "Hey, what happened to Katani?"

"She went up to Kazie's room with Kara-Lee," Avery said, dejected.

A concerned Maeve studied her friend. She wanted this trip to be filled with drama —but only the good kind!

Just then, Mr. Ramsey returned to the table with Mr. Madden and Andie in tow. They'd gotten up to order more sparkling water. "Hopefully this last glass will do the trick," Mr. Ramsey said weakly.

"You might want to order a couple more, just to be safe!" Avery offered, glad that the spotlight was off of her for a minute. She avoided looking at her dad and Andie. She'd never felt weird about having divorced parents before—a lot of kids at school had parents who had split up, and it had happened a long time ago. But it was totally weird to see her dad with Andie on this trip. And it seemed as if Kazie's only plan for this vacation was to totally invade her territory.

"Looks like he's not shreddy to pound some sick waves, huh, Ave?" Mr. Madden looked at Avery with a wink, but she just barely cracked a smile.

Charlotte felt bad for Mr. Madden. She knew he was probably thinking that Avery would be more excited to see him. And she was . . . until Andie and Kazie showed up. *Some kinds of surprises aren't really fun!* Charlotte realized. *Poor Avery's still in shock.*

"Sick waves?" Mr. Ramsey asked.

Avery's smile slipped into a little laugh. She forgot that sometimes she had to translate for her dad, the snowboarding Snurfman. "Sick means good, Mr. Ramsey."

"But I'm sick . . . ," his voice trailed off.

"That's sick like bad," Avery explained.

Mr. Ramsey turned to Avery's dad. "I bet you never get seasick, Jake."

Andie burst out laughing. "You clearly don't know Jake!" She smiled and grabbed Mr. Madden's hand. Maeve thought it was sweet, but the look on Avery's face was anything but sweet!

"They had just built a brand-new half-pipe in Telluride, and of course the Snurfman had to be the first to ride it," Andie said when she was done laughing. "And he got motion sickness!"

Mr. Madden squeezed Andie's hand and made a pained

face. "Sometimes you gotta blow when it's time to go!"

"The back-and-forth motion of going up one side of the pipe and coming back down made him lose his lunch. We had to throw out a brand-new snowboarding jacket!"

"Ewwwww!" said Isabel.

"This is where it helps to own your own ski and snow-board shop," Mr. Madden told her.

Avery couldn't believe her ears. *Andie wasn't even there that day!* That had happened a few years ago when Avery and her brothers, Scott and Tim, had come out for spring break to visit her dad.

Charlotte saw the scowl deepening on her friend's face. She had to step in. "Avery, that doesn't happen to you, right? 'Cause you're a pro."

Avery shrugged. "Yeah, I guess."

"Avery's too modest," Andie exclaimed, "I'm sure she told you girls that she took fifth in the Snurfer competition last winter. And she was up against some serious competition. Girls who snowboard almost every day."

Like Kazie, Avery thought.

"Yeah, Ave, now I bet you're shreddy for the waves!" her dad said. "It's been what, two years since last time we surfed up a big one?"

"No talk of waves, please!" Mr. Ramsey begged them.

"Dad, I think you're getting worse," Charlotte worried.

"Talk to Dr. Madden. I operate under the 'total pre-paredness' credo," Mr. Madden replied. "I have some motion-sickness patches in my room. Just put them on your wrists and you'll be fine in no time."

"They work wonders," Andie assured him. "Look, I'm wearing one right now, just to be safe." She pulled up the sleeve of her fuchsia dinner jacket to show off the tiny patch.

"They're in my cabin," Mr. Madden told them. "It's a bit of a trek, but I prefer to think of it as an adventure."

"I'm always up for adventure!" Maeve said.

Avery shrugged. "Sure, let's motor." At least she wasn't hanging out with Kazie.

The World's Smallest Cabin

Mr. Madden led everyone through a maze of hallways, elevators, and stairwells until they reached a dimly lit hallway with a small door at the end.

"This is weird," Maeve shivered.

"I feel like we're in a maze, Dad," said Avery.

"That's what happens when you make plans at the last minute. You get what's available." Mr. Madden got out his key and opened the door to his cabin. The room was so small that they all couldn't even fit inside! "It's the smallest cabin on the boat," he told them proudly.

"You can say that again!" Mr. Ramsey squeezed in between Avery and Charlotte.

"No one usually wants it," Mr. Madden explained. "Actually, when I made my last-minute reservations, they told me all they had was Andie and Kazie's luxury stateroom, and it was only for two people . . . but you know Jake the Snake." He winked at Avery. "I went through about twenty people on the phone before someone finally offered me the economy stateroom."

"More like the economy closet," Avery remarked. "If you had taken another cruise, you'd have a nicer room."

"Yeah, but then Andie, Kazie and I wouldn't get to spend time with you!" her dad responded. "Anyway, I don't plan on spending much time down here."

Mr. Madden unzipped a bright red canvas bag that was almost as long as the room itself. He started tossing clothes everywhere looking for the motion-sickness patches.

"He normally keeps his skis in there," Andie explained, looking over Avery's head from out in the dimly lit hallway.

"It looks like your dad is the one who taught you to pack, Avery." Isabel giggled. Maeve and Charlotte laughed, and even Avery couldn't help cracking a smile. Her father's wad-up-your-clothes-in-a-ball-and-shove-in-the-nearest-bag technique did look awfully familiar.

Maeve looked around the room, admiring what Mr. Madden had done with it. "It might be small, but you've made it really homey."

Isabel agreed. "That poster in the corner is wicked cool."

Everyone checked out the poster, which featured a girl in a yellow jacket on a bright red snowboard, who appeared to float in the air nearly perpendicular to a half-pipe.

Avery stared at the poster. *It couldn't be . . .* She looked at her dad, who followed her gaze and nodded.

"Yeah, that's you at the Snurfer," he said, referring to the competition he held for snowboarders in Colorado every year. "It's a sick shot, right? I've got one for you, too." He pulled a rolled-up poster out from beneath a mountain of brightly colored shirts and handed it to Avery.

"Avery, that's you?' Maeve asked, shocked.

Avery nodded. She always talked about snowboarding with her friends, but they had never gotten a chance to see her in action.

"You're practically flying!" Charlotte exclaimed.

"Your brother always says you're good, but we didn't realize how good!" Isabel added.

Avery had to admit, the poster was awesome. But if her dad thought it made up for the Kazie surprise, he was sorely mistaken!

"Aha! Got it!" Mr. Madden held a small white envelope above his head, victorious. "One order of seasickness patches! This should fix you right up!"

He handed the envelope to Mr. Ramsey, who ripped it open and placed the small, tan square gingerly on the inside of his wrist.

"Let's hope this is the cure," Mr. Ramsey looked around the room with a weak smile.

Mr. Ramsey Flus the Coop

"Your dad isn't seasick," Dr. Weber told Charlotte, "he's got a bad case of the flu." He plucked the thermometer out of Mr. Ramsey's mouth and peered at it over his wire-rimmed glasses. "One hundred and one."

Charlotte and her Dad were in the onboard infirmary. They had left Mr. Madden in his tiny room, then said good night to Andie, who wanted to go check on her daughter Kazie, Kara-lee, and Katani. After that, Mr. Ramsey only made it up one set of stairs before panting that he had to sit down! Charlotte had felt his forehead and insisted that they find the ship's doctor.

Avery, Isabel, and Maeve wouldn't hear of going back to their cabin without Charlotte and Mr. Ramsey, so all four girls navigated the hallways until they found the little white room with a plaque on the door reading ALOHA CRUISES INFIRMARY, DR. STEPHEN WEBER, MD. When the group entered the office, a nurse passed out masks and gloves. They didn't want any contagious diseases being passed around the ship.

"Will he be okay, Dr. Weber?!" Maeve wanted to know.

"Call me Dr. Steve. And yes, he'll be fine."

"I just need an aspirin," Mr. Ramsey insisted. He tried to sit up in bed but was too weak.

"You just need some rest, Dad." Charlotte played with the elastic on her mask nervously.

"Listen to this young lady," Dr. Weber instructed him. "She's smart."

Charlotte's lip started to tremble. *It's only the first day of vacation and my dad is sick!* When he got sick at home, she always brought him tea and ordered pizza or something for dinner. But this was different. They were miles from land! "Is he going to be better soon?"

Dr. Weber patted Charlotte's gloved hand. "He won't be better tomorrow, but he'll be better in a few days. Don't worry. We'll take good care of him here."

"Thank you, Dr. Steve!" Isabel exclaimed.

Maeve thought if she were casting a part for a ship's brave doctor healing a band of sailors after a pirate attack, she would give the part to Dr. Steve. He had kind brown eyes behind his silver wire-rimmed glasses, lots of curly salt and pepper hair, and his tone was both reassuring and calm.

Maeve squeezed Charlotte's shoulder. "Don't be upset! Your dad's going to be okay!" She loved her mask. It made her feel like she was on *ER*.

"This is like a full-on hospital," Isabel added helpfully. The little white examination room opened onto a hall lined with equipment, several patient rooms, and nurses in blue scrubs.

"You're right," Dr. Steve told them, "it *is* a hospital. You can't always get to land right away if you're sick at sea, so we have to be able to accommodate, well, anything. And we have to be *extra* careful with anything contagious."

"But you've seen this before, right?" Charlotte asked as a nurse wheeled her dad into a room with a large glass window.

Dr. Steve smiled warmly, taking off his gloves. "The flu? I sure have. It's pretty common for people to get sick after long airplane flights, since the air you're breathing is recycled through the plane. Give it a few days and your dad will be right as rain," he assured the girls. "For now, we'll be calling in one of our onboard child-care assistants to supervise you girls."

"Oh, we can supervise ourselves—" Maeve started, until Charlotte elbowed her.

A pretty young woman with an oval face and dark brown eyes entered the sickroom. She was wearing a khaki uniform, and her black hair was pulled back into a loose ponytail.

Dr. Steve handed her a file folder, which the woman tucked under her arm. "Girls, this is Marisol. She'll stay with you while Charlotte's dad is here in the infirmary."

Marisol smiled, which lit up her entire face. "Hi, girls! I know this isn't *exactly* what you were expecting out of your cruise, but I'll try to make it as fun as possible. Promise."

Isabel perked up at Marisol's lilting Spanish accent. "*¿Está usted de Mexico?*" she asked politely.

"I'm not from Mexico," Marisol explained, "but I'm half Mexican. *Mi familia* lives in California."

"In Hollywood?" Maeve asked excitedly.

"No, San Diego—"

"Can you surf?" Avery wanted to know, but Marisol shook her head.

"Well, at least I know you girls are in good hands!" Mr. Ramsey chuckled. He could see and hear the girls through the glass.

"You sure you'll be okay, Dad?" Charlotte asked, pressing her hands up against his window.

"I'll be fine," Mr. Ramsey insisted. "Everyone's right, I

just need some rest. And I'll rest better knowing you girls are out there having fun." He smiled warmly at Marisol.

"How can I have fun when I know you're in here sick?" Charlotte asked, not convinced.

"Charlotte, this is very important. I need you and Isabel to be my eyes and ears for the parts of the trip that I'll be missing. So you two are on assignment."

"You can come visit your dad any time you want," Marisol assured her. "In the meantime, I'll be your chaperone."

Captain Bob burst into the room. "I 'eard we had a man down, but he's in good hands. And so are you girls! Marisol could fight off a bucketful o' scurvy dogs!" he declared.

"Hey, it's not the dogs' fault they have scurvy," Avery protested.

Maeve and Isabel stifled a giggle. Avery loved all animals, especially dogs.

"Scurvy toads?" asked Captain Bob.

"Not any better," Avery responded. Even Charlotte was laughing now.

"If ye have any problems—you need anything—you call me. Star-111 on any ship phone." With a quick salute, he was off.

Avery and Isabel looked at each other and started to giggle. Captain Bob was one crazy boat Captain. Avery wondered if he really thought he was a pirate.

After blowing her dad a kiss, Charlotte followed Marisol and her friends out into the corridor.

"Okay, so let's figure out who's who," Marisol said. She opened the file folder that Dr. Weber had given her. "I'm going to guess that you're Charlotte," she said, looking at Charlotte, "since your dad is the 'man down.'" Charlotte nodded. "And . . . Avery, are you the surfer?" Avery raised her hand and waved. "I bet that's Maeve with the gorgeous red hair, who's bound for Hollywood?" Maeve smiled and nodded. "And you're Isabel with the fabulous *papagayo* shirt?"

Isabel smiled. Katani had helped her sew the parrot design. "I love birds."

"Me, too," Marisol confided. "Now where's Katani?"

Postcards Home

Katani was still hanging out with Kazie and Kara-Lee. She had no idea how much their trip had suddenly changed. When Andie walked Katani back to her room that evening, it was a shock to find a strange woman in the room instead of Mr. Ramsey!

"Jake and I will do whatever we can to help out," Andie offered Marisol after the girls had explained what had happened.

After Andie left, Katani showed Marisol her planner. "I've got everything all scheduled, so we'll be easy on you. And . . ." Katani waited for everyone's attention. "I brought back presents for the BSG!"

"Oooh! Presents!" Maeve jumped up and tried to peek in the little plastic bag Katani was carrying.

Katani held it up out of reach. "These are for everyone

to share for the rest of the trip!" Then she let Maeve reach into the bag.

"Postcards!" Isabel exclaimed.

"I bought these on the way back from Kazie's room," Katani explained. "There's a mail slot we can drop them in, and they get picked up every day when we dock!"

"Thanks, Katani!" Charlotte gushed, picking out a card with a waterfall for Sophie. *This is the perfect way to end a whirlwind day*, Charlotte thought. *Writing to one of your best friends.*

Ma Cherie Sophie,

    Bonjour from Hawaii! I'm so lucky my dad is a travel writer! Except he has the flu so he will be spending most of the trip in the infirmary. I know I'll still have fun, but I can't help worrying about my dad. Anyway, ma cherie, I'll be writing tons since I'm helping him out with his assignment (after I write this postcard I need to research endangered species in Hawaii!). I'll find time to send you a longer letter when I get home. I miss you!

                      Au revoir,
                      Charlotte

Dear Kelley,

    Cruising is awesome and Hawaii is so beautiful! I met some cool new people—*Crazie Kazie and Kara-Lee. We're all totally stylin' and we call ourselves the Kgirls! Rockin', right? The best part is . . . you're a Kgirl, too! Miss you tons!*

Love,
Katani

Dear Sam,

This dream trip has been nonstop drama since we got on board! Avery's dad showed up with his girlfriend and they are too sweet! And the captain plays a pirate on board—I sooo have to ask him for some acting tips! Also, I learned the hula. I think I was up onstage dancing longer than anyone else!

XOXO,
Maeve

Dear Elena Maria,

So I have to admit, I was nervous getting on the ship! Not only is it bigger than our house, it's bigger than, like, a hundred of our houses! Luckily Hawaii is beautiful, so I got over being scared pretty much right away (even tho I think the captain is really a pirate!). Can't wait to show you my drawings!

Adios,
Isabel

Dear Scott,

　　If you knew Dad was going to show up on the cruise with Andie and Crazie Kazie, I wish you wouldn't have kept it a secret. Which means if you didn't know, well, "Surprise!"

　　Why me?

Later,
Avery

P.S. The pool has three huge waterslides! And there's a whole mini golf course, and a basketball court, too. Totally sweet.

CHAPTER

5

A Mysterious Voice . . .

Charlotte opened her eyes. Something was moving. *My bed is rocking! Actually, scratch that.* The entire room was moving! She bolted upright and smacked her head against the porthole behind her.

"Ow!" She looked out the porthole to witness the sun peeking up over the horizon, turning the sky orange and pink. Turning back to the room, she saw the outline of Isabel sitting up in her bunk.

"I almost forgot where we were," Charlotte whispered.

"Me too!" Isabel exclaimed, and then clapped her hand over her mouth. "Me too," she said, whispering this time.

Charlotte checked her watch. "It's kind of early, but I was thinking about visiting my dad before breakfast. Want to come?"

"Sure," Isabel nodded. "Anyway, we're not supposed to go anywhere alone."

"Right," Charlotte agreed. She made up the sofa bed and

folded it back into its original position. The springs creaked loudly. She looked to see if she had woken anyone up.

Isabel noticed her checking around the room. "I don't think you're in danger of waking anyone! It would take a hurricane to wake them."

Avery was snoring in the top bunk across the room. Her covers were bunched up around her, and her foot was hanging off the side of the bed, dangling in midair. Beneath her, in the lower bunk, Maeve slept with a pink satin sleep mask over her eyes.

Isabel crept down off the top bunk, still careful not to make a sound. Katani was curled up on the bed below her own. "Avery seemed pretty upset at Katani going off with Kazie and Kara-Lee last night."

"Avery seems pretty upset about a lot of stuff right now. Although if I were in her shoes, I'd probably feel the same way," Charlotte admitted.

"Do you know if she and Katani talked about it?" Isabel asked. She didn't like her friends to be upset at all, but to be upset with one another was the worst.

"I don't think so," Charlotte replied. "I was so wrapped up with my dad being sick . . . and then we all got excited about the postcards. Anyway, they'll work it out."

"I'm sure you're right," Isabel decided. "After all, isn't that what good friends do?"

Charlotte stashed her journal in her book bag and motioned for Isabel to follow her. "Totally. Kinda like how they come along when you visit your sick dad in the infirmary."

Isabel gave her friend a hug. "I'm sure he's feeling better already." Isabel knew what it was like to have a sick parent. She'd moved to Boston so her aunt could help care for her mother's multiple sclerosis. "We should ask Marisol before we leave, though." Isabel reminded her.

Charlotte nodded and knocked lightly on the door to the adjoining cabin. No one answered.

"Maybe she's still asleep?" Isabel whispered.

Charlotte gently pushed the door open.

The two girls turned to each other, wide-eyed. Marisol was gone!

A-Mazed!

"I think we've been down this way before," Isabel said, confused.

"That's funny," Charlotte wondered. "Because I was just going to say that this doesn't look familiar at all."

"We probably should have brought our map." After leaving a note for the rest of the BSG, Charlotte and Isabel set off to find the infirmary on their own and to ask about Marisol.

Charlotte sighed. "I thought I was paying attention to where we were going last night, but all these hallways look exactly the same."

"It's not your fault!" Isabel assured her. "You had plenty of other stuff on your mind. I'd say let's just go back to the room, but we've turned around so many times, I don't even know how to get back there!"

"Okay. My dad always says that when you're lost,

you should just stop and think for a second," Charlotte decided.

She and Isabel studied the green and gold carpet, which extended twenty feet in either direction. There were doorways at either end.

"I think that we need to go that way—" they said simultaneously, each pointing in the opposite direction.

They both burst out laughing. When Charlotte caught her breath, she pointed in the direction that Isabel had wanted to go. "Since you're the artist, you probably remember what things look like better than I do. So I vote your way."

The girls headed off down the hallway and through the door. The passage continued for another ten feet before it turned a corner into another hallway.

"If only there was a sign!" Charlotte sighed, defeated.

Isabel smiled and pointed over Charlotte's head. "Um, Char?"

A sign over Charlotte's head read STAFF QUARTERS.

"Izzy, you're a genius!" Charlotte cried. "Someone here can tell us where the infirmary is!"

"So do we just knock on a random door?" Isabel peered at a little placard beside one of the cabins. "These have names on them," she said.

"Maybe we can find Marisol's room!" Charlotte cheered. "Maybe she went back 'cause she forgot something."

"This one's hers!" Isabel knocked lightly on a door near the end of the hallway, but no one answered. "Do you think she already went back to our room?" she asked, trying to keep the rising panic out of her voice. What if they never found their room again? *What was that number Captain Bob told us to call? Star-100? Or Star-101?*

"Okay, let's try one more time." Charlotte knocked at Marisol's door, this time more loudly. "Hello? Anyone home?"

"*¿Hola?*" Isabel added, just in case.

A reply came from beyond the door. But it wasn't the reply the girls were expecting!

"Help me," a faint voice cried.

Charlotte and Isabel looked at each other.

"Did you hear that?" Isabel asked, grabbing Charlotte's hand.

Charlotte swallowed nervously. "I think it came"— she pointed at the door with a shaking finger—"from in there."

"Maybe she's sick?" Isabel asked nervously.

Or in trouble, Charlotte thought. She didn't want to say it out loud, just in case it was true.

Breakfasting Up

"I hope Charlotte and Isabel aren't upset that we left before they came back," Maeve said, stretching her arms up in the air.

"We waited a whole half hour! And I'm so hungry, I could eat a whale," Avery complained. "If I ate whale. Which I don't. But I don't know if I even have the energy to make it all the way to the dining room."

"You just have a little jet lag," Katani countered. "Besides, Charlotte and Isabel are probably with Marisol. We're being totally responsible—we left a note and we're walking together—so I think we're cool." She turned to discover that Maeve and Avery weren't following her, and so she snapped her fingers. "Earth to the BSG!"

"Maeve's on Planet Boy," Avery mumbled.

Katani watched as Maeve peered at her reflection in a hallway mirror and fluffed her red curls. "Maeve, you look amazing. I know you look amazing because I helped you pick out your outfit," Katani said proudly.

Maeve was wearing a magenta and pink sundress with tiny flowers on the straps as a swimsuit cover-up. They were planning on hitting the pool after breakfast and before horse-back riding. Maeve twirled around, modeling her dress. "Did you see that boy I was *hula*-ing with last night?"

"Maybe if you're lucky he'll be at breakfast," Katani pointed out.

"Which we're never going to get to if we don't motor," Avery added.

Maeve smiled dreamily. Maybe he would be at breakfast! Should she go up and just ask him his name? Was that too forward? What if he'd already had breakfast and was getting ready to leave? Maeve started walking faster, passing by her friends.

"Whoa, slow down," Katani instructed her. "We're supposed to stick together, remember?"

"Yeah, I don't think Maeve is the one who needs reminding," Avery remarked.

Katani stopped in her tracks. She didn't know what was going on with Avery, but she was going to find out. "And *what* does that mean?"

"It means you went off with Crazie Kazie and Kara-Lee last night instead of sticking with your friends!"

"Ave, you can't mean that. Kazie and Kara-Lee don't have anyone their own age to hang out with." Katani was shocked. Avery was the one who always reminded her to be friendly to everyone!

Maeve stared at her friends, wide-eyed. "Um, why don't we just go have breakfast and we can talk about this stuff later?" she suggested. She looked at Avery, who shook her head and just plowed on.

"So Kazie and Kara-Lee can hang out together." Avery couldn't believe that Katani had no idea that hanging out with Kazie wouldn't make her happy.

Is Avery telling me who I can and can't hang out with? Katani was getting annoyed. "I'm just being friendly," she retorted.

"Well, there are a million other people you could be friendly with!" Avery griped. A little part of her wondered, *Why am I acting like this? I must just need some food really badly. . . .*

Katani stared at Avery in disbelief. "I don't get it, Ave. You and Kazie should *obv* be BFFs! She's totally into the same things you're into. I wouldn't mind having Kazie for a sister."

Avery's mouth dropped open. *Who said anything about sisters?* "Well, congratulations!" she yelled. "You can have her!" And with that, she stormed off down the hall.

Katani turned to Maeve, stunned. "What was that all about?"

"She just doesn't like Kazie." Maeve had known that Avery was upset, but she hadn't realized *how* upset. "We better go find her, though. We're not supposed to go off alone!"

"Right," Katani agreed, but when they found Avery, she wouldn't even look at Katani.

"The dining room is just through that door, there," Katani told Maeve. "So . . . whenever Avery calms down, come find me at Mr. Madden and Andie's table, 'kay?"

Maeve could smell the aroma of fresh waffles and bacon. It smelled so good! "Okay . . . but if you see that boy with the cute smile, find out his name for me?" Maeve put an arm around Avery's shoulders as Katani disappeared into the dining room.

Discovered!

Charlotte and Isabel stood frozen outside of Marisol's stateroom. They were both sure they heard a voice ask for help, and then . . . a crackle! But what to do now?

"Do you think we should go get someone?" Isabel asked. She looked around nervously, but the hallway was empty.

"Hang on. Let me see if I can hear anything." Charlotte pressed her ear against the door. "Nope, nothing."

Isabel bit her lip. "I'm going to knock one more time. If we don't hear anything, we go for help."

"Okay." Charlotte moved aside.

"Here goes nothing." Isabel knocked three times quickly on the door.

"Come in!" said a high-pitched voice.

Charlotte and Isabel looked at each other.

"What now?" whispered Charlotte.

"We go in!" replied Isabel, but she didn't look entirely convinced. The voice wasn't bright and cheery like Marisol's, but crackly, like someone with a cold. Was Marisol sick now too? She took a deep breath and turned the door handle. The lock turned with a *click*.

"Here goes nothing," Isabel whispered. She pushed at the door, which swung open with a creak, to reveal . . .

Nobody.

"The ship must be haunted . . . ," Isabel moaned. Just then, she heard a scratching sound and grabbed Charlotte's arm to bolt down the hall!

But Charlotte peered around the door, too curious to run away. "Izzy, look!" The excitement in her voice calmed her spooked friend.

The girls stepped into Marisol's room and Isabel followed Charlotte's pointing finger to a corner near a small closet.

"A parrot!" Isabel cried. Her eyes lit up with relief and delight. She loved birds, she drew birds, but she had never been this close to a parrot before! "It's an African Grey!"

"How do you know that, Izzy?" Charlotte asked.

"'Cause I draw bird pictures and that's what he looks like!" Isabel replied.

The gray bird's white face was flecked with small amounts of red, and he bobbed his head up and down excitedly as he stared at the girls from his perch on top of a folded-up ironing board.

"It looks like he's dancing!" Isabel bobbed her head back and giggled.

"Help me! Help me!" the parrot squawked.

Charlotte tiptoed toward him. "Um . . . Polly want a cracker?"

The parrot tilted its head and looked at Charlotte, confused. She halfway expected him to say, *"Is that the best you can come up with?"*

"¡Hola!" squawked the bird.

"Oh, you speak Spanish, do you?" Isabel gently approached the perch, careful not to spook the bird. *"¡Hola! Un papagayo bonito?"* she asked in a soothing voice. The parrot started bobbing up and down again.

"Ooh, he likes that!" Charlotte whispered. "But where do you think Marisol is?" Isabel was too enraptured by the parrot to worry about their new chaperone.

"Izzy!" Isabel said, pointing to herself.

The parrot started to scoot sideways on his ironing board perch toward Isabel. She leaned down to inspect him more closely when he hopped on her shoulder!

"He likes you." Charlotte smiled.

Isabel blushed. "I guess I've always been studying birds, just in case . . ."

"In case we happened to meet one on our cruise?" Charlotte grinned at the thought.

"Yeah, well, this wasn't exactly what I imagined," Isabel giggled.

"Franco hungry!" the parrot squawked. "Franco *bonito!*"

"Aha, your name is Franco!" Isabel exclaimed. "Franco, nice to meet you!"

Suddenly, the bathroom door burst open and Marisol hurried out, carrying a bag of birdseed and wagging a finger at the parrot. "Franco, *qué pasa . . .*"

She dropped the birdseed on the floor and her face went white when she saw Charlotte and Isabel!

"*¡Oye!*" Marisol exclaimed, putting her head in her hands. "*Lo siento . . .* I mean, I am so sorry! I didn't think you'd be up yet, *ay, qué tonto . . .* what am I going to do?"

"It's okay," Isabel soothed her. "You're not foolish! We just wanted to visit Charlotte's dad, and got lost . . . and Franco told us to come in," Isabel explained. "We're so glad we found you!"

Marisol's eyes darted from the girls to the parrot and back to the girls.

Franco made a clucking sound and rammed his head against Isabel's ear. "Franco love Izzy!" the parrot exclaimed.

6

Kgirl Reunion

Katani entered the dining room alone, taking in the feast of sights and sounds. A huge buffet was set up in the middle of the room, piled high with exotic tropical fruits, as well as traditional eggs and bacon and even a waffle bar. She searched the room for a familiar face.

"Kgirlllll!" a voice shouted over the crowd.

Katani turned and saw Kazie weaving through the crowd, her blond pigtails thwacking unsuspecting passersby.

"I saved you a seat!" she exclaimed, grabbing Katani by the hand.

Kazie had a knack for snaking through the mob of hungry people. She brought Katani back to her table, where Mr. Madden, Andie, and Kara-Lee were finishing up breakfast.

"The Kgirls are back and ready to blast off!" Kazie announced.

"Kazie, why don't you let Katani hit the buffet first," Andie suggested.

Mr. Madden laughed. "You'll learn pretty quick that Kazie's like an instant pick-me-up."

Mr. Madden was right, Katani thought. She was sad that Avery couldn't see that. *All she needs is some time*, Katani thought. Meanwhile, she was going to enjoy her new friends.

"Where are the other girls, and Marisol?" Andie inquired, looking around.

"They'll be here soon," Katani replied, explaining Charlotte and Isabel's note.

Kara-Lee smiled. "Before they arrive, I could go for seconds on breakfast. Shall we?" The Kgirls hooked arms and stormed the buffet.

Family Matters

Maeve and Avery walked together all the way from the dining room up to the top deck without really thinking about where they were going. While Avery brooded, Maeve chattered about all the movies she'd seen recently, and how much fun it was to learn the *hula*. She even shared her theory that her dance partner could be secretly related to Fred Astaire. Maeve figured her bubbly happiness about the cruise had to wash over onto her friend eventually. At least it might take her mind off things.

But when they found themselves at the pool—with its three waterslides, a swim-up juice bar, and a view overlooking the ocean—Avery simply sat down in a lounge chair and sighed. Maeve realized her nonstop-cheerful technique was failing miserably.

"Are you okay?" Maeve asked.

Avery shrugged. *I have no idea if I'm okay!* Right now, looking out at the ocean, everything felt pretty okay, and she knew Katani was one of her best friends . . . so why had she blown up at her?

"I don't know," Avery finally replied. "I'm hungry, but I don't even want to eat."

Wow! Avery, who had boundless amounts of energy, *never* felt like not eating! Something was definitely wrong. Maeve knew she had to make her friend laugh, pronto. The pool was empty except for a tired-looking lifeguard and one older couple in bathing caps. Most of the passengers must have gone to the dining room for breakfast.

"I know what will make you feel better!" Maeve smiled.

"What?" Avery asked.

Maeve took off her cover-up, revealing a matching magenta and white swimsuit. "Look out beloooow!" She took a flying leap into the pool and did an impressive cannonball, spraying water everywhere.

Avery burst out laughing. "Sweet!"

Maeve resurfaced, her red curls flattened to her head. "Told you I'd make you laugh!"

The older couple must have decided they had other places to be—away from giant splashes—and gave the girls a little wave as they toweled off.

"Watch this!" Avery announced. She took a running

jump at the pool, clothes and all! "CANNONBALL!"

Avery hit the water with a tremendous splash. She swam to the surface, and the girls paddled over to the edge, looking out over the side of the top deck onto the ocean. The sun had risen but was still low in the sky, its rays twinkling off the tips of the waves.

"I can't believe you got your hair wet," Avery said. "What if that cute boy shows up?"

"Then he'll see that I'm having fun with one of my best friends," Maeve replied.

Avery smiled. The one thing about Maeve was that even if she was boy crazy, her heart was always in the right place.

"Actually, Ave," Maeve continued, "you should think about that yourself."

"Think about what?" Avery asked, confused. "I hope you're not talking about boys—" *That's the last thing I'd need right now, on top of everything else!*

Maeve cut her off. "I mean that you shouldn't let other people get in the way of having fun. It's not your style, anyway. Weren't you the one who added amendment number four to the Tower rules: 'We should have as much fun as we can'?"

"Oh," she replied, realizing Maeve was right.

"You're on a tropical fantasy vacation with your best friends. Think about how fabulous that is!"

"Yeah, it *is* totally coolio," Avery admitted.

"This is too beautiful a place to let anyone ruin it for you," Maeve continued. "My mom sometimes says, 'The only person who can ruin a beautiful day for you is your-self.'"

Avery stared out over the water. It was a perfect day: blue skies, shining sun, gulls crying and dipping in and out of the waves looking for food. *So what if Kazie's the most annoying person on the planet and won't leave me and my friends alone? I'm still with my best friends . . . for a whole entire week . . . on an amazing cruise . . . in Hawaii!*

"It'll be okay," Maeve reassured her.

Avery nodded, and then looked back out at the waves. She saw something leaping out over the white-crested caps, making tiny little arcs, over and over again.

"Maeve, look! Dolphins!" Avery pointed at a family of dolphins frolicking in the surf alongside the ship. They were having so much fun! *And I'm going to have fun too,* Avery promised herself. *At least, I'll try!*

Maybe Maeve was right. Maybe it would be okay after all.

Friends of a Feather

Isabel scratched Franco's neck. "Marisol, is he yours?"

Marisol hadn't said much since she'd discovered the girls with the parrot. Charlotte wondered where he came from, and especially how he wound up in Marisol's room.

Finally, Marisol opened up. "*Sí,* Franco is mine. Well, sort of . . . excuse me." Marisol strode over and held out her finger. Franco hopped off Izzy's shoulder with an apol-ogetic look.

"Pineapple!" He squawked.

"Not now, *escapista*!" Marisol muttered, opening the closet and shooing Franco into a birdcage hidden behind a rack of clean Aloha cruise uniforms. She left the closet door open and sat down on the bed with her head in her hands, sniffling quietly. "Girls, you won't tell anyone, will you? I'm so, so sorry I wasn't there this morning. Why did I think I could pull this off? I mean, trying to hide Franco on this ship! When they assigned me to stay with you . . . I thought if I got up early enough I could still take care of him . . . but what if he escapes again when I'm not here? I'll lose my job! But I had to take him with me. I did . . ." Her voice trailed off.

She raised her head, and Isabel saw tears running down her cheeks.

"You can trust us," Isabel said. "We promise not to tell! But why are you hiding him?"

"Is there some way we can help?" Charlotte asked.

Marisol shook her head slowly. "No, no . . . this is not your problem, girls. It is mine. And I know it seems *loco*, crazy, but I can explain—"

"Pineapple!" the parrot interrupted.

Marisol sighed and wiped her eyes before picking up the bag of birdseed she'd dropped and filling a bowl inside the cage. "Want pineapple!" Franco complained, but devoured the food, anyway.

"There *was* pineapple, but you ate it all already," Marisol scolded him before turning back to the girls.

"On my twenty-first birthday, I got an e-mail from my

aunt Consuela's neighbor who said my aunt was forgetting things, like to pay her bills or how to get to the grocery store . . . and there was no money to hire a caretaker. So I dropped out of school to care for my aunt."

Isabel and Charlotte nodded but said nothing.

Franco finished up his plate of food and reached through the bars with one foot. Holding the cage with his beak, he was able to slide the lock out and squeeze through the door!

Looking extremely pleased with himself, Franco did a funny crabwalk across from the closet bar to the ironing board, then nudged Isabel's elbow with his head. She made a fist with her hand and held it out, letting Franco hop back onto her arm. He crawled back up her shoulder.

"Franco, what am I going to do with you?" Marisol sighed.

"Tell us about your aunt," Isabel prompted as she stroked Franco's gray head.

"My aunt Consuela is—was—an actress," Marisol continued. "As the former star of many *telenovellas*, she was very particular about who visited with her those last days. She didn't want anyone to see her looking less than her movie star self."

Marisol retrieved a framed picture from her bedside and handed it to Isabel. The black-and-white photograph showed a beautiful young woman, her head thrown back in laughter, holding up a young girl wearing a party dress. "That's me with my aunt Consuela when I was a little girl."

"She's beautiful," Charlotte murmured, looking over Izzy's shoulder.

"Aunt Consuela died just a few weeks after I dropped out of school." Marisol's eyes filled with tears. "But not before she made me promise to find someone to take care of her beloved parrot, Franco."

Franco heard his name and tilted his head to one side. "Kiss kiss Consuela!"

Isabel patted Franco's head, consoling him. "I bet he misses her."

Marisol smiled sadly. "He does miss her. I get along all right with him, but not always. Actually, Isabel, he doesn't let just anyone hold him. You're the first person he's taken a liking to since my aunt died!"

"Love Izzy!" Franco crooned.

Isabel smiled to herself. While she loved birds, she hadn't ever really had a chance to handle one in person. She was secretly delighted to know that she was a sort of "Bird Whisperer."

"I didn't think you were allowed to have pets on the ship," Charlotte remarked cautiously. "Avery wanted to bring our dog, Marty, along, but my dad said that it was against the ship's rules."

"You're right," Marisol whispered apologetically. "I'll lose my job if they find out Franco's here. But I really had no choice! See, I needed money . . . you know. My parents and sister and two uncles all work for the cruise line. They got me this job, which is the best one I've ever had, and I love it . . . but with all the travel, I couldn't leave Franco at home! And he bit every single person who tried to take care of him, so . . ."

"What's going to happen to him now?" asked Isabel, concerned.

Marisol looked embarrassed. "Well, I tried to sell him — though Consuela would have been *muy furioso* — and then one woman who came to look at him told me about this famous bird sanctuary on Maui."

"We're going there, right?" Charlotte remembered Maui from their itinerary.

"Yes. Near the end of the cruise. My family thought I was crazy. They said I should just release Franco into the wild," Marisol told them.

Isabel's eyes went wide. "You can't do that! He's a pet, not a wild animal!"

Charlotte remembered their conversation at dinner from the night before. "My dad said parrots are an invasive species on Hawaii! One parrot flock got to be such a problem, the authorities wanted to kill them."

Marisol looked horrified. "I didn't know that!"

Charlotte nodded. "I need to research the story for my travel journal. It's sad that some people just abandon their pets when they can't take care of them. That's how we found Marty," Charlotte explained. "He was a stray and had been eating garbage."

"I could never abandon Franco," Marisol cried. "But that's what my family thinks I did . . ." she lowered her voice to a whisper. "No one knows he's on board but us."

"And no one will," Charlotte reassured her.

Suddenly, Isabel had an idea. "You should take him back to our room until Mr. Ramsey gets better! I know that Maeve, Avery, and Katani can keep a secret, and you won't have to sneak back and forth anymore."

"Great idea!" Charlotte agreed. "And, it's a bigger room with a huge closet."

Marisol looked worried. "I don't want to get you girls involved. After all, it's my job to look out for you."

"But you won't have *any* job if someone finds him here, right?" Isabel pointed out. "Plus, if they catch him, they might let him go . . . and, and . . ."

"He could get killed," Charlotte finished quietly, shuddering at that horrible thought.

"So, *qué piensas*?" Isabel asked in Spanish. "What do you think?"

"When everyone's on shore leave in Kauai enjoying the activities planned on the island," Marisol plotted, "the ship will be pretty much empty . . . except I'm your chaperone, so I'll probably be with you . . ."

"Just carry him to our room late tonight," Charlotte said. "We can hide him in a pile of towels or something."

"We'll bring back food from the dining room for him," Isabel said. "And keep him company."

"I still don't know . . ." Marisol hesitated, clasping and unclasping her hands. Fresh tears pooled in her eyes.

Isabel hugged her. "I'll draw a picture of him for you. That way, when he's at the bird sanctuary, you'll have something to remember him by."

Charlotte was pretty certain that Isabel would be

drawing more than one portrait of Franco, since Marisol wasn't the only one who would want a memento of the bird.

"Okay, I think you girls have me convinced . . . almost." Marisol checked her watch. "¡*Ayyyy!* We're beyond late! Your friends *must* be awake by now. I am a *chaperón terrible*," she said, switching the words around and pronouncing them in Spanish.

"No, you're the best chaperone ever!" Isabel assured her as Marisol grabbed a map from a pile of papers on her desk and traced the route to the infirmary for the girls. They agreed to meet Marisol and the rest of the BSG outside the infirmary after visiting with Mr. Ramsey. Then they'd go to breakfast together. Hopefully there would still be some food left!

As they turned to leave, Isabel stole one last look at Franco—who was staring right at her from inside the closet!

"*Hola*, Izzy!" he called after her.

"*Hasta*, Franco!" she called back, closing the closet door gently, then following Charlotte into the hallway.

"Do you think we're going to be able to keep Franco a secret?" Charlotte wondered.

"We will," Isabel replied with confidence. *We have to,* she thought to herself. *Franco's life depends on it!*

Secrets to Keep

By the time they reached the ship's infirmary, the sun was up and shining through the windows. Charlotte and

Isabel waved to Mr. Ramsey through the glass window.

"Can we come in?" Charlotte pleaded.

"You'll need masks and gloves," her dad said, coughing.

There was only one nurse in the whole infirmary this early, and the girls managed to find her after knocking on the wrong door and waking up a poor passenger who was there with an allergic reaction to the chlorine in the ship's pool.

Charlotte wasn't happy about wearing a mask, but she was pleased that her dad looked a little better. However, he still wasn't the dad who had surprised her and her friends with a weeklong cruise around the Hawaiian Islands. He had announced it over pizza at one of the BSG's famous sleepovers after getting the approval of everyone's parents.

"So how are you feeling?" Charlotte mumbled through her mask, wishing she could give her dad a big hug.

"Better than ever," Mr. Ramsey croaked, but Charlotte could tell he meant the opposite.

Isabel poured him some water out of a bottle near the bed and set the glass down on his bedside tray. "Do you want us to bring you anything? Something to read?"

Mr. Ramsey took a sip of water, coughed into his fist, and shook his head. "I'm mostly sleeping. What about you two? Are you having fun? Are you taking notes on cruise life for the article?"

"We are," Charlotte promised, "but it would be more fun with you. So get better fast!"

"I'm working on it," he replied. "And Marisol is taking care of you?"

Charlotte and Isabel shared a look.

"That's a definite yes," Isabel assured him. Marisol was taking care of them—and a parrot, too!

7

What to Do, What to Do?

The dining room was filled with the delicious smell of bacon and freshly baked muffins. Avery inhaled deeply and her mouth watered. Her appetite was back about a million-fold after the morning detour to the pool with Maeve, and she needed energy, fast! Especially if she was supposed to go horseback riding for the first time in her life later that morning.

"I'm hitting up that buffet!" Avery declared as she took in the colorful display of fruit, eggs, waffles, and bagels. "What do you think, Maeve? Two or three waffles?"

"Slow down!" Maeve told her. "First, let's find a place to sit." She searched the room and spotted Katani across the room. "C'mon, this way."

Maeve dragged Avery over to discover Katani, Kazie, Mr. Madden, Andie, and Kara-Lee seated around a huge table, finishing up breakfast. Yellow hibiscuses, Hawaii's state flower, adorned the tables.

Mr. Madden stood up to give his daughter a hug. "Hey kiddo, we wondered what happened to you."

"Where's Charlotte, Izzy and Marisol?" Avery asked as her dad gave her a big squeeze, which for some reason made Avery feel a twinge of embarrassment.

"And a good morning to all y'all as well!" Kara-Lee replied.

Avery ignored her and asked again. "Shouldn't Char and Izzy be here by now?" She looked to Katani, avoiding Kara-Lee and Kazie's eyes.

Katani almost gasped at Avery's rudeness. But she reminded herself that Avery was still freaked out from having her dad and his girlfriend show up unexpectedly.

"Oops, Avery, lost your friends?" Kazie teased, laughing.

Maeve looked from Avery to Katani to Kara-Lee to Kazie. *We can't be getting on each other's nerves on day two of our tropical fantasy cruise!* she thought. *This situation calls for some improv!*

"Well, at least they're together!" Maeve chirped brightly. "Now, Kara-Lee, I want to hear you talk talk talk! One day I might have to do a Southern accent and yours is like pancakes with extra syrup on top."

"Aren't you the sweetest!" Kara-Lee declared.

Avery had had enough of the mutual-appreciation society. "Speaking of syrup," Avery interrupted, "I'm grabbing some of that buffet."

"That's my girl!" Mr. Madden said with a twinkle in his eye. He smiled at her lovingly and then went back to talking with Andie.

The only girl he seems to notice is his girlfriend, Avery thought, then caught herself. *Remember the dolphins. Let's up the fun factor!*

Watermelon, pineapple chunks, and waffles—with fresh juicy strawberries—helped her feel less cranky. But even when she sat back down and savored the sweet taste of the fruit, Avery still couldn't get around one thought: *Two seconds on the boat and suddenly Katani's all BFF with Kazie. Why can't Katani, who can see through everyone, see how totally annoying Kazie is?* And Kara-Lee, well, she didn't have anything against Kara-Lee really, except that she was totally hogging Katani's time.

Avery put her head down and dug into her waffles and eggs.

"Slow down, Avery," Katani joked. "It's not going anywhere!"

"She's gonna need all the energy she can get for our *gnarly* day," Kazie declared. "Up high for horseback riding!"

She held her palm out to Avery to get a high five, but Avery didn't even look up. Maeve was horrified! *What happened to our talk by the pool?* She knew Avery was upset, but she had never seen her be mean to anyone! Maeve looked at Mr. Madden, but he and Andie had their heads together and were discussing something. *Good, the lovebirds missed it!* Maeve slapped Kazie's palm instead.

"What are all y'all planning on doing?" Kara-Lee asked the table. She was staring down at an activities brochure.

Katani leaned over Kara-Lee's shoulder. "We should

make a list." Katani loved lists—she was always being pulled ten different ways, so lists helped organize her time and effort.

"Item *numero uno* has to be karaoke! There's a competition when we hit Maui," Kazie exclaimed.

"Definitely!" Kara-Lee declared. "I love to sing! Don't you girls?"

Avery shoved a wedge of pineapple in her mouth. "I just want to snorkel and surf," she muttered to Maeve in between bites.

"The sights below the surface of the water must be *fantabulous*," Maeve agreed, envisioning colorful fish—and maybe even mermaids! *I wish I turned into a mermaid when I went swimming . . .* , Maeve imagined. "Can I see that schedule?" she asked.

Kara-Lee handed her the brochure, pointing out, "Snorkeling's not until the day after tomorrow."

"Hey, this bike ride tomorrow looks fun." Maeve read out loud: "'A leisurely bike ride through historic Hilo and nearby volcanic craters.'" Her eyes grew wide. "Um, is that safe?"

"The volcanoes are as chill as you are," Mr. Madden explained. "Ave, are you shreddy to hang ten? Check it out—surfing, day four!"

"I was born shreddy," Avery replied.

"We can carve up the waves together," he added, giving her a surfer salute: thumb and pinky extended, the rest of the fingers curled closed.

So my dad is *planning on spending some solo time with me.*

Avery swallowed the lump in her throat. She felt bad that she hadn't really made an effort to hang out with him since he'd shown up the night before.

"Yeah, Avery only snowboards, like, twice a year and she totally shreds," Kazie laughed. "Can you imagine what she'd be like if she could hit the runs every day?"

And Kazie ruins the moment once again, Avery thought. Her dad would tell her that Kazie was trying to be nice, but Avery could smell an insult from a mile away. *If only I lived in Colorado like Kazie, I might be a supercharged A-plus boarder too!*

"Just wait till you see how I shred a wave," Kazie told everyone. *"Gnarly."*

"Gnarly" seemed to be Kazie's new favorite word. *And my dad smiles every time she says it!* Avery noticed.

Katani had gotten the brochure from Maeve and was busy copying activities into her planner. Kara-Lee looked impressed. "I don't know how I'm going to manage all of this and not be plum tuckered out," she commented.

"Totally!" said Kazie. "I might hafta hit that buffet for thirds. I need to keep up my energy!" Kazie jumped up from the table and hopped over to the line of people waiting to fill their plates.

"Make sure your eyes aren't bigger than your appetite!" Andie called after her.

Mr. Madden smiled at Andie and gave her hand a squeeze. Maeve caught the gesture out of the corner of her eye. *It's nice to have a touch of romance around the breakfast table!* she thought. Although judging by the look on her friend's face, Maeve was sure Avery didn't feel the same way.

Katani finished her list. "Okay, this is what I have so far." She slid the list across the table to get everyone's input.

girl

Day 1: Yesterday. Honolulu. Arrival.

Day 2: Today. Kauai. Horseback riding.

Day 3: Tomorrow. Hilo. Volcanic bike tour.

Day 4: Day after tomorrow. Kona. Snorkeling and Surfing

Day 5: Maui. Beach day?

Day 6: Maui. shopping???

Kara-Lee studied Katani's list. "You're missing the most important thing!'

"What?" Katani asked, confused.

Kara-Lee took the pen from Katani's hand and scribbled something on the list. She handed the napkin back to Katani. "Now it's perfect!"

Katani looked back at the list.

Day 5: *Maui. Beach day? AND KARAOKE COMPETITION!*
Day 6: *Maui. shopping???*

"The Kgirls are fixin' to rock the mic!" Kara-Lee declared.

"*Kgirls?*" Maeve said.

Kazie had returned with a plate full of waffles. "All our names begin with the letter 'K'," Kazie said, shoving a forkful of pancake into her mouth, "so we're the Kgirls Club!"

Avery's eyes looked like they were about to fall out of her head. As for Maeve, she wasn't exactly sure how she felt either. Katani was a BSG and now she had her own club with Kazie and Kara-Lee!

"We're going to *krush* the competition in karaoke!" Kazie continued. "That's 'krush' with a 'K'."

Maybe Avery's right, Maeve thought. The Beacon Street Girls were supposed to be on this cruise together. It didn't seem right that Katani was going off and forming a club with other girls and leaving them out. *This trip seems to be getting more and more confusing every minute*, Maeve worried.

"Katani, you don't like to sing," Maeve said.

"But I looove karaoke!" Katani blurted out. Except that wasn't entirely true. She didn't mind listening to a karaoke performance, but her friends knew her voice was terrible. But Kazie and Kara-Lee were so excited about performing, she just couldn't let them down!

"I can totally rock a harmony like no one else," Kazie bragged, "so we're a shoo-in to win."

"Yeah, a shoo-in," Katani added weakly. Maeve gave her a weird look, but let it go.

There was a lull in the conversation as everyone finished breakfast and stared at the empty, sticky plates littered with pineapple rinds and waffle crumbs.

Maeve held her stomach. "I don't really feel that much like horseback riding, especially after I ate so much. Can't we just hang out by the pool instead? We could have a BSG pool party!" she exclaimed. "Speaking of the BSG, where are—?"

"Horseback riding will be fun," Katani interrupted. She was relieved that the conversation had turned to something she was *definitely* good at! "Maeve, you mostly just hang on and listen to the instructor. These trail horses know what they are doing. And Isabel and Charlotte are probably with Marisol. They wrote in their note they were going to visit Mr. Ramsey."

"With everything I ate, my horse is gonna hafta do a ton of work," Avery said, sipping on a glass of water. "I probably just gained three hundred pounds."

Maeve laughed at Avery's exaggeration. Everything Avery ate got burned off in about three seconds!

Avery figured horseback riding couldn't be any harder than shredding up the slopes snowboarding, or weaving a soccer ball across the field to score a championship-winning goal. Still, she wished she had made time to go riding with Katani and Kelley when they had invited her to go along. But soccer practice and homework always got in the way.

"Since Mr. Ramsey isn't feeling well, Andie and I are going to tag along and be your chaperones," Mr. Madden informed them. "The activity directors wanted you to stay with your child-care assistant, but I told them, 'No way!' All Mr. Ramsey has to do is sign some forms after breakfast, and it'll be official: Meet your new 'Shore Leave Chaperone.' Call me your SLC!"

"Awesome!" yelled Kazie. "The Kgirls take on the jungle with Jake the Snake!" She high-fived Katani, and Mr. Madden turned to Avery with his palm outstretched.

Avery slapped her dad's hand lamely. *Great, quality time with Crazie Kazie, and a personal escort from my dad . . . and Andie*, Avery thought, cringing.

"Hey guys, sorry we're late!" Charlotte said, rushing in with Isabel and Marisol.

"Where have *you* been?" Maeve wanted to know. "We were ready to send out a search party!"

"We were . . . um . . ." Isabel grasped for the words. She didn't want to keep secrets from her friends, but she couldn't tell them about Franco with Mr. Madden and Andie there!

Charlotte finished her friend's sentence. "We were visiting my dad in the infirmary, like we said in the note. We had a lot to talk about."

Isabel smiled at Charlotte as if to say, *Good save.*

"They needed my help to find the infirmary," Marisol stammered, sweeping her long dark hair back from her face. "You have my *deepest* apologies that I wasn't there to accompany the rest of you to breakfast! I promise it will never happen again."

"No worries!" Jake Madden waved a hand in the air. "We came, we saw, and we conquered that buffet! What's your name, Marianne?" he squinted at her name tag.

"Marisol."

"Nice to meet you, Marisol, I'm Jake Madden, Avery's dad, and I'll be taking the chaperone-baton for the day. You are off the hook!"

Andie smiled at Marisol. "Thanks so much for helping out with this unexpected situation. But we've arranged to take the girls on all of their offshore excursions until Mr. Ramsey gets better."

"It's a pleasure to meet you," Marisol told them. "This is very good. I see that the girls are all together and safe, so I'll just get back to work and meet you all when you return."

Isabel smiled to herself and waved as Marisol left the dining room. She knew exactly what sort of work Marisol had to do—she had to get Franco ready for his new cabin! Isabel didn't know how she was going to contain her excitement all day.

"So," Katani said, rising from the table, "I'd better get ready for horseback riding! Who's coming with me?" She looked at Avery, who wasn't meeting her eye. She wanted to repair this rift between the two of them, and fast. "Ave, I can give you some pointers on riding, if you'd like," she offered.

Avery shook her head. "I'm still finishing my breakfast."

Katani sighed. *Her plate's empty!* she thought, but knew better than to push it. She hoped Avery would come around eventually. She turned to Maeve. "What about you, Maeve?"

"I think I'll stick with Avery," Maeve replied. Maeve knew that Katani's feelings were hurt, but Avery needed her more right now. "You go ahead, and we'll catch up."

Kazie jumped out of her chair. "Kara-Lee and I will come! We'll make it a Kgirls-only event!"

Kara-Lee followed Kazie's lead. "That sounds fabulous!"

Katani felt uncomfortable with "Kgirls only." The BSG never thought of themselves as an exclusive club or clique. They were just good friends. "You guys should come too, after you eat," Katani confided to Charlotte and Isabel, then waved good-bye and followed Kazie and Kara-Lee out of the dining room. Mr. Madden and Andie also excused themselves from the table, telling the girls that they would meet them on the dock.

Charlotte waited until everyone was out of earshot. "The Kgirls Club?" she asked Avery and Maeve. "What's that?"

Avery pushed her empty plate away and rolled her eyes. "You don't want to know."

The Lucky Cap

The dock was a flurry of activity! A mix of passengers, crew, and locals rushed around, although no one seemed to go anywhere.

Maeve pushed her sunglasses on top of her head. "Everyone looks like a tourist."

"That's because everyone *is* a tourist," Avery replied.

"Including you!" Charlotte added. After breakfast, the BSG, minus Katani, had returned to their room to get ready for shore leave. Of course it took Maeve a dozen tries to pick out the perfect sunglasses to go with the perfect tank top and capris.

Maeve lowered her sunglasses—pink tortoiseshell— and beamed the crowd with her best Oscar acceptance smile. "I always try to blend in whenever I go," she said. "It's a sign of a great actress."

"But, Maeve," Isabel asked her, "I thought you wanted to be a star? Don't stars always stick out wherever they go?"

Maeve waved one hand dramatically. "Details, details!"

Charlotte and Isabel burst out laughing, and even Maeve couldn't keep a straight face.

Avery looked around for Katani, Kazie, and Kara-Lee. She refused to call them the Kgirls! "Okay, they left breakfast before we did, so why are we here before they are?"

"I see them!" Charlotte cried out, spying Katani in the

crowd. She jumped up and down and waved her arms until Katani spotted her and waved back. "They're coming this way."

"Great," said Avery under her breath. She wanted to stamp her feet or something. Ever since Kazie showed up she just hadn't been herself at all. Usually, Avery wanted everyone to join the party—the more, the merrier—and now, here she was, wishing that the newcomers would just go away.

Katani jogged up, followed by Kazie and Kara-Lee. They all wore variations on the same outfit—T-shirts and jeans with fabric *leis* threaded through their belt loops. Each girl had her hair braided with ribbons, just like Kazie wore, and the look was topped off with baseball caps.

Maeve studied her friend. "Katani, I thought you hated baseball caps?"

Katani smiled nervously and touched her head, which was adorned with a green Savannah Sand Gnats cap she must have borrowed from Kara-Lee. "Oh, you know me, always on the cutting edge of fashion. Caps are totally *in* on a cruise. "

"Just last week you said they were sloppy," Avery insisted.

"But it works here in Hawaii. Total protection in the tropical sun, don't y'all think so?" crooned Kara-Lee. "Aren't these belts precious?" she continued. "Totally Katani's idea!"

Avery noticed that Kazie was wearing a Boston Red Sox baseball cap . . . one that looked eerily familiar.

"Where'd you get that cap?" she asked suspiciously.

Kazie shook her head, sending her blond braids swinging. "Jake the Snake found this in the house and . . . hey! You're a Red Sox fan, aren't you?"

"Yes," said Avery, seething. "That's my lucky cap!"

"Then you're out of luck, I guess?" Kazie said, laughing. "How lucky can it be if you forgot it?"

Avery looked like she was going to snatch the cap right off Kazie's head! Maeve thought quickly. "Ave, I bet you've got a ton of Red Sox caps at home," she said, putting an arm around her.

"Yeah, and I only have this one!" Kazie exclaimed. "There he is! Jake the Snake, our SLC!" Kazie yelled over the crowd, waving her arms frantically. "Over here!"

Avery watched as Mr. Madden and Andie weaved through the crowd toward the girls. She didn't know who made her more furious: Kazie, who had practically stolen her cap, or her dad, who had just given it away. She didn't leave the cap for Kazie. She *forgot* it. There was a big difference!

"Seriously *gnarly* day for shredding up the horse trail, dudes!" Mr. Madden remarked.

You don't even know the half of it, Avery thought. She needed to talk to her dad about the baseball cap situation, and soon!

"Looks like everyone's here," Andie reported.

"Why don't we snap a quick pic before we take off to parts unknown!" Mr. Madden motioned everyone to gather together and pose in front of the dock.

"Jake, the girls don't want to stop for a picture," Andie said.

"We need to capture the moment! C'mon, everyone smoosh together so I can get all of you! Now say fleas!"

"FLEAS!" yelled everyone.

Mr. Madden snapped the photo. "Sweet!"

Avery tugged at her dad's sleeve. "Um, Dad, you got a sec?"

"Always!" Mr. Madden put his digital camera back in its carrying case. "What's up?"

"Why did you give Kazie my Red Sox cap?" she asked.

"You must have left it after a trip—" he started to say.

"Then you could have just shipped it back to me!" Avery countered.

Mr. Madden knelt down to Avery's level. "I just thought you and Kazie could use the Sox as a way to, y'know, bond."

The problem isn't that we have nothing in common, Avery thought, *the problem is that I don't like her! And on top of that, no matter where I go, or what I do, she's there to mess things up: Dad, friends, vacations, the Snurfer competition . . . there's Kazie cracking jokes at me.* But there was no way she was going to make her dad understand all that.

"I just can't believe you'd give away something that was mine," she said finally in an angry whisper. "That's my cap. Not hers. And you didn't have any right to—" Avery could feel the tears welling up in her eyes. She knew it wasn't really about the stupid cap , but she couldn't help herself.

"Whoa whoa whoa, hang on a second there, Ave," her dad said. "I'll buy you a new one just like it, okay? I just kinda thought you and I, well, I thought we were on the same wave."

"Same wave?" Avery asked.

"It's not what you wear, it's how you tear. Am I right?" He held up his hand for a high five.

Avery couldn't believe it. *He's taking Kazie's side! He knows how much I love the Red Sox.* She swallowed back tears. He was not going to see her cry. And Kazie wasn't going to see her cry, either.

"Ave, don't leave me hanging! Am I right?" He showed her his outstretched palm.

Avery slapped him five. "You're right."

But there wasn't anything right about this situation. Nothing at all.

8

Horsing Around

The twelve-passenger van pulled up to the riding stable in a cloud of dust. The girls piled out of the vehicle one by one. The last was Isabel, who looked a little green.

"That was the bumpiest ride I've ever been on," she moaned.

"Total roller coaster!" Kazie cheered.

Avery snorted. *Does Kazie think she's helping?* "Isabel doesn't like those either."

Charlotte stopped writing in her journal long enough to witness the exchange. She knew what being blindsided by your dad felt like. For a while before the Valentine's Day Dance, she thought her dad was dating Avery's mom! But that turned out to be a big misunderstanding, and there definitely wasn't anything iffy about Mr. Madden and Andie's relationship. Charlotte had a feeling that Avery was going to have to learn to get along with Kazie one way or another. So the real problem was how to even begin to make peace between the two of them!

"Isabel, are you sure you're okay?" Charlotte asked, but she was looking at Avery.

"I hope no one else on this trip is going to end up in that infirmary!" Maeve insisted.

"I just need a second," Isabel said. "Then I'll be fine."

"If you're not feeling well enough to go riding, I can hang back with you," Avery offered. They had arrived at the stables and Kazie was pointing at each of the horses in turn, trying to get Katani to pick out the biggest and strongest one for Kazie to ride. *Who does she think she is, a cowgirl?* Avery wondered. *Wait, make that cowgirl with a 'K'* . . . She chuckled at her little joke.

Isabel shook her head. "I'm fine, Avery! Promise." She'd been riding before in Texas at her sister's big *quinceañera* party, and she wasn't going to miss out on this opportunity for anything!

A man in jeans and a red T-shirt that read KAUAI ISLAND STABLES in big, bold letters walked up to them. "Hi, everyone! I'm Kai Paele. I'll be your riding instructor and guide for today. Has anyone here ridden before?"

Andie, Isabel, Katani, Kazie, and Kara-Lee raised their hands, along with several other strangers in the crowd.

Charlotte whispered to Isabel, "Does riding a camel or an elephant count?"

Maeve looked around and noticed "that boy" from the ship with the cute smile. His hands were stashed firmly in his pockets. *Phew! I won't be the only beginner . . . and I can finally find out his name!* Maeve tried to catch his eye, but the guide cleared his throat and Mr. Madden pointed at Maeve to pay attention.

"Just a few pointers. You keep calm, your horse stays calm. If you feel like you're going too fast, pull back on the reins. There's no need to worry if you're new to this. Our horses here are so gentle that you could let a puppy dog ride 'em," Kai continued.

For the first time that day, Avery smiled, thinking of Marty wearing a little cowboy hat and boots, riding a horse!

"And they know the trail, so you'll be able to sit back and enjoy the sights that Mahaulepu has to offer. It's a popular tourist destination, but also sacred to native Hawaiians, and home to many species of rare and endangered plants and animals."

Isabel clutched her bag close to her chest. She was thrilled that she had remembered to bring her sketchpad to draw all the local wildlife.

"Excited?" Charlotte asked.

Isabel nodded. "I hope we see some birds!"

"Like African Greys?" Charlotte whispered.

Isabel giggled. "Hopefully not until we get back on the ship!"

"Now if you'll all follow me," Kai said to the crowd, "I'll get you saddled up and ready to go!" He motioned for them to follow him over to the barn.

Andie walked alongside Avery. "Ave, I'm shocked that you haven't been riding before! You're so athletic!"

Avery shrugged. "I just never really thought about it before. It kinda seems like the horse does all the work and the rider just sits there!"

"Well, I bet you're a natural," Andie said brightly, putting her hand on Avery's shoulder.

Out of the corner of her eye, Avery noticed Kazie glaring at them. "Maybe." Avery shrugged, and then a weird thought occurred to her. *Andie is acting like my mom!* That was something Avery was not prepared to deal with. *I already have a mom*, Avery thought as she ran ahead to catch up with Charlotte and Isabel. *And why doesn't Andie get that crashing my vacation was a terrible idea?*

Welcome to the Jungle

The line of horses ambled along the trail that ran through the jungle under a canopy of trees, shielding the riders from the morning sun. Birds chirped and insects buzzed, providing them with a sound track to the ride. Isabel tried to take it all in. Kai was right, Mahaulepu was spectacular—a virtually untouched natural resource. She heard a rustling in the bushes and craned her neck to see if she could spot anything.

"As you can witness for yourself," Kai told them, "Mahaulepu is host to some pretty spectacular native plants, animals, and birds."

A ducklike creature with a black and white head and speckled black and white feathers waddled out of the bushes.

"That's a—" Kai started to say.

"A nene!" Isabel blurted out. She covered her mouth and blushed red. "Sorry!"

Kai smiled. "No, no, that's good! Not many people have heard of a nene or could identify one on sight!"

Kazie laughed. "A *nay-nay*? It sounds like a name you call someone."

"The nene is Hawaii's state bird," Isabel said.

"That's right," Kai turned in his saddle and smiled at Isabel. "It's been brought back from near-extinction. We're lucky even to see one!"

All the riders *ooohed* and *ahhhed* as the gooselike bird poked around in the bushes, looking for something to eat.

Avery noticed that Kazie looked like her wings had been clipped. No one thought her joke about the bird's name was funny.

"Is there a conservation program or something to help Hawaii's native birds?" Avery asked, perking up a little. She had always been into the environment and saving the planet. Maybe the Green Machine ecology club she'd started at school could take up the nene as their next cause!

"Yes," Kai answered, obviously pleased that these tourists cared about Hawaii's wildlife as much as he did. "There are several programs. I can provide more information if you like after the ride. Thanks to dedicated conservationists, the nenes are slowly coming back!"

Isabel balanced her sketchpad against her horse's mane, trying to get the small black and white goose on paper before it disappeared into the jungle thicket.

"Isabel, you're amazing," Charlotte remarked. "I can barely get a picture with my camera and you're sketching on horseback!"

Isabel was proud that she remembered everything her cousins in Texas had taught her about riding. She stroked her gray mare's neck to keep her calm, and held up the drawing to show her friend. "It's rough, but I can fill it in when we get back." Then she clicked her tongue and squeezed her legs to tell her horse to walk forward.

Charlotte tucked her camera back in her pocket. "I got a photo, but it might be a little blurry."

Charlotte wasn't just trying to shoot pictures like a tourist. She wanted to capture the feeling of being here on horseback, riding through Mahaulepu's ancient jungle trail. Her father always reminded her that his goal as a travel writer wasn't just to list the pros and cons of going to a certain place, ticking off details, but to make the reader feel like he or she was *there*. A travel writer's job was to evoke the sights and the sounds of being somewhere else. And since her dad was sick in the ship's infirmary, Charlotte knew it was her job now.

The girls caught up to Kai, who had paused under a tree with branches that stretched out like arms draped with fernlike leaves and bright red flowers.

Twisting jungle branches capture red fireworks of flowers, Charlotte thought, hoping she'd remember to write it down later when she had a free hand.

As they crossed over the small creek running past the base of the tree, a royal poinciana, Kai had called it, Avery held tight onto her horse's neck. She still wasn't sure about this riding thing. She loved horses, but leaving the walking up to someone else wasn't something she was used to. It reminded her of the time her brothers always kidded about when she was three years old and her dad was pushing her in the stroller and she yelled out, "Lemme walk!"

Avery looked for her dad to remind him about it, but he was taking a picture of Andie smiling on her horse. He'd already taken about a million pictures of her, and only one of Avery. *Spending time together seems to mean spending time with Andie,* she fumed. *I don't even know whether I'm jealous or angry or just upset!* Avery exploded inside. *One second Kazie's on my nerves, then Dad's acting weird, then Andie's pretending to be my mom . . . I wish that I had never come on this trip!*

Spooked

Up ahead on the trail, the Kgirls' horses ambled side by side. Kai was right—the horses seemed to know their way through the jungle without any help from their riders. Katani relished the feeling of moving in tune with her horse's gait.

"You've got a great seat, Katani," Kara-Lee remarked in her Southern drawl.

"Excuse me?" Kazie said. "Did I hear you right?"

Kara-Lee's eye grew wide. "Oh, I am so sorry! That's a compliment: It means Katani's a good rider!"

Kazie burst out laughing. "Ha! Sweet seats all around!"

Maeve's horse was a few steps behind, and Maeve

wasn't feeling all that confident in her seat. She wobbled and grabbed her horse around the neck to steady herself. Knowing how to ride a horse was practically a necessity as an actress, especially if she wound up stranded in one of those flowering trees, waiting for Indiana Jones, played by her idol Simon Blackstone, of course, to come galloping in on an Arabian horse . . . *a world-famous stallion that's in Hawaii because he was smuggled in on a ship along with crates full of gold and jewels!*

Maeve's fantasy was rudely interrupted when her horse (a plain-looking, lazy, brown and white pinto) took an extra-large step over a rock, jostling her already-sore rear end. Riding was trickier than she had expected. And it was hard to look good doing it, as humidity was not a friend to those with naturally curly hair!

As Maeve tugged at a knot in her red mass of curls with one hand while trying awkwardly to hold on to the saddle with the other, she realized the boy she had been dancing with the night before at dinner was riding right behind her! *Just my luck* . . . Maeve thought, but quickly regained her composure. "Hello, *hula* partner!" she cooed.

He rode up next to Maeve and smiled, exposing perfectly white teeth that gleamed in contrast to his tan skin. His hair fell in thick, brown waves to his shoulders. *He looks like a surfer out of a summer movie,* thought Maeve. She worked up her most bewitching smile.

"I don't believe we formally met the other night. I'm Maeve."

He smiled again, and her heart did a little leap. "I'm

Chad," he responded. "Um, I think my horse wants to be first. He keeps passing everyone. Excuse me!"

Tall, good-looking, and polite! Maeve thought as Chad and his horse went bouncing past.

But then Maeve's lazy horse picked up the pace for the first time all morning! It was as if he didn't want to be left behind. "Whoa!" she shouted, but it didn't seem to work.

"Pull back on the reins," Chad suggested, laughing. He sounded sort of like Maeve's brother, Sam, when he got stuck in a high-pitched giggling fit, but of course Chad was *sooo* much cuter. Maeve pulled on the reins, and her horse slowed, right next to Chad's.

"Are you doing okay?" he asked. "You were looking a little wobbly there," he said, sounding half concerned and half amused as he shook in his saddle, imitating her.

Maeve brushed aside her suspicions that this boy acted like her little brother. Boys just took longer to mature than girls. Those were the facts of life. "First-time jitters. I've never been horseback riding before."

"Neither have I," Chad confessed. "But I learn quickly. I live in California, so I'm mostly the surfing type."

Maeve was right! He was a surfer boy! "California! As in Hollywood?" she asked.

"Los Angeles," he replied. "My parents took me and my friend Will on this trip to celebrate my birthday. It's in a couple of days."

"Happy early birthday!" Maeve said. She wondered how old he was going to be. He was tall, so maybe fourteen? Just as she was about to ask, another kid—Chad's friend Will, she guessed, rode up and gave Maeve a thumbs-up.

"Rad moves, horse girl!" he said.

"Shut up!" Chad shoved at his friend. "We can't wait to try out a coupla of moves we've been practicing on these *rad* Hawaiian waves. Do you surf?" he asked.

"I do now!" she exclaimed. Will looked confused, but Chad laughed. *He gets my sense of humor!* Maeve blushed. "Actually, my friend Avery's the only one of us who's even been to Hawaii before, and she's a pretty good surfer—" She looked around to introduce Avery. "Where'd she go?"

Chad gently tugged at his reins, slowing down his horse. "That's not her, is it?" he asked, pointing behind him.

Avery was about fifteen feet behind the group on her horse, which wasn't moving at all. "Ave, are you okay?" Maeve called back.

"He won't budge," Avery responded. Her dark brown horse's nose was buried in a nearby bush, and he chewed happily on the leaves.

"I'll get help!" Maeve yelled back.

Avery sighed. Great, everyone was now going to see than she had no idea what she was doing on horseback. *Didn't Kai say these horses knew what to do? It's more like they do what they want!*

"Giddyap?" Her horse didn't move, except to shake his mane and make a *whuffing* sound as he poked around for more food. "Oh, c'mon, please?" Avery begged.

Maeve called ahead. "Excuse me! Kai!" Kai couldn't

hear her over the buzz of the forest, so Chad put his fingers in his mouth and whistled.

That got Kai's attention! "We need your help back here!" Maeve explained.

Kai raised his arm, signaling all riders to stop. "Hang on, we've got a small situation."

"Situation?" Mr. Madden asked.

Avery could hear everyone discussing her up ahead. *Great, Dad didn't even realize I was gone*, she thought. *He probably would have noticed if it were Andie!*

"Sometimes the horses get a little fussy," Kai said. "It's important not to let them start eating the vegetation, or they won't stop! Just hold on." He turned his horse around and galloped back toward where Avery was stuck.

Avery realized everyone had stopped and turned to look at her. There hadn't been a sport yet that she wasn't able to conquer, but it looked like horseback riding was going to be the first. There was nothing more embarrassing than having to be rescued! It made her look so helpless— her worst nightmare. And naturally, it had to happen in front of Kazie!

"Kai to the rescue!" Kazie whooped.

Avery just knew the K's were all laughing at her. She dropped her reins on the horse's neck just as a bird burst out of the bush he was chomping on!

The horse took off at a gallop! She grabbed for the reins and held on tight as her horse took off down the trail, shooting past the entire group of riders. Everything was rushing past her in a blur.

"Pull back!" Avery heard everyone yell. Maeve and Chad were shouting loudest of all. *And is that Kazie's crazy laugh I hear?* Avery finally managed to grab the reins and pull back, and the horse suddenly came to a halt.

Kai caught up with her. "Well, that was quite a scare. Looks like your horse got spooked by that bird. You okay? You did a super hero job of catching him up."

Avery caught her breath and waited for her heart to stop beating a million times a minute. She was terrified, but she wasn't about to let anyone know! "I'm fine."

Kai looked skeptical. "Okay, but how 'bout you ride up here next to me? You'll be my riding buddy!"

Katani rode up alongside Avery and the guide. "Slapping the reins against your horse's neck is a cue for him to go faster," Katani warned her. "So you've got to be careful. Also, if you sit back and concentrate all of your weight in back, it'll be an easier ride. Here, look at me."

Avery didn't want Katani's tips! Or anyone else's, for that matter. She just wanted this ride to be over—NOW. *Humiliation. That's what this is.*

"Chill out, Katani," Avery muttered through gritted teeth, "I'm fine. Go back to the Kgirl club."

Katani bit her lip. It was clear that Avery wasn't fine at all. She stared at her for a long second then pulled her horse back and let Avery continue on.

Oblivious to Avery's embarrassment, Kai continued the horseback tour. "Now what we've got coming up here are rock formations and the caves of Mahaulepu," he said.

"You'll see some ancient petroglyphs carved on the rock faces."

"What's inside the caves?" Charlotte asked.

"Cave wolf spiders," Kai replied.

"Ewwwwww!" everyone groaned.

Spiders? Avery perked up a little. Maybe the rest of the ride wouldn't be so bad after all. "Tell me more about these wolf spiders?" she asked Kai, ignoring the Kgirls, who of course preferred to ride a safe distance away from the creepy caves.

CHAPTER

9

A Sight for Sick Eyes

ater that evening, all the girls paraded through the maze of hallways to the infirmary, eager to show off their party attire and tell stories about their day to Mr. Ramsey. The evening's dinner theme had been "Tropical Black Tie." Maeve stopped to admire herself in a mirror as they passed by the ship's lounge.

I could wear this dress to the Oscars, she decided. It had been a fairy-tale day so far. She almost fainted at the sight of Chad in a tuxedo and floral bow tie, and he said she looked like a "movie star." Maeve knew it was destiny that landed them both on the same cruise!

Avery doubled back to retrieve her. "Maeve, your reflection will always be there, but visiting hours are only for another thirty minutes!"

Maeve blew herself a kiss in the mirror and they caught up to the rest of the girls.

Avery had been feeling pretty good ever since she managed to actually spot one of the endangered wolf spiders near the end of the ride and earn Kai's eternal gratitude for promising to start a save-the-nenes-and-wolf-spiders campaign as soon as she got back home. The rest of the BSG weren't sure how AAJH would feel about this new plan for the Green Machine club, but knew better than to argue. Maybe the spider thing would pass.

Katani looked down at her watch. "I don't want to be late to meet the Kgirls at the pool."

"Nope, wouldn't want to be late for *that*," Avery said. She sounded cheerful, but Charlotte knew better. Even a new environmental cause wasn't enough to dissolve the tension building between Avery and Katani.

"C'mon, guys, it's just this way," Charlotte said, motioning them forward. There wasn't anything she could do about that tension right this second!

"Everyone's invited to hang out with us," Katani insisted, "just so you all know." She wished the BSG would just give the Kgirls a chance. Kazie and Kara-Lee were the coolest people Katani had met in a long time, but her best friends kept forcing her to choose who to hang out with! *I can spend as much time as I want with the BSG when we get back home*, Katani told herself. *My only chance to hang out with the Kgirl Club is now, on this cruise. And it's not my fault nobody wants to hang out all together, is it?*

None of the girls said anything more. Instead they followed Charlotte in silence as she led them up a small stairwell. They turned left, then right, and then went up another flight of stairs. Suddenly they were standing in front of a door that read INFIRMARY.

"Okay, I'm all turned around. I can't believe you and Izzy didn't get totally lost coming here, Char," Maeve remarked.

Charlotte smiled at Isabel. "Oh, we did!" She held open the door to the infirmary and the girls tiptoed in, not wanting to wake anyone who might be resting.

"Charlotte, Isabel, so nice to see you again," said Dr. Steve. "I just checked on your father. He's doing much better."

"Is he well enough to leave?" Charlotte asked hopefully.

"Not quite," he said, "but here are some masks and gloves so you can go visit him. He's awake." He handed out blue paper masks to all of the girls.

"Does this come in pink?" Maeve asked. Dr. Steve laughed and shook his head. "Oh well, still *très dramatique!*" Maeve quipped to Charlotte.

Charlotte didn't answer. She looked befuddled as she struggled with the ties on her mask. Isabel came over to help her. "Just pretend it's Halloween! Or you're on Maeve's TV drama," she said.

Dr. Steve opened the door to Mr. Ramsey's room. "You can go in now."

The girls filed into the small room, where Mr. Ramsey was propped up on a pillow, reading a book. "Well, there's a sight for sick eyes."

Charlotte rushed over to her father's bedside and gave him a quick hug. "When can you leave?"

Mr. Ramsey sighed. "Careful, there. I'm still contagious!

I need to stay for another couple of days. But they're tak-ing great care of me here. I'll be right as rain in no time."

"But without the rain part," Avery said seriously. "There's still surfing to do."

"Gotcha," Mr. Ramsey replied. "Marisol stopped by before dinner to fill me in on everything you've been up to."

Isabel and Charlotte shared a quick look. Not *every-thing* they were up to, they were sure about that! When they got back on the boat after horseback riding, Marisol had been there to greet them, and let them know that a certain someone named Franco had been delivered safely to Mr. Ramsey's closet. They'd been in such a hurry to get ready for dinner, though, that they hadn't yet had a chance to tell the rest of the BSG!

"You guys are going easy on Mr. Madden and Andie, right?" he teased.

"They've been just lovely!" Maeve exclaimed. "It's so delightful to have a dash of romance in the trip."

Mr. Ramsey looked at Maeve with a bemused expres-sion. Of all Charlotte's best friends she was definitely the quirkiest.

Avery groaned. She was tired of Maeve's romance obsession, although the more she watched her dad and Andie, the more she realized that Maeve was right. It was one thing visiting her dad in Telluride and seeing him there with Andie, but seeing them together, here, just a few months later, was just too weird to handle.

"It's been great, Mr. R., but we're ready to have you back," Avery added. "Y'know, back to normal."

"Don't worry, we're having a really amazing time," Katani added. "Kazie and Kara-Lee are way fun. They're practically like Beacon Street Girls now!"

If Katani thinks Kazie's ever going to be part of the BSG, Avery thought, *I'll start calling her Crazy Katani!*

"Oh, good," Mr. Ramsey responded. "But I have to confess, I'm a little concerned about my article. While I can write about my excellent care in the infirmary and the competence of the shipboard doctors, I don't think that's what they're looking for in my piece."

He started folding the corner of the page in the book he was holding back and forth. Charlotte knew this was something her dad did only when he was nervous. "It's okay, Dad, Isabel and I totally have you covered."

Charlotte held out her journal. "I've started a piece about the feral parrot problem, and I jotted down some observations about today's horseback riding trip through Mahaulepu. I'm also taking lots of photos."

Isabel retrieved her small sketchpad from her purse and handed it to Mr. Ramsey. "These are just quick drawings, but I'll turn them into larger sketches."

Mr. Ramsey's whole face lit up with astonishment. "Girls, if I weren't contagious I'd give you both giant bear hugs!" He coughed into a napkin. "Excuse me—*cough*—this is—*cough*—just wonderful . . . very creative!"

Flipping slowly through every page of Charlotte's journal, Mr. Ramsey kept nodding and smiling. "Charlotte, I do believe you inherited the Ramsey writing gene!" He was equally mesmerized by Isabel's sketches. "It looks like this bird could just fly off the paper! And you drew this on horseback?" He handed the sketchpad and journal back to the girls. "Thanks to you two, I can stop worrying about my article and concentrate on getting better."

"Which means you're one step closer to recovery," Dr. Steve said from the doorway. "But for now, Mr. Ramsey needs his rest." He held the door open while the girls said their good-byes and filed out of the room.

Charlotte untied her mask and breathed a sigh of relief. "Well that's one less thing to worry about."

"One less thing?" Maeve asked. "Is there something else to worry about?"

Isabel took a deep breath. "There's something that Charlotte and I have been meaning to tell you guys."

"Actually, it would be better to show you," Charlotte continued. "But it's back in the room."

Katani checked her watch. "I'm totally late to meet Kara-Lee and Kazie at the pool. You can show me later, right?"

"Yes, but . . . ," Isabel started.

"It won't take long. And it's kind of important," Charlotte finished.

Katani shook her head. "I'm beyond late. Why don't you guys just come to the pool and we can do that later?"

All four girls shook their heads. *We have to feed Franco, first!* Isabel was thinking. Of course Avery wasn't interested, and Maeve was too intrigued by whatever it was her friends had to show them all to take a detour up to the pool.

Katani sighed. "Listen, I told them I was coming, so I'm going to just go meet them and I promise to catch up with you guys real soon." She waved and took off down the hallway.

Charlotte was in shock. "Didn't she hear me say this was important?"

"I don't know," said Isabel. She was just as confounded as Charlotte was at Katani's behavior.

Maeve sighed. "Listen, I like Kara-Lee and Kazie. I do! But this whole Kgirl club thing? It seems kinda like a clique."

"She did just invite us to hang out with them," Isabel said, defending Katani. She could see Maeve's point, but she didn't want to take sides.

"You're right, Izzy. But did she really want us to come?" Charlotte wondered. "I don't want to sound mean or anything, but she's been spending way more time with them than us. We were supposed to stick together so my dad could get all our different perspectives on cruise ship life!" Charlotte was feeling energized by her dad's enthusiasm for her writing. *But how am I supposed to fill in for him if the BSG can't even get along?*

Finally, they get it! Avery thought. "Kazie is trouble. I've been trying to warn you guys all along!" she exclaimed.

"Okay, this is our room," Isabel declared, cutting off an argument before it could get started. "Prepare yourself for something pretty cool."

Inside the room, Isabel instructed everyone to change out of their nice clothes and into jeans and T-shirts.

"What sort of surprise do you have to dress down for?" Maeve wondered.

"Just trust us," Charlotte instructed her.

Once everyone was changed, Isabel led them over to the adjoining door to Mr. Ramsey's stateroom. She knocked first, but Marisol wasn't back yet. She'd been called away for a staff meeting while the girls visited with Charlotte's dad.

"Ready?" Isabel asked. Maeve and Avery nodded. Isabel looked to Charlotte.

"Whenever you are, Izzy!" Charlotte stepped aside.

Isabel opened the door.

"FRANCO LOVE IZZY!" Franco declared.

"Aaaaaaaaaaaahhh!" Maeve screamed.

"Aaaaaaaaaaaahhh!" Franco screamed back, imitating Maeve.

Avery burst out in a fit of giggles. "Maeve, that was so awesome! You totally freaked! And freaked out this poor guy—"

"His name's Franco," Isabel said. It obviously hadn't taken him long to not only escape his cage, but get out of the closet as well.

Isabel retrieved the escape artist bird from his haphazard perch on Mr. Ramsey's travel radio and carried him over to her friends. "Franco, please meet Avery and Maeve."

Maeve caught her breath and turned her head to one side to get a better look at the parrot. He bobbed up and down on Isabel's arm, clearly excited at all the activity, then turned his head to one side, just like Maeve! "Didn't anyone tell you it's rude to mimic people!" she scolded.

Franco bowed his head, looking ashamed. "Franco bad!"

Avery giggled again. *This trip suddenly got a whole lot better!* "So who does he belong to? Is he ours?"

"I wish!" Isabel sighed. She explained the situation with Marisol, the promise she made to her aunt, and how she snuck out that first morning to take care of Franco. "She's taking him to a bird sanctuary in Maui," she finished sadly.

"The important thing is that he's somewhere safe," Avery reminded her friend. "Remember that story your dad told us about, Char? About those poor feral parrots on Maui?"

Charlotte nodded. "Mhmm. We can't let the cruise people set him loose."

"We're really helping Marisol out!" Isabel added. "She could lose her job if they caught her with a bird on board." Isabel showed Avery how to hold her arm so Franco would perch there. The parrot gingerly stepped off Isabel's shoulder and onto Avery's outstretched arm.

Maeve wasn't convinced. "But aren't birds noisy? And messy?" she protested.

"We can take care of everything!" Avery exclaimed.

"He'll be the newest member of the BSG! Our very own onboard Marty!"

"At least until we get to Maui," Charlotte chimed in. "But no one can know he's here."

Avery giggled. "So he's *exactly* like Marty!"

"Marty smelly!" Franco squawked, sending Avery into such a fit of giggles, Franco flapped off her arm and landed right on Maeve's shoulder!

Maeve squeaked in surprise and tried to shake the bird off her shoulder, but he would have none of it. "Get him off!" she begged Isabel. "What if he . . . what if . . ."

That's when the unspeakable happened. "Oops!" Franco said happily, hopping from Maeve back to Isabel. All the girls stared at the drippy white blob running down the front of Maeve's T-shirt.

"Ewwwwww!" Maeve screamed.

"Yuck," Charlotte agreed.

Avery wasted no time in running into Mr. Ramsey's bathroom and retrieving a giant roll of toilet paper, which she tossed to Maeve in a perfect football throw that would have made her brother Scott proud. Unfortunately, Maeve didn't even see it coming! But Franco did, and snatched at the end of the white paper, flying up toward the ceiling to perch on the curtain rod with paper trailing down from his beak as the roll spun across the floor and under the bed!

"Um, at least you changed out of your nice dress . . . ?" Isabel tried to cheer up Maeve as she crawled around on the floor, bunching up the runaway paper.

Charlotte took the wad from Isabel and wiped at Maeve's shirt.

"I'll get her a new shirt!" Avery shouted and returned with the first thing she found in Maeve's giant suitcase.

"But that one doesn't *match*!" Maeve wailed dramatically, finally coming out of her state of frozen shock.

"There are things that don't match jeans?" Avery said with a baffled expression, staring at the lacy blue and purple striped shirt she had grabbed.

Maeve looked so tragic, and Avery so confused, that Charlotte and Isabel couldn't keep in the laughter. When Franco dropped the last of the toilet paper and started laughing along too, with a weird, almost robotic-sounding *ha-ha-ha*, even Maeve stopped feeling sorry for herself and joined in!

Operation Feed Franco

Once everyone had calmed down, and Maeve had found a clean, *matching* shirt (thankfully she had brought enough clothes for an extra week of cruising), Avery got down to business.

"I think it's totally cool that we're helping out Marisol," Avery began. "But for now, we need to figure out Operation Franco. Number one: Who cleans up after him?"

"We take turns," Isabel suggested. "If only Katani were here to make a schedule!"

Avery was too happy about the parrot to feel upset that Katani wasn't here. "She can help with a schedule when she comes back. Let's keep going. Two: What are we going to feed him?"

"Franco hungry!" the parrot squawked. Suddenly his wings were a blur as he flew down from the curtain rod to Isabel's shoulder.

"Will he warn us before doing that again?" Maeve stuttered.

"We have plenty of birdseed," Isabel started to say, finding the bag Marisol had left with the cage in the closet. But Franco had a different idea.

"Pineapple! Love pineapple!"

Maeve smiled. "I like pineapple too, but—"

"Pineapple!" the parrot insisted.

"See Maeve? He can order his own dinner!" Isabel declared.

Charlotte looked in the mini-fridge in her father's room. "Except we don't have any pineapple."

"And the dining room is closed," Avery added.

Isabel thought about it for a moment. "If he eats pineapple, I'm going to find him pineapple," she said with a determined look on her face. She tried putting Franco back into his cage in the closet, but he climbed across her back from one shoulder to the other to avoid her hands.

"Franco sad! No go! No no no!"

"He's kind of overdramatic," Maeve commented.

"You're one to talk!" Avery laughed.

"Marisol told us her aunt who owned him forever was an actress," Charlotte said.

"In *telenovelas*!" Isabel added.

"Oooh! A parrot *de amor*," Maeve crooned to Franco. "I like you better already!"

"I guess Franco will just have to come with us," Isabel decided.

"He can't come with us," Charlotte cautioned her. "What if he gets caught?"

"Oh, no!" squawked Franco.

"Oh, no, is right!" Maeve said, then sighed. "Great, now you've got me talking to a bird!"

"Franco love Izzy," Franco cooed, and Isabel melted inside.

"How could you say no to a face like that?" she pleaded to the other girls.

"So where are we off to?" Avery asked, ready for a parrot adventure.

Isabel thought it over for a second. "Maybe we can take him to the upper deck? Sometimes people have snacks before bed. There may be leftovers."

"That idea just might work!" Charlotte agreed.

10

Pineapple, Pineapple Everywhere

They made it to the upper deck without being seen. The night was cool and clear, the moonlight casting shadows along the deck.

"I have to say, that's a pretty good disguise, Izzy," Charlotte whispered.

Franco poked his head out between two buttons of Isabel's bulky raincoat. She hadn't wanted to pack the jacket in the first place, but now she was glad her Aunt Lourdes had insisted.

"¡Hola!" the bird said.

"Not a peep!" Isabel whispered. Franco bobbed his head up and down and then pulled his head back through the jacket so he was hidden from sight. Isabel hoped that meant "yes."

"Jackpot!" whispered Avery. The tables next to the lounge chairs were littered with empty glasses garnished with uneaten wedges of pineapple.

"Pineapple!" squawked Franco.

"Shhhhh!" Isabel cautioned the demanding bird.

"We're on it!" Avery whispered. She, Maeve and Charlotte went from table to table, collecting the fruit in wadded-up napkins from the abandoned drinks. When they had gathered as much pineapple as they could hold, they brought it all back to Isabel and started feeding the parrot through the buttons in the raincoat.

Franco was in food heaven. "Franco love pineapple!" he exclaimed. His curved beak made small work of the triangle-shaped yellow slices, and soon they were all gone.

"I love me pineapple as well!" a voice bellowed out. *Oh, no!* The girls turned to see Captain Bob at the other end of the deck, *coming right toward them!*

Isabel glanced around. "Omigosh! There's nowhere to hide!" she whispered frantically. "What are we going to do?"

"Keep that bird quiet and follow my lead," Maeve replied.

"Shhh, Franco!" Isabel warned him.

Maeve adjusted Isabel's raincoat and motioned for everyone to huddle around their friend. "Hey, Captain Bob!" she called out coolly as he approached. "Beautiful night, isn't it?"

"It is!" Captain Bob replied. He looked at Isabel's raincoat, confused. "Was it raining?"

"Oh, Izzy just caught a chill." Maeve smiled.

"Charlotte's dad is still sick, so we don't want to take

any chances," Avery continued in a rather professional-sounding voice.

Charlotte and Isabel looked at each other, amazed. They knew Maeve was an improv pro, but Avery?

"Captain Bob, shouldn't you be, I don't know, like steering the ship?" Maeve asked.

Captain Bob tipped his hat to them. "Aye, but me first mate has it handled. After me grub I like to take a stroll abovedecks. It's better than walkin' the plank!"

"Walk the plank!" screeched Franco from inside the raincoat.

Captain Bob raised an eyebrow. "Did one of you just say something?"

Charlotte, Maeve and Avery crowded around Isabel, who smiled uncomfortably. "Quiet," she mumbled.

"Excuse me?" Captain Bob puffed out his chest.

Maeve erupted in a fit of laughter. The girls looked at her confused, but she motioned for them to follow along. "Oh, Captain Frawley." Maeve waved a hand like she was explaining something perfectly simple, even though she didn't know yet what she was going to say!

"Isabel and Avery," Maeve started slowly, buying herself some time . . . "They, well, umm." A light went on in Maeve's eyes. "They're just practicing being, you know . . . ventriloquists!

"That was Isabel's voice I just heard?"

"Of course! I mean, sometimes it is," she declared.

"Izzy's getting pretty good at it," added Charlotte. Maeve was putting on an Oscar-worthy performance, so she was going to do everything she could to help!

"That's pretty amazin'," Captain Bob admitted. "Can ya do it again, girl?"

Everyone stared at Isabel. She cleared her throat. "Um, sure . . . hang on." She opened her mouth and nudged Franco under her jacket, willing him to saying something—anything! But Franco didn't say a word!

Isabel coughed. "I'm, uh, new at this, so it doesn't always work," she explained.

"Practice makes perfect!" Captain Bob advised her.

"That's what I've been telling her," Maeve said. "But does she listen?"

Avery rolled her eyes and shoved Maeve playfully. "Anyway, thanks, Captain Bob! Have a great night!"

"Same to you girls!" he said, and tipped his hat and started to walk off.

"G'night, Captain Smelly!" Franco cried from his hiding spot.

Captain Bob whirled around. "Sorry!" Isabel said, muffling her laughter.

As Captain Bob left, he surreptitiously sniffed his armpits. The girls waited until he was out of earshot and collapsed into laughter.

Captain Smelly

They safely got Franco back to the room without anyone noticing. Charlotte couldn't believe they'd had such a close call—with Captain Bob, of all people. "Throwing your voice, Maeve, that was brilliant!"

"Excuse me," said Avery, "but I believe Izzy and I are the ones with the voice-throwing ability."

A knock came at the door. Everyone froze. *Have we gotten caught after all?*

"Quick! We'll hide Franco in the closet!" A panicked Isabel opened the doors and thrust the bird in among Katani's neatly unpacked shirts.

The girls held their breath as a key card *beeped* and the door swung open.

Everyone breathed a sigh of relief as Marisol let herself and Katani in.

"That pool is *da bomb*!" Katani gushed. "You guys should totally come with us tomorrow. You'll see how . . ." Katani's voice trailed off as she noticed that no one was saying anything. "What's up? Spill."

"You know that surprise we had?" Charlotte asked.

Katani flopped on the bed. "Oh, yeah! Can you show me now?

"Surprise!" Isabel opened the closet door, and Franco hopped out—right at Katani!

"Surprise!" Franco repeated.

Katani's eyes grew wide as she stared from the bird to the inside of her closet—half of her clothes had fallen off their hangers and the rest were all tangled in a ball! "*Where* . . . on earth," she said slowly, looking each girl in the eyes, "did you get a parrot? And *what* did he do to my closet!?"

"His name is Franco," Marisol said, eyes flicking from Katani and back to the other girls. As she repeated her story, Charlotte started picking up Katani's clothes and hanging them up again.

"Franco, this is Katani," Isabel introduced when she was done with the story.

"Styliiiin'," cooed Franco.

Katani smiled, but had some questions. "Listen, I love animals, I do! But we're here as guests of the travel magazine and the cruise lines! Isn't it against the rules to have animals on board? What if they throw us off the cruise? And what are you feeding him?"

"I brought some pineapple for him—" Marisol started, taking a Ziploc bag out of her pocket. She stopped when she saw the girls' amused faces. "What? *¿Qué paso?*"

Maeve motioned for Avery, Isabel, and Charlotte to join her, and the girls reenacted the scene from the top deck with Captain Bob.

"Captain SMELLY?" a disbelieving Katani protested. "He did not!"

"Did so!" Isabel said proudly. "And Avery and Maeve, you should have seen them!"

"Smelly!" Franco squawked. Katani started giggling and Avery smiled. *It's good to be back with my friends—all of my friends,* she thought, looking at Katani.

"*Captain* Smelly!" Katani told the parrot, and soon all of them were wiping tears off their cheeks. Everyone except Marisol.

"I'm happy you're having a good time with Franco, but we must be more careful or I will lose my job for sure," a concerned-looking Marisol warned the girls. "Captain

Bob may be goofy, but he's also really smart. You know that staff meeting I had to go to? He wanted to talk to us about proper onboard conduct, and he reviewed several passages from our employee manual . . . including one about what to do if an animal is discovered on board. I guess my neighbor from the staff quarters thought she heard scratching."

Isabel's face was perfectly straight now. She took a deep breath. "What does that mean?"

"Well . . . usually the only animals you find on a cruise ship are rats. That's what everyone was worried about."

"Ewww!" Maeve gagged.

"Oh, no!" squawked Franco.

"But they might go looking. It's a good thing I moved Franco here, girls. You have my sincerest thanks for keeping him safe."

"And we'll make sure he *stays* safe!" Isabel promised, scratching the bird's gray-feathered head.

Postcards Home

Dear Kelley,

We went horseback riding through the most gorgeous Hawaiian jungle and I totally thought of you! It was sooo much fun. Unfortunately, that's where the fun ends, as I have surfing and karaoke to look forward to—not! I'll have to do some serious shopping to make up for it! I promise to buy you something nice. Miss you tons!

TTYL,
Katani

Ma Cherie Sophie,
   Dad is doing much better, but he's still not shipshape. (Ha!) I can't say this trip has turned out the way I expected it to, but my dad says that adventure is the best part of travel. Remind me to tell you our parrot story. It's super top-secret, so I don't dare write it out on this postcard! Hawaii is beautiful, but not so très chic as Paris . . .

Au revoir,
Charlotte

Dear Sam,
   One day when I'm rich and famous, I'm taking you to Hawaii! I might even let you drag me to the Pearl Harbor memorial . . . but seriously, I'm loving every minute of this vacation! I'm going to learn how to surf! I'll teach you when I get home. Promise!

XOXO,
Maeve

Dear Elena Maria,

    There's a funny story behind this picture. I'll fill you in when I get home!

                    Adios,
                    Isabel

Dear Scott,

    T-minus two days till I'm shredding the waves. Can. Not. Wait. Andie and Dad are being, well, you know. GROSS. Don't even get me started on Kazie. I'm just thinking of carving it up! And saving the nenes and wolf spiders. Did you know Hawaii has more endangered species per square mile than any other place on the planet? So sad!

                    Later,
                    Avery

Part Two
New Family, Old Friends

11

Supercollider!

"Those track pants have to be here somewhere," Avery mumbled as she rummaged through her backpack on the top bunk. Everyone else was all ready to go on the bike ride through the lava fields in Hilo. "I can't find anything!" she complained.

"Maybe if you learned to pack neatly instead of just shoving everything in, you'd be able to find what you're looking for," Katani responded. Not only was she ready, but her outfit was fully coordinated from the laces in her sneakers to the ribbons in her hair.

"Ha-ha-ha!" squawked Franco. Marisol had let them bring him in their room while they all got ready, since it made him happy to be out of his cage.

Avery stuck out her tongue at Franco and dumped the contents of her backpack on the floor. Oops! Everything landed on Maeve.

"Hey!" Maeve yelled. She ducked, but not in time to avoid a flyaway pair of track pants. "Watch it!"

Avery hopped off her bed and retrieved the runaway pants from her friend's head. "Finally! I was looking for those."

Maeve piled all of Avery's belongings back onto her bunk. "Katani, I need your opinion. What does my outfit say to you?" She was wearing a pink top, denim leggings, pink socks ,and sneakers.

Franco whistled at her from his perch on the edge of Isabel's bunk. "Cuuuute!"

"I agree," said Katani, giving a thumbs-up. "Our little parrot friend may have a future in fashion!"

"How is Franco doing?" Charlotte asked.

Franco began to bob up and down at the sound of his name. Isabel scratched between the feathers on his head. "Franco, are you going to be good while we're gone today?"

"Good, good!" the bird insisted.

"I think the question is, will Franco be quiet?" Avery interjected.

"Franco want pineapple!"

"There's a shocker!" Maeve declared. She was in front of the mirror, putting the finishing touches on her look.

Isabel checked their mini-fridge. "Franco, you finished all the pineapple last night!'

"Want pineapple!" he insisted stubbornly.

Katani checked her watch. "We don't have time to get down to the dining room and sneak some out," she said. "We're supposed to meet everyone down on the dock in half an hour."

"We'll find you more pineapple," Avery assured the parrot.

"There's only one problem," Isabel said as she closed the room service menu. "There's no pineapple on the menu."

"No pineapple? Impossible!" Maeve declared.

"Want pineapple!" Franco repeated.

Charlotte studied the room-service menu. "Hang on, I have an idea." She picked up the phone on the nightstand next to her sofa bed. "Is this room service? What sort of garnish comes on your tropical fruit smoothies? Mmm-hmm. Good," Charlotte said into the receiver, "then we'll have five." She hung up the phone.

"Five fruit smoothies?" A quizzical Maeve asked. "But we already had breakfast."

"I ordered five fruit smoothies," Charlotte explained, "that come with pineapple wedges!"

"Ha-ha-ha!" laughed Franco.

Just then, the phone rang. Charlotte picked it up. "Dad? Hi! We're just getting ready for . . ."

"Pineapple!" Franco squawked.

"Oh, um, that was . . . Avery," Charlotte fumbled for words.

"How come we always take the blame?" Avery whispered to Isabel, smiling.

"Yep, we're doing fine," Charlotte continued, a little louder than usual to cover up Franco's chirps. "Marisol's taking us to the tour bus in just a few minutes, then Mr. Madden and Andie are chaperoning again . . ."

As Charlotte finished explaining their plans to her dad and hung up the phone, room service arrived and Maeve carried the smoothies in on a silver platter, handing them out like she was giving out Academy Awards.

"Ready to go?" Marisol asked, stepping into the room from her new cabin. "What's this?" She stared at the smoothies.

"We're cruising in style!" Maeve handed Isabel her tall, frothy orange drink and Franco nipped the pineapple right off the rim before it was even out of Maeve's hands!

Isabel laughed. "See, Franco? Everyone loves you! Everyone gives you pineapple!" She leaned into Franco's face and made a kissing sound.

"Say, '*Dame un beso*, kiss kiss!'" Marisol suggested, laughing.

Isabel tried it, and to her surprise, Franco kissed her back!

Maeve shuddered. "Franco can have *all* of my smoothie. I've suddenly lost my appetite!"

It took all four remaining pineapple wedges to lure Franco into his cage and keep him there while Charlotte shut the door with two locks . . . the normal one, and one from Katani's suitcase.

"I hate to see him locked up like that!" Isabel sighed, but she knew it was the only way to keep him out of sight.

"Don't worry, I'll check on him whenever I have a free minute," Marisol promised. "Now let's get you out to the bus!"

Hello, Hilo!

An hour later, the girls hopped off the bus in front of Volcanic Bike Rentals—Where Fun Flows Like Lava! Mr. Madden and Andie wore matching red ATS shirts and khaki shorts, which Maeve pronounced "über cute." Avery was worried that Maeve was right. *My dad and Andie act like they're on a crash course toward . . . the m-word.* Avery gulped back a bitter taste that suddenly rose into her mouth. She didn't even want to think "marriage," it was just too scary! At least she had time. Those things . . . the w-word, weddings, took years to plan, right?

Mr. Madden clapped his hands, interrupting Avery's thoughts. "Round up!" Everyone gathered around. "I don't know if we've met, but I'm Jake Madden—"

"We know who you are, Dad," Avery complained.

"Aka, Jake the Snake!" Kazie blurted out.

"That, too. Now I know our illustrious members of the BSG—"

"Don't forget the Kgirls!" Kazie interrupted again, elbowing in between Mr. Madden and Andie. Avery couldn't believe it! They had been out here for, like, two minutes and already Kazie was demanding to be the center of attention.

"Yup, of course. But I haven't met these righteous dudes." Mr. Madden walked over to where Chad was standing with his friend Will. He held out his fist in a surfer salute, his thumb and pinky sticking out like the letter *Y*. "Jake Madden. The Snurfman. Jake the Snake."

Chad returned the surfer greeting, and then introduced

his friend. "This is Cowabunga Will and I'm his surfing partner in crime, Chizzam. Though the girls know me by my alter ego, Chad."

I have got to learn this insider surfer lingo! Maeve sighed as "Chizzam" smiled and waved at her. She made a quick mental note: *Remember to look cute while bike riding.*

After a quick safety demonstration, everyone was fitted for a bike and helmet, and they began their descent into the lava fields of Hilo. Avery pedaled as fast as she could, wanting to break off in front of everyone to get some peace and quiet. It was a perfect day for a ride. The air was warm with a slight breeze that kept it from being uncomfortably hot. She had to admit, biking through a lava field? Kind of awesome.

In the distance she could see forests made of ferns, and large, round craters where she was sure she could rock out some of her mountain biking moves. Avery was admiring the expanse of black rock in front of her when she caught a blur of pink whizzing by.

Kazie!

"You snooze, you lose!" Kazie yelled.

"I was just enjoying the scenery," Avery yelled back. "*Everything* isn't a race."

Kazie laughed. "That's what you say when you can't keep up!"

Exercise normally cleared Avery's head, but right now her thoughts were charging ahead like a runaway train. *Kazie beat me? No way!* She pushed herself harder and pulled ahead of the pink whir. Looking back, she flashed

Kazie that same surfer sign her dad had used. Only now, instead of "hello," it meant "See ya later!"

Kazie's face was taut with effort as she willed herself to go faster. She caught up with Avery. "Pretty good . . . but not good enough! You're as slow as your scaredy-dog Marty." Kazie pulled ahead by a nose.

That one hit close to home. *How dare she insult Marty!* Avery's feet blurred as she inched closer to Kazie. "Nope, I think you're just used to people running away from your Frankencat, Farkle!'

"Farkle has *ten times* the courage of your cute widdle puppy dog!" Kazie yelled, as Avery started to pass her.

"That 'cute little puppy dog' has more friends than Farkle, you, and your mom all put together!" Avery almost couldn't believe the words coming out of her mouth as she pedaled faster through the black rock. It was like everything that had happened over the past few days was boiling out of her like, well, lava from a volcano. Kazie may have stolen Katani, her Red Sox cap, and her dad's attention, but she wasn't going to let her insult her dog or take this race!

Surf Lingo 101

"I definitely like horseback riding better," Katani complained as she and Maeve pedaled slowly over the trail winding through the lava fields.

Maeve wiped a bead of sweat that trickled down her face. "I don't know how Kazie and Avery do it; they're practically flying up there! I can barely make it up this hill."

"The ground is flat here, Maeve," teased Chad as he and Will sped by.

"Hmmm . . . I know what I need!" Maeve announced to Katani. "A challenge! Think I can catch up to Chad?"

Katani nodded and waved her on. Maeve pedaled as fast as she could, but only managed to reach Mr. Madden. Chad, aka "Chizzam," was pulling farther and farther ahead with Will.

"Having fun?" Mr. Madden asked.

"I can't tell," Maeve admitted. "So how do you get a surfer name like Jake the Snake? Are there more secret thingies like that sign you made? Is surfing, like, a secret society?"

"Whoa, whoa." Mr. Madden looked like he was trying to figure out which question to answer first, and finally settled for a shrug. "Someone's got to give you a surf name. The rest? Just go with the flow."

"That's it? You've got to be kidding!" Maeve was hoping for some real insider information, but it looked like it wasn't going to be that easy to break into the surfing mainstream.

Mr. Madden laughed. "That's the best part of shredding—whether it's a powdery white slope or a raging surf or something like the lava fields—you're just out digging nature and getting your sweat on. Speaking of which, I'm going to sprint on ahead—"

"So, how did you and Andie meet?" asked Maeve before he could take off.

Mr. Madden slowed down. "She started working in my store—"

"Love at first sight!" Maeve said dreamily.

"Not exactly. We just found out we had *mucho* in common." He started to pedal faster.

"That is so romantic!" Maeve said. "You're, like, on the same wave."

"Right on! She shreds, she's competitive but also loves to have fun. But in the end, we like to go fast! Get ready for takeoff!"

Mr. Madden shifted gears and tried to speed up again, but Maeve chattered on. "Chad likes to surf. You know, I think Chad and I have a little of that instant-connection thing going too," she confided.

"He's that Chizzam dude totally tearing it up on ahead, right?" he asked. "Tell you what, I will fly on by and put in a good word for you—"

"You're the best! But Chad's really into surfing, so I thought if I had a couple of tricks up my sleeve that might totally surprise him, y'know? I'm an actress, so it won't take much. Try me!"

Mr. Madden glanced one last time at everyone racing up ahead. "Sure," he said with a sigh.

Maeve clapped, then grabbed her handlebars as the bike started to wobble. "I'm so lucky I caught up to you, Mr. Madden!"

"Me too," he said as he slumped in his seat, "me too."

Slowpokes

Katani pedaled past Andie, who was taking photos of the lava fields. "Hey Katani, are you the last of the pack?" Andie asked, putting her camera away in its carrying case.

"Pretty much." Katani waited as Andie hopped on her bike and rode next to her. "You don't have to slow down for me."

"It's more fun to ride together," Andie told her. "Besides, it looks like your friend Maeve has stolen Jake's attention!"

Jake turned around and gave his girlfriend a mournful look. She waved happily and gave him a thumbs-up. "He's used to girls like Kazie and Avery," Andie confided. "And from what I've seen of Maeve, she's another kind of girl entirely!"

"You got that right." Katani laughed. Andie didn't even know the half of it! Maeve was probably reenacting scenes from Katharine Hepburn movies in the hopes that Mr. Madden knew some of the lines.

"It's so beautiful here!" Andie suddenly gushed. "Jake got me this new camera a couple weeks ago and I'm not sure if I'm using it correctly. We might end up with photos of my fingertips."

They rode on in silence, the warm tropical wind at their backs. Katani remembered visiting Jamaica with her grandmother. *I would love to go on a cruise with Grandma Ruby one day!* Katani's grandmother was the principal of her school and always seemed to know how to handle tricky situations. Katani could have used her advice on this trip, that was for sure. The craziness with the Kgirls, and Avery's issues with Kazie . . . well, it was a ton to deal with.

Andie finally broke the silence. "I have to thank you, Katani, for being such a good friend to Kazie this week.

She's so enjoyed spending time with the *Kgirls*. What a clever name!"

"Thanks, but . . ." Katani hesitated a minute. Her grandmother wasn't here. Who else could she talk to?

Andie steered around a bumpy piece of terrain. "But what? Are you worried about something?"

Katani took a deep breath. "I dunno."

"When Kazie's worried, she won't tell me a thing." Andie smiled. "We talk for hours when she's angry or excited, but if she's nervous, she just clams up. Like after the last snowboarding competition, I had to pretend it was no big deal right along with her, even though we were both biting our nails as the judges read off the scores!"

"No way Kazie gets nervous!"

"Of course she does. It happens to everyone. So. Between you and me: What's the matter?" Andie urged.

"It's just this singing thing," Katani confessed. "I totally can't sing at *all*, and Kazie and Kara-Lee want to do karaoke with me!"

"You girls will be great! Don't worry about it."

"Uh . . . you haven't heard me sing," Katani replied jokingly. "Besides, you're good at everything!"

Andie laughed. "Katani, you've never tried my cooking!" Andie mouthed the words "Bad, very bad!" and Katani couldn't help laughing. Avery had told her about the horrendous meal Andie had cooked for her in Colorado.

"Anyway, that's what makes friendships fun," Andie said. "Trying new things together."

"But what if they don't want me in the club anymore when they find out what a terrible singer I am?" Katani worried. "You won't tell them, will you?"

Andie smiled and slowed down, coasting on her bike. "Your secret's safe. But I promise you that the Kgirls like you for you. Not for the stuff you can do, or the competitions you can win, but for you. Trust me on this one."

Suddenly Katani felt relieved. Of course Andie was right . . . definitely!

Stop and Smell the Volcano

Avery was beginning to get tired, but pushed herself as hard as she could. She really wanted to stop and check out some of the scenery, like the mist pools that the guide had told them about back at the bike shop. But if Kazie was making this into a race, Avery was going to win! She kicked it into high gear and everything blurred as she sped by.

All of a sudden, she hit the smooth surface of a volcanic rock that had tumbled onto the path a little too hard and started to lose control! *Whoa! Don't panic! Squeeze the brakes.*

Slowing down, Avery finally regained her balance. *Close one.*

Kazie seized the moment and sped past. "Have a nice trip?"

I would if you'd just go home, Avery fumed. Her knuckles turned white where she gripped the handlebars, and she pedaled like her life depended on it.

Not too far behind Avery and Kazie's mad race,

Charlotte studied the scenery. "What do you think, Izzy?"

Isabel shook her head. "It's amazing!"

The Hilo Lava Fields were like no place Charlotte had ever seen, and she had traveled a lot! The charcoal-colored ground stretched toward the horizon, and bits of vegetation snuck in through the cracks, peppering the countryside with flecks of greenery. She slowed down her bike long enough to snap a couple of pictures.

Isabel followed suit, trying to soak in the scenery and commit it to memory so she could paint it later. The small clouds of steam escaping from the ground in the distance actually looked like dragons breathing inside their caves. She could almost see the scaly beasts curled up beneath the black stone.

"This is like being on another planet, don't you think?" she asked Charlotte.

"Brilliant!" Charlotte paused to scribble the phrase down in her journal, along with all the other words that were swimming around in her head: *On another planet . . . desolate, bleak, barren, monolithic stones and winding paths.* A volcano rose up on the horizon, towering over the fields. "Isabel! That's Mauna Kea!" she exclaimed, as she put her book away and got back on her bike.

"The volcano?" Isabel asked.

Charlotte nodded, and then saw her friend's concerned expression. "It's dormant. That means that it's not in danger of erupting."

"I didn't think we'd be biking out here if that thing

was about to explode," Isabel said confidently.

"Right now I think the only volcanoes that are in danger of erupting are Volcano Avery and Volcano Kazie." Charlotte sighed.

Isabel feared Charlotte might be right. "Hopefully those two will stay dormant for the rest of the trip!"

Crash Course

Avery and Kazie flew over the lumpy ground of the lava fields.

"No way you're gonna beat me, Short Stack," gasped a winded Kazie.

"Watch me!" yelled Avery.

If there was anything that might possibly be worse than insulting Marty, Kazie had hit it right on the nose. *No one calls me short and gets away with it! No one.* Avery fumed as she barreled ahead of Kazie.

That's when the terrain started to slope downward. Avery didn't think the decline was that bad, but soon realized her mistake as she started to lose control of her bike again! The frame rattled as she tried to hold on and steady herself. She pumped her brakes, but the gears just scraped together in a high-pitched squeal!

"WATCH IT!" screamed Kazie.

Kazie slammed into Avery's bike from behind, sending both girls flying over their handlebars and down the hill. They landed in a tangled up heap, sending up a cloud of thick black dust.

"Did you see that?" Charlotte yelled to Isabel. The

girls raced faster than they thought possible to help their friends. Chad and Will were already off their bikes, trying to help Kazie and Avery up.

"Dude! DUDES! Are you okay?" asked Chad.

"It was like, WHAMMO!" Will replied, imitating the crash with his hands.

Kara-Lee pedaled up. "Is everyone all right?" Her voice sounded more high-pitched and squeaky than normal.

"Go back and tell Andie and Mr. Madden," Charlotte instructed her. "Hurry!"

Isabel rushed over to Avery. "Are you okay?"

Avery felt around. Her left elbow was killing her. "I'm banged up, but I don't think anything's broken," she said as she wiggled her hands and feet. Avery's bike, on the other hand, was toast. The fender was bent into the tire, tearing the rubber! "Wish I could say the same for the bike *she* ruined." Avery pointed at Kazie, who was sitting up, cradling her knee.

"I ruined?" Kazie yelled back. "If it wasn't for you, I'd still be cruising through the lava fields. You totally owe me a pair of pink track pants!" Kazie yelled, poking at the hole in her knee, which revealed a huge red bruise that was sure to turn black and blue in a matter of hours.

"Are you hurt?" Charlotte asked, offering Kazie a hand.

Kazie hoisted herself up. "Cuts and scrapes, thanks to Short Stack. Tell your friend she should learn how to ride."

"Don't you *dare* call me *short*!" Avery reached for Kazie

like she wanted to knock her down again, but Isabel managed to hold her back.

Mr. Madden pulled up, followed by Andie and Kara-Lee. ". . . It's a *disaster*!" Kara-Lee was frantically explaining.

Mr. Madden jumped off his bike and ran toward his daughter, grabbing Avery's hand and looking at her, then Kazie. "Are you guys okay? What happened?"

Andie wasn't quite as fast, but she made it to Kazie soon after and gave her daughter a gentle hug.

"Kazie crashed into me!" screamed Avery.

"You crashed into *me*!" hissed Kazie.

"Okay, everyone just calm down," Andie suggested, backing off. "You're lucky you both didn't get seriously hurt."

"If I was lucky, Short Stack would know how to ride!" Kazie yelled.

"I told you, *don't* call me that, you, you . . . vacation crasher! Why did you have to come on this cruise, anyway?" Avery screeched, fighting back tears.

Avery and Kazie faced off, and then ran at each other. Mr. Madden grabbed Avery while Andie held Kazie back.

"What the heck happened?" asked Mr. Madden. "I thought we were all having a gnarly vacation together, then—"

"IT'S HER FAULT!" Avery and Kazie yelled in unison, pointing at each other.

CHAPTER
12

Matching Band-Aids

A very sat in a hard plastic chair in the infirmary while Dr. Steve shined a penlight in both of her eyes. The doctor turned to Mr. Madden. "She's perfectly fine, just a few bruises."

"Let's check you out, Kazie." He knelt in front of Kazie and performed the same tests, asking her to bend both her arms and legs, then prodding her stomach to see if anything hurt. "Just a few bumps and bruises here, too. It's a good thing you were both wearing helmets. I want you girls to take it easy, okay?" Dr. Steve plastered Kazie's knee with a Band-Aid featuring a smiling dinosaur. He'd used the same goofy Band-Aid for Avery's arm.

Avery and Kazie both nodded, avoiding each other's eyes. Dr. Steve turned to Mr. Madden and Andie. "If there are any more problems, I'll be here."

Mr. Madden shook Dr. Steve's hand and held the door open for Andie. "Ave, Kaz, c'mon."

Avery followed her father and reached the doorway

at the same time Kazie did. Kazie paused at the threshold. "Oh, please, after you," she gushed, her voice dripping with sarcasm.

Avery crossed her arms, covering up the silly dinosaur Band-Aid, and refused to budge. "No way! I don't know what you're gonna do to me behind my back."

Andie whirled around. "That's it! Both of you girls are going to end up grounded in your cabins for the rest of the trip if you don't pull it together *right now* and behave."

Kazie groaned. "But it wasn't my fault! Avery—"

Avery scowled. "Me?"

Mr. Madden put a hand on each girl's shoulder. "If I were you, I would not want to miss this once-in-a-lifetime opportunity to shred up some waves tomorrow. So . . . I think we need to have a little talk. But let's get out of this hallway, first."

Parent Talk

Avery, Kazie, Jake, and Andie were packed like sardines into Mr. Madden's tiny cabin. Andie and Mr. Madden sat on the bed, while Kazie took the only chair.

Figures, thought Avery, who had to sit cross-legged on the floor. Kazie's knee was poking her shoulder, but there wasn't any room to adjust.

"We're all here—" Mr. Madden started, and then stopped. He opened his mouth and then shut it and looked at Andie.

Andie nodded. "We're here because Jake and I are worried."

"Yeah, that's exactly it," Mr. Madden agreed. "Worried." They looked at the girls, waiting for one of them to say something.

Kazie broke the silence. "Okay, well, it's not like this was my plan."

"Yeah," Avery said. "My plan was to just be on vacation with my friends. I mean, it's nice you're here, Dad, but . . ."

Avery shifted uncomfortably, whacking her head into Kazie's knee. "Owww," she complained.

"I'm supposed to be helping Kara-Lee with karaoke right now," Kazie groaned.

"It's just that . . ." Mr. Madden trailed off again. He took a deep breath. "We were sorta hoping you two would be friends. But, y'know, you can't force it." He laughed awkwardly.

Avery watched her dad fumble over his words. If there was anyone who always had something to say—especially something funny to say—it was her dad. As much as she wasn't used to seeing him with Andie and Kazie, she really wasn't used to seeing him like this.

"You girls are a lot alike," Andie took over. "And well, we thought that would be a good thing. You seemed to be bonding that week in Colorado . . . anyway, you're both good sports and part of being a good sport is being *civil*. We certainly didn't think you'd get so competitive you'd injure yourselves trying to outdo each other!"

"Exactly," Mr. Madden said, squeezing Andie's shoulder. "That's exactly it."

The more Avery thought about it, the more she realized she didn't mind that her dad showed up and surprised her on the trip. *But why did he have to bring Andie and Kazie too? Things were better when it was just the two of us!*

She glanced at Kazie, who looked like she might be thinking the same thing. Avery remembered Colorado, and Kazie definitely hadn't been as crazy there as she was now. What was wrong with her? *And what's wrong with me?* Avery looked back at her dad. "I'm sorry for worrying you."

Kazie reluctantly agreed. "Me too, Snurfman."

"Are we done here? 'Cause my foot's asleep," Avery said from her cramped spot on the floor.

"So we're good?" Mr. Madden asked. "One whiff of trouble, and no surfing tomorrow. Got it?"

I cannot miss surfing! Avery thought. *Not for the world.* She hadn't been surfing with her dad in ages, and she couldn't wait to attack the waves next to Jake the Snake. She hadn't even told him yet that she had her own surfer name, now! When the BSG did that scavenger hunt on Cape Cod, she managed to get in some surfing practice and earned the name Aloha Jedi.

Mr. Madden counted them down. "One, two, three, shake!"

Avery shook Kazie's hand. *Maybe Aloha Jedi can be nice to Crazie Kazie for a couple of days,* Avery thought. But deep down her feelings were much more confused.

Pooling Around

"Cannonball!" Avery screamed and took a flying leap into the pool. She tucked her knees into her chest and hit the water with a huge splash!

After the painful lecture from both Andie and her dad, Avery had returned to the cabin. Everyone wanted to know what happened, but Avery avoided her friends' questions and suggested they hit the pool instead. The girls made sure Franco had plenty of pineapple, then Marisol walked them up to the top deck.

The trip to the pool quickly became a "Who Can Make the Biggest Cannonball Splash" contest with another group of kids. It was no surprise that Avery was ahead.

Isabel grabbed her sketchpad out of the way of the flying water. "That's a perfect ten, Ave!" she cheered.

"Way to go!" Charlotte applauded as Avery emerged from the depths of the pool, grinning.

A black-haired boy in blue and white swim trunks shook his head skeptically. "You're so small. How do you make a splash that big?"

Avery shook the water from her hair and shrugged. "Years of practice. C'mon, Maeve, you're next."

Maeve waved Avery off. "I think I'm getting plenty soaked just watching you guys!" *If Chad were here, though . . . ,* she thought, imagining impressing him with a gigantic surf-girl worthy cannonball. For some reason, though, the Chad in her fantasy morphed into Riley, her number one crush back home. *I wonder if he's written any new songs since I've been gone?* she found herself thinking.

"You're no fun!" Avery looked around. The black-haired boy sized up the distance to the pool, and took a flying leap. He barely made a splash.

Avery laughed. "I told you, practice!" The boy stuck his tongue out at her and exited the pool. "Okay, Katani, you're up!"

Katani made her way to the edge of the pool and got ready to jump when someone tapped her on the shoulder. It was Kara-Lee. Kazie was hanging back, arms crossed over a pair of pink overalls that covered up her scraped knee.

"What's going on?" Kazie asked. For the first time since Katani had met her, Kazie didn't look happy.

"Oh, Avery just organized a little cannonball contest before we all headed down to dinner," Katani said. She worried that it sounded more like an excuse than an explanation.

"So why didn't you invite us? " Kara-Lee wanted to know.

Katani shrugged. "I don't know . . . it just sort of happened."

But the truth was she did know. *I didn't mean to exclude the Kgirls! I just wanted to spend some time with the BSG.* She hated the feeling that she had to choose between the two groups.

"I guess I just didn't think you'd be interested," Katani concluded.

"Yeah, okay." Kazie shrugged. "I didn't really want to swim, anyway. I'm still sore because *somebody* had to crash into me. See you at dinner."

"We'll catch up at dinner?" Kara-Lee said apologetically, turning to follow Kazie.

Katani watched her new friends leave, wondering why being a good friend to one group meant being a bad friend to the other. *Friendship shouldn't be so hard!* she wanted to shout after them. *What happened to silver and gold?*

Going Bananas

After dinner, Katani and Kara-Lee walked through the aisles of Bananas, the boutique that Carla, the ship's greeter, had recommended she check out at the beginning of the cruise. Avery's dad had taken her to the on board arcade after dinner, and Kazie was mini-golfing with her mom. *Maybe some Dad-time will help Avery calm down,* Katani hoped.

Kara-Lee tried on a necklace with an ivory-colored seashell pendant. She admired herself in the mirror. "I don't get it. Why is Avery making things so difficult for Kazie? What did Kazie ever do to her?"

Katani bit her lip. "I don't think it's that simple, Kara-Lee."

Kara-Lee turned to Katani. "What do you mean?'

"It's hard to share things," Katani explained. "I have three sisters, so I should know! And, well, I guess Kazie and Avery don't want to share their parents." When she said it like that, it made perfect sense.

"But Kazie's totally cool," Kara-Lee reminded her. She unhooked her necklace and tried on another one made out of tiny iridescent shells. "I mean, you obviously think so.

We wouldn't be the Kgirls if that wasn't the case. So why doesn't Avery give her a chance?"

Katani felt torn. She liked Kazie, but Kara-Lee obviously didn't know Avery like Katani did. "Yes, but Avery thought she was going to go on this cruise with her friends and whammo! Here's her dad who shows up with his girlfriend and her daughter . . . totally interrupting *her* cruise, with *her* friends. That's got to be weird." Katani surmised. "And by the way, you should get that necklace. It's beautiful."

Kara-Lee tilted her chin up to admire the necklace. "I think I will." She turned to Katani. "Y'know, as an only child, I used to dream that someone would show up with a brother or sister for me."

Katani laughed. "I have more sisters than I know what to do with! But no matter how much we fight sometimes, I really do love all of them," she confessed. "My friend Charlotte's like you, though . . . it's just her and her dad."

"Kazie's only got her mom," Kara-Lee mused. "Are you going to get this?" she asked, running a finger alongside a scarf with yellow flowers Katani had been admiring.

"No, I'm saving my money," Katani answered. "I want to get something really nice for my sister, Kelley."

"That's so sweet!" Kara-Lee smiled. "What did you have in mind?"

Kara-Lee and Katani left the boutique, chatting about the things Kelley might like—something horse-themed, maybe. Charlotte and Isabel waved from the bookstore.

"Hi," Isabel waved them in. "Listen to this! In one

story I just read, there was this snow spirit, Poli'ahu, who lived on Mauna Kea and got in a fight with her sister, the volcano spirit, Pele . . ."

"But she didn't know it was Pele at first because Pele disguised herself and entered this competition to see who could sled down the side of the mountain the fastest," Charlotte gushed.

"Everyone said Poli'ahu won," Isabel continued, "so Pele got all upset and made the mountain erupt and destroyed the sledding slope!"

"Poli'ahu fought back with blizzards, covering the whole mountain in snow and ice," Charlotte finished. "In the book it said myths like this probably explained geology. But I think it's just a cool story!"

Katani and Kara-Lee looked at each other. Those two fighting sister spirits sounded eerily familiar!

Charlotte glanced at her watch. "We better go, Izzy." She turned to Katani and Kara-Lee. "We're meeting up with Maeve then going to visit my dad."

"Bye!" Isabel waved as they headed out the door.

Kara-Lee and Katani decided to walk through the Atrium. The evening was winding down and people were talking quietly on the plush maroon sofas in the lounge.

Kara-Lee unwrapped the necklace and put it on as they walked through the huge mirrored lounge. "We totally forgot to check out clothes for the karaoke competition!"

Katani was hoping Kara-Lee would have forgotten, as the deadline to sign up was drawing near. Kara-Lee and

Kazie were over-the-top excited about participating, but Katani was dreading it! "Oh. Right."

"What do you think we should sing? " Kara-Lee asked.

"Oh, I don't know," Katani said. "The last time I had to sing in front of a crowd I was with Nik and Sam."

Kara-Lee's eyes grew wide. "Really? You know Nik and Sam? I love them!"

Katani told Kara-Lee about their fateful trip to Big Sky Resort and how they had run into Nik and Sam at the airport and ended up friends.

"They have that new single out!" Kara-Lee exclaimed, "'Three Hours Till You.' It's perfect! You know how it goes, right, Katani?"

Kara-Lee began humming a verse. *Even her humming sounds better than my singing,* Katani thought. "Yeah, I know it."

"I know that they each take a verse and then sing the last one together, but since there's three of us we can each take one and all sing the refrain," Kara-Lee decided. "I reckon we could even win!"

Kara-Lee hugged Katani, who couldn't believe she just blew the perfect opportunity to tell Kara-Lee that she couldn't sing. "Three Hours Till Total Humiliation!" Katani cringed.

Out of the Infirmary and into the Fire

Charlotte, Isabel, and Maeve were now experts at navigating the maze of hallways to the infirmary. "Left at the ladder!" Charlotte called out as the girls hooked a sharp left and crossed through the long, green-carpeted hallways.

"You know, that crash this morning was pretty scary." Isabel remarked. "I'm really glad Avery and Kazie didn't get badly hurt."

Maeve caught herself in a reflection of the glass that covered the fire extinguisher and stopped to fluff her hair. "Actually, girls, you know what's scary? This whole Kgirls Club."

Charlotte doubled back to retrieve Maeve. "As scary as your obsession with running into Chad?" she asked, dragging Maeve away from the glass.

Maeve laughed. "Nothing wrong with a girl wanting to look her best!"

"I actually think Kazie's pretty fun," Charlotte admitted. They turned right and continued down another long passageway. "But I see why Ave got upset."

"And I think that Katani didn't make it any easier by forming a whole other club," Isabel continued.

"Now instead of us doing stuff all together, it's like we're in competition with each other," Maeve sighed. "Not the sort of drama I was looking forward to on vacation."

"And not what the BSG is all about," Charlotte concluded.

When they reached the infirmary, Charlotte turned to Maeve and Isabel. "Let's not talk about this in front of my dad, okay? The only thing I want him to worry about is getting better."

"I'm sure our Hawaiian myths will keep him happy and entertained!" Isabel promised Charlotte as they opened the door.

Dr. Steve looked up from his desk. "Aha, here for our patient?"

"Is he doing better?" Charlotte asked.

Dr. Steve nodded. "He is, but we're not letting him go until his fever is completely gone." Dr. Weber handed a pile of masks to Charlotte. "You'll still need to wear these to visit your dad. I don't want any of you getting sick." He pointed to Mr. Ramsey's room. "He's reading; just knock before you go in."

It took almost thirty minutes to catch Mr. Ramsey up on the BSG's goings-on—well, most of the goings-on—they left out their pineapple-loving parrot and glossed over Avery and Kazie's crash. When Charlotte retold the myth of Pele and Poli'ahu, it made her dad laugh so hard he coughed up some of his bland, mushy dinner!

"I'm so glad you girls have me covered," he told them. "If it weren't for you, I'd be in a serious writer quandary!" Charlotte beamed inside at the compliment.

Trouble at Sea

"I'd love to head out to the deck so I can see the stars while I write in my journal," Charlotte told her friends as they walked back toward their stateroom.

"Ooh, can I come?" Isabel asked. "I know my drawings of those fighting snow and volcano spirits will be so much better if I'm breathing Hawaiian air for inspiration!"

"Artists!" Maeve shook her head. "I am one hundred percent *wiped out* from biking, so I'll see you guys later!"

Maeve let herself into their room only to discover a forlorn Katani sitting on the sofa bed and looking out the porthole. Franco was resting on top of Charlotte's suitcase. He blinked twice at Maeve's entrance and went right back to sleep.

"Looking for your love lost at sea?" Maeve joked.

Katani shook her head. "Although I wouldn't mind being lost at sea right about now."

Maeve sat down next to her friend on the sofa. Katani wasn't one to mope. "What's up?"

"The Kgirls signed up for the karaoke competition." Katani sighed.

Maeve wanted to ask why Katani wasn't going to perform with the BSG, but she knew that Katani needed a friend and not a lecture. "And you didn't want to?" she guessed.

Katani looked at Maeve and laughed. "Um, my voice, remember?"

"Well, maybe they can't sing either!" Maeve offered brightly.

Katani ran her hands through her hair. "Nope, they can, and I can't, and Kgirl karaoke is gonna be a complete disaster."

Maeve jumped up. "You just need to be a little creative. What song are you singing?"

"Three Hours Till You," Katani told her.

Maeve raised an eyebrow. "The new Nik and Sam? Really? I love that song!" Maeve sang the first verse.

> *"Even though I know it's true*
> *The way you feel about me,*
> *the way I feel 'bout you,*
> *Only three hours —*
> *Three hours till you."*

Katani applauded as Maeve took a bow. "Now, if you can teach me to sing like that in the next two days, I think we're set."

Maeve shook her head. "No, no, no, like I said, we're going to make you sing like *you*. But you're just going to do a little doo-wop."

Katani looked at her blankly.

"You know, just the *uh-huhs*, the *oh yeahs, oooh ooohs*. That sorta thing. When I point, you doo-wop!"

"*The way you feel about me —* " Maeve belted out. "Now say, 'Oh yeah.'"

"*Oh, yeah!*" Katani sang, getting into it.

Franco's eyes sprung open. "Oh, yeah!" he squawked.

Maeve laughed and clapped along. "*The way I feel 'bout you —* "

"*You-ooh-ooh!*" Katani and Franco sang together. The parrot bounced up and down on his suitcase perch to the rhythm of the girls' clapping.

"*Only three hours —* " Maeve sang. "*Three hours till youuuuuuuu —* "

"*Oooh-oooh!*" sang Katani.

"*Oooh-oooh!*" echoed Franco.

"*Oooh-oooh!*" Katani sang, thinking, *Maybe with Maeve and Franco's help, I won't crash and burn in front of the whole ship.*

CHAPTER
13

The Calm Before the Storm

I saw an eel," Kazie bragged.

Everyone was gathered on the beach after a peaceful snorkeling expedition, gobbling down a picnic lunch. Soon it would be time to board the bus and head over to Ke'ei Beach for surfing.

"You did not see an eel," Avery scoffed. "I was right next to you the entire time."

"It was one of the times I was way ahead of you." Kazie smiled.

Avery fumed. Kazie's voice sounded polite, but Avery knew better. She took a deep breath to hold in a comeback. "The first sign of a fight, both of you are back on the ship. No ifs, ands, or buts!" Andie had pronounced that morning at breakfast while Avery's dad nodded along. No way was Avery going to miss her chance to surf.

Avery and her dad had learned to surf together in Hawaii just a few years ago, but Kazie had never tried it before. *There's no way Kazie can fake her way through surfing.*

It really wasn't anything like snowboarding—not at all, Avery thought as she tossed back the rest of her juice.

Her dad walked over and sat down in the sand next to her. "Shreddy, champ?"

"Never been shreddier," Avery said. She shot a look at Kazie, who was waving her arms around wildly while talking to Kara-Lee and Katani.

"You need to keep your weight back," she heard Kazie explain. "That's the secret to staying up on a board."

On a snowboard, yes . . . Avery thought, *but not on a surfboard!*

"Let's get going, kiddo. I want to be the first off that bus, and first on a board."

Now we're talking! Avery grinned up at her dad.

Katani sat with Kazie and Kara-Lee, anxious about surfing for a whole different reason than Maeve, who was practicing her surf stance on her towel! Katani wasn't trying to impress anyone—she just hoped she wouldn't look totally uncoordinated next to Kara-Lee the cheerleader and Kazie the pro snowboarder.

Suddenly Katani noticed that Kazie had stopped chattering on and on about how to stay up on a snowboard and was tapping her foot anxiously. She remembered what Andie told her about Kazie getting nervous sometimes. "What's wrong?"

Kazie stopped tapping her foot and started fidgeting with one of her braids. "Oh, nothing. Surfing better be like snowboarding, 'cause I've, uhhh, never surfed before."

Kara-Lee waved her off. "And you think we have?"

"I don't like being clueless," Kazie confessed.

"You'll be in good company," Katani reminded her.

"And you'll catch on quickly," Kara-Lee assured her.

"There's one thing you should know about Ave; she's a great sport," Katani told Kazie. "It's like, the first thing that her dad taught her. If you ask, I'm sure she'll help you out."

"No way! She might be a good sport to *you*, but not to *me*." Kazie tossed her braids back.

"Have you given her a chance?" Katani mumbled.

"It doesn't matter how well you surf, Kaz, we're just out here to have fun," Kara-Lee added brightly.

Katani hoped Kara-Lee and Kazie would remember that when it came time for karaoke!

From Hawaii to Broadway!

Maeve was packing up the remnants of her lunch when she felt a tap at her shoulder. She turned to discover none other than Chizzam himself!

"Chizzam!" Maeve held out her hand in the surfer salute she'd seen Mr. Madden use. "Ready to surf?"

"Dude!" Chad returned the signal and broke out into that crooked grin that made Maeve melt. Or was that the ninety-degree heat? "You sound like a total landshark. Say it like this: 'Let's get ripping!'"

"Since I really *am* a newbie, um, *landshark*," she reminded him, "you're going to have to stay close and give me some pointers."

Chad sat down next to Maeve on the picnic blanket. "If you're not a surfer, what are you?" he teased.

"I'm an actress!" Maeve declared. "Or at least, I want to be one."

Chad's jaw hung open. "No way! My grandmother used to be an actress. Well, she's still an actress, I guess. She has this whole 'if you're born an actress, you die an actress' thing. It's pretty funny."

Maeve couldn't believe it! First a cute boy who lived in Los Angeles, and then his grandmother's an actress? This was destiny!

"What has she acted in?" Maeve asked.

"She did a lot of Broadway musicals," he said. "You know—" He started to sing in a rather squeaky high voice:

> *"What do you go for,*
> *Go see a show for?*
> *Tell the truth*
> *You go to see those beautiful dames!"*

Maeve ignored the fact that his voice obviously hadn't broken yet and gasped. "*Fame!* I love that musical!"

"My grandmother always sang that to me and my, like, one hundred girl cousins. Anyway, 'cause of her, everyone in my family is a huge Broadway fan. My cousins star in every musical at school. But I mostly just watch them."

"You should totally try out next time!" Maeve exclaimed.

Chad shrugged. "Guys think it's weird, so let's keep it a secret that I like musicals, okay?"

Maeve was about to burst with happiness. He trusted her with a secret! "Of course, to my grave," she promised solemnly.

Surf's Up!

Avery stepped out of the bus and onto Ke'ei Beach. The sand was soft and warm under her bare feet. The sun's reflection off the ocean was blinding, but the waves were perfect! She slipped her sunglasses out of her backpack and put them on.

"Have you surfed before?" Annika, one of the surf pros assigned to their group, asked Charlotte, Isabel, and a very happy Avery.

Avery whooped her "yes" as the other two shook their heads nervously.

"Generally beginners want a longboard," Annika replied gently, steering the girls toward a row of long, round-nosed boards.

"That's funny, I would have thought shorter was easier," Charlotte confessed.

"The longer it is, the easier it is to maneuver," Avery pointed out, inspecting every board in the row. "A lot of people pick shortboards. Or the ones with the prettiest designs," Avery added, giggling at Isabel, who was checking out a bright green board that had a scarlet macaw etched on its surface.

"What?" Isabel asked. "Isn't it beautiful?"

Annika helped Isabel pick out a longboard with a fun starburst pattern. As the girls walked away with their boards, Avery looked over her shoulder to see Kazie and Andie moving from board to board, looking uncertain. Kazie stopped in front of a sleek, expert-level shortboard, and then caught Avery looking at her.

"Ready to shred!" Kazie shouted.

Mr. Madden put an arm around Andie's and Kazie's shoulders. "Surf Betties! I'll be right next to you. You'll be rippin' those waves in no time."

Avery was stunned. Surfing was the one thing she was supposed to do with her dad—the one time she figured Kazie and Andie wouldn't get in the way. Her dad saw Avery's stunned look, and shouted over, "What do you say, Ave? Shall we show these ladies how to rip it up out there?"

"I don't know, Dad. I'm planning on hitting the break, and they're total landsharks, no offense," Avery replied carefully.

"That's why we need to look out for each other!" her dad looked to her for support. "You were a landshark once, too."

"I'm no *landshark*!" Kazie protested. "Did you forget who's the snowboarding champ, here?"

"Nope." Avery turned away and carried her board over to the BSG, who were struggling into their wetsuits in the changing rooms. *So much for Dad-time*, she thought. *But I'm still going to find the sickest, gnarliest waves and totally rip up this beach.*

"I'm melting!" Maeve complained as Isabel zipped up her wetsuit.

"It'll get cooler once you're in the water," Avery told her.

"What Maeve actually wants to know is will she *look* cooler once she's in the water," Isabel joked.

"We can't wait to see your moves, Ave," Charlotte enthused as they ran over to the big group gathering on the sand, suited up and ready to rip.

"A lot of you are beginners, so you probably shouldn't try to stand up on the board today," Annika reminded them, fingering the big, red whistle that hung around her neck. "And that's fine. Learning to paddle through the water, finding the right wave break and owning it takes time. So for now just paddle out—not too far—and have fun. We're all around if you have any questions, and I believe we've got a few experienced surfers with us today—do you mind raising your hands?"

Avery proudly raised her hand, as did her dad, Chad, and Will. She glanced over at Kazie, who had been looking right at her but suddenly looked away.

"You pros are responsible for being my helpers today." Annika winked. "Now get out there and have fun!" They all grabbed their boards and ran toward the water.

"Number-one rule, kids!" Mr. Madden shouted. "Don't turn your back on the ocean. Number two—"

"If in doubt, just stay out!" Avery chimed in.

"Nice job, snurfette. That's right—if you're not sure about a wave, wait for the next one."

Avery splashed into the water, impatient to get started. "Catch you out there, Dad?" she shouted, hoping he'd changed his mind about sticking with the landsharks. *Can't he hear those crashing waves calling?* But Mr. Madden waved her off. "I'm gonna give Andie a few pointers, first. I'll be out there in a few!"

"You and your friends can stick with me, if you want," Andie told Kazie, who bit her lip and looked first at Mr. Madden standing right next to her mom, then at Kara-Lee and Katani, and finally over at Avery, swimming out into the deep water. The Kgirls waited for her cue. "C'mon, Kgirls, let's do it," Kazie decided, her blond braids bobbing wildly as she strode away from her mom and into the ocean.

Charlotte, Isabel and Maeve waded into the water carefully. Maeve waved to a young, muscled lifeguard floating on a Jet Ski labeled HAWAIIAN WATER PATROL in big red letters on the side.

"If I need to be rescued, I hope *he* rescues me!" Maeve sighed. Charlotte playfully shoved Maeve, who lost her balance and fell face first into the water!

"Ohhh, now you're gonna get it, Char!" Isabel laughed as Maeve got up and lunged for Charlotte. The trio was soaking wet before they even made it out to the wave break.

Avery sat in the water straddling her board, waiting for the perfect wave. Back on the beach, she could see her dad and Andie heading into the surf together. She watched as her dad showed Andie how to paddle and balance on her board. She remembered how her dad had taught her to surf. She had tried to stand up on her board too soon, but her dad was right behind her to catch her when she flopped right over, promising that he'd be there every step of the way. And he had been, she thought, until Andie and Kazie showed up.

A wave rose up behind her and Avery paddled along the lip. As it began to crest, the wave turned into a small tube. She stood up on her board and carved it up inside the cave, darting back and forth. As the water collapsed in on itself, Avery slid toward the beach, skidding to a beautiful stop.

"Shweeet, Avery!" Chad's friend Will screamed as Chad gave her a double surfer salute.

"Call me Aloha Jedi!" Avery shouted, then looked over to see if her dad had caught her perfect landing, throwing out a *"Cowabunga!"* Or *"Rockin' ride, Snurfette!"* But he was too busy splashing around with Andie as he tried to pull her out into deeper water.

Just Like Dancing

Maeve, Charlotte, and Isabel floated on their boards about twenty yards from the beach, watching each wave pass by and making excuses for why it wasn't the right one.

"Too small," Isabel joked.

"Too big." Charlotte hesitated.

Maeve watched Chad and his friend Will trade waves with Avery, zipping effortlessly in and out of the water.

"Yo, Aloha Jedi! Pull a roundhouse!" Cowabunga Will shouted to Avery.

"Nice 360!" Avery slapped Chizzam a high five when he coasted in after twisting around full circle on the biggest wave yet.

As Chizzam paddled back out to the break, he called out after Maeve. "Hey! Maeve! Don't be a Beach Bunny!"

"Being a bunny doesn't sound all that bad," Charlotte mused. She and Isabel giggled, but Maeve shook her head, her red curls flying back and forth. Charlotte recognized the look on Maeve's face: It was the look she got when she was dead-set on doing something.

"Maeve?" Charlotte asked.

"It's time to stop being Goldilocks!" Maeve declared. "This wave is just right!"

Isabel and Charlotte watched in awe as Maeve paddled furiously into the new wave. As it rose, Maeve had a flash of courage and hopped up to a standing position on her board, keeping her legs bent, her head low, and her arms out. She wobbled, but regained her balance! *I can't believe it! MKT is surfing!*

Maeve surfed right into the shallow water, and just when she knew she was going to fall over, managed to leap off her board in triumph. She heard applause coming from the beach. Avery, Chad, and Will were clapping furiously and giving her the surfer salute!

"That was surftastic, dude!" Chad cheered louder than anyone else. Maeve shook out her hair happily, sending water droplets spraying everywhere.

"Hey!"

Maeve whirled around to see that she had soaked

Kara-Lee, who was standing right behind her. "Whoops! Sorry!" Maeve apologized.

Kara-Lee smiled. "Well, I guess that's why they call it a wetsuit. I had no idea you were so good at this!" Kara-Lee gushed.

"Neither did I," Maeve admitted, "I never even tried surfing until today."

"Well, you're just a natural," Kara-Lee told her.

"I think it's all balance," Maeve confided.

"Katani tells me that you take dance classes, I bet that's what makes you so good," Kara-Lee replied.

Maeve paddled back into the water, motioning for Kara-Lee to follow her. "Hmmm, I think you're right!" *It did feel just like dancing!* She could see why Katani liked Kara-Lee. Maybe there was hope for peace between the BSG and the Kgirls after all.

Surfing with the Duke

Chad and Will splashed over to teach Maeve and Kara-Lee some moves, so Avery paddled out past the break toward the seawall, where the waves were sicker and only the serious surfers were carving it up. She watched as a teenager from their group bit it on a ten-footer, trying to commit to memory the way the waves broke and their timing. Straddling her board, she floated in the water, waiting her turn.

The lifeguard on the Jet Ski hummed up beside her. "Kid, this isn't for random standers. This is big kahuna business. The waves are truckin' today."

Avery nodded, appreciating that he was warning her that only experienced surfers rode these waves since they were big and fast. "Chillax, I'm a total gidget."

He gave her the thumbs up. "Righteous! But be careful." He swerved out of the way and continued his patrol. Avery waited in the break, watching how each wave crested and curled toward the seawall. This part of Ke'ei Beach was famous—surfing legends like Duke Kahanamoku had ridden these same waves. Duke was famous not only for his Olympic gold medals and fame that got people into surfing all over the world, but also for his sixteen-foot-long wooden board that weighed more than a hundred pounds!

"Are you shreddy?"

Avery whipped around—*Oh, no!*

Kazie straddled her board in the water next to Avery. "I'm ready to hang ten. What about you, Short Stack?"

Avery gulped back an angry comeback about the Short Stack thing, and managed to swallow a mouthful of salt water. "Kazie, you shouldn't be out here!" Avery coughed.

Kazie shrugged. "Why not? You're out here. And as far as I can tell, you're just hanging."

If she knew what she was doing, Avery thought, *she would know I'm waiting for the right wave!* She looked her in the eyes. "Kazie, I've been surfing a ton of times. This is like hitting a double black diamond when you've never been on a snowboard before." Avery looked around for help, but everyone was surfing the safer part of the beach.

"And I've hit more double black diamonds than you even knew *existed*. Cowabunga, dude," Kazie shouted, paddling into the next wave.

As it began to peak, Avery realized the wave was going to be a monster. *Why did Kazie go and do something so stupid and dangerous?* she wondered. The cold grip of fear washed over Avery when she realized that Kazie was doing exactly what the two of them had been doing since they met. They were competing to see who would be the best.

Except that this time, Kazie was in way over her head.

The Big One

"Sweet move, Surf Bunny!" Mr. Madden called out as Maeve sailed in for another perfect landing.

Maeve curled her hand into a fist with her thumb and pinky extended—the surfer salute. "Banzai, dude!"

Mr. Madden laughed. "Everyone looks like they're having a righteous time."

Andie searched the water, concerned. "Except Kazie and Avery. Jake, I can't find them."

Mr. Madden scanned the horizon. "There they are." They watched as both girls approached a giant wave. "Andie, I thought you said that Kazie hadn't surfed before?" Jake asked nervously.

"She hasn't." Andie replied. Andie watched in horror as the wave grew larger. "Jake?"

"I'm on it!" He paddled furiously toward the girls. Andie followed close behind.

Behind them, Annika blew her big red whistle, and the lifeguards leaped into action.

Panic!

"Lean back!" Avery cried out. "Steady, don't tip forward!" Her instructions were falling on deaf ears as the look on Kazie's face suddenly turned to sheer panic.

"I can't stay up!" Kazie yelled over the water. She wasn't even trying to stand anymore, just clinging to her board in sheer terror.

"Just hang on!" Avery yelled back. What had she been thinking? Of course Kazie was going to follow her to the more dangerous part of the beach in an effort to one-up her! She wanted to blame Kazie, but Avery knew she would have done the exact same thing. *She's out here because of me,* Avery realized. *If something happens to her, it's all my fault.*

A tube formed in the giant wave, and the sound was deafening. Avery struggled to stay upright.

"AVERY! HELP!" Kazie screamed. Her board went out from under her and the wave swallowed her whole.

"KAZIE!" Avery watched helplessly as Kazie's board shot out of the wave— without Kazie! *This is all because of our stupid competition thing. I just wanted my dad to myself.* Avery bit back tears as she cut back through the wave, diving beneath the water again and again, searching for Kazie's pink wetsuit.

Andie and Mr. Madden saw the wave come crashing down and the board pop out. Kazie was no longer in view!

Andie tossed her surfboard aside and dove into the water, swimming toward her daughter.

"Andie, wait!" Mr. Madden cried out. "The lifeguards are on it! The wave's too big!" He tried to paddle after her, but his surfboard leash got tangled up with another surfer's. Soon Andie was yards ahead of him, heading right into the path of an enormous wave on her own.

14

Monster Waves

very could hear the hum of a Jet Ski arriving, so she took another deep breath and dove again, scanning the murky depths for any sign of Kazie. She spotted a flash of blond braids near the surface and jumped away from her board, grabbing the back of Kazie's wetsuit. Avery hauled Kazie to the surface and propped her up on her board. Kazie coughed and sputtered, trying to catch her breath.

"Are you insane?" Avery yelled at her as they bobbed up and down in the swells together. "You don't belong in these waves!"

Kazie spat out a mouthful of salt water and wiped her mouth with the back of her hand. "Why do you think I'm called Crazie Kazie?"

Avery stared at Kazie for a moment, then gave her a half hug—it was the best she could manage while treading water—as relief spread all through her. "I'm glad you're okay," she gulped back a sob.

"Me too," Kazie replied.

Avery had Kazie grab the back of her surfboard so she could tow Kazie toward shore. The rescue Jet Ski roared up behind them, but Kazie and Avery both waved him off. "We're fine!"

As they paddled in, Avery's head felt like it was swimming faster than the rest of her.

"I guess I was really stupid out there," Kazie muttered. "Thanks."

"No biggie. We make an okay team," Avery declared.

"You mean we make a great team when you're coming to my rescue," said a sheepish Kazie.

"Well, yeah," Avery agreed with a smirk. "But let's not do *that* again!"

"Deal," said Kazie. "Hey . . . we can agree about some stuff."

They walked together out of the surf and into a crowd of worried friends.

"What happened?" Kara-Lee asked. "Why would you do that, Kazie?"

"Are you okay?" Isabel wanted to know.

Questions bombarded them, but Kazie wasn't listening. She looked frantically around the beach. "Where's my mom?"

"I thought she was with my dad?" Avery wondered, then saw her dad struggling with his surfboard, while this other guy shouted at him.

"She's been with him, like, the entire trip!" Kazie complained.

Weird, thought Avery. *Does Kazie feel the same way I do about my dad and Andie?* But she didn't have time to worry about that now.

"Dad!" Avery shouted from the shore.

"We're okay!" Kazie waved.

"Where's Andie?" he called to them frantically.

Then they all saw her—swimming toward the seawall! Suddenly, she was sucked into the current of a monster wave like a bit of crumpled paper spiraling into a storm drain. The wave rose up, hovering with the weight and anger of a blue avalanche, before crashing down angrily upon the place she'd just been.

"Mom!!!" Kazie screamed.

Surf's Down!

Mr. Madden dove beneath the surface of the water and swam as quickly as he could toward the place where Andie had disappeared. Kazie rushed toward the water, but Avery managed to hold her back.

"But my mom—"

"Stay here!" Avery shouted. "My dad's out there, and look—the Jet Skis!" Two lifeguards were already roaring into the giant waves.

Charlotte saw that Kazie was completely still and speechless. "Don't worry," she urged in what she hoped was a soothing voice. "It's going to be okay."

Kazie's lip trembled as they watched Mr. Madden splash in the waves just ahead of the jet skis, swimming against the current.

"Look!" yelled Isabel. Everyone watched as Mr. Madden grabbed Andie and they struggled against the water. He hooked his arm around her and started to paddle toward the closest Jet Ski. A crowd had formed on shore, watching the daring rescue.

"What's going on?" Katani demanded to know. Isabel put an arm around Charlotte, and Maeve chewed on her fingernails. Avery motioned for everyone to be quiet and pointed toward the water.

Maeve's favorite young lifeguard had pulled Andie onto a special body board. Mr. Madden hopped up on the seat behind him and leaned down to hold Andie's hand as they zoomed back into shore.

"Make way!" The lifeguard shouted, and the crowd scattered.

Someone must have notified the cruise lines, because Captain Bob came running over with a signature green and gold Aloha Cruise Lines towel. Mr. Madden laid Andie down on it. Sea water dribbled out of her mouth.

"MOM!" Kazie yelled, running toward her mother and kneeling on one side as Mr. Madden gently tilted her head back and held his ear close to her nose and mouth.

A lifeguard tried to elbow Mr. Madden out of the way, but he held his ground. Without hesitating for even a second, he placed his mouth over Andie's and blew in air.

At that moment, Andie started coughing up sea

water onto Mr. Madden and the fancy towel. The life-guard squeezed Kazie's shoulder. "Your mom'll be fine. Thanks to your dad's quick action."

"He's *not* my dad," Kazie snapped defiantly as she broke free of his grasp and wrapped her arms around her mom.

"Why were you in that deep? You don't even swim that well!" she yelled as she hugged her mom, angry and relieved.

Andie sat up slowly, breathing in long, ragged breaths. "Kazie?" she asked.

"Oh, Mom. You're okay, I'm right here." Tears stung at her eyes. "It's my fault," Kazie moaned.

Avery shook her head, shoving her way through the quickly forming crowd to get closer. "Hey. Hey! It's going to be okay. Your mom is okay."

"It's all my fault," Kazie said hoarsely.

Avery shook her head. "This is *our* fault."

Kazie gave her a weak smile and both girls stood in silence while Mr. Madden and the lifeguards helped Andie stand.

Avery felt an arm around her shoulder. It was her dad, who leaned down and hugged her. "Dad, I'm so sorry, I am so, so sorry!"

Her dad quieted her. "Everyone's okay. That's what's important." He squeezed Avery's hand and then got down on one knee by Andie, who hugged Kazie again and then looked back at Jake with a surprised expression. *What's Dad doing?* Avery wondered.

"I have a question for you, Andie," he stated solemnly.

"I'm okay," Andie assured him.

Mr. Madden laughed nervously. "That wasn't the question." Mr. Madden gently took her hand in his.

Mr. Madden swallowed the lump in his throat. "Will . . . will you marry me?"

Romance Shock

Avery shook her head wildly. *This is NOT happening!* Beside her, Kazie had her hands over her face, but she couldn't cover up an expression of pure shock as Andie smiled and nodded, tears streaming down her cheeks. "Of course I'll marry you!"

The beach erupted in applause as Mr. Madden helped Andie to her feet. He took her in his arms, dipped her, and kissed her!

How romantic! An awestruck Maeve beamed from the sidelines.

"I thought I'd lost you," Jake Madden told Andie in a voice just loud enough for the ring of onlookers closest by to hear. "And well, it made me realize that I don't want to waste another single minute waiting to spend the rest of our lives together!"

As romantic as, as . . . a movie! Maeve thought, hoping against all hope that one day, a major movie star would propose to her in exactly the same way. *Only he'll have a fresh-cut rose and a diamond ring and a flock of doves will rise up in the air as we embrace!*

While everyone crowded around to congratulate the newly engaged couple, Maeve squeezed her way through to wrap Avery and Kazie in a three-way hug. "Was that not the most romantic thing you've ever seen?" she gushed.

Avery and Kazie exchanged a look that could only mean one thing: *Who is this girl?*

"You're going to be sisters now!" Kara-Lee exclaimed.

Charlotte leaned over to Isabel. "Well, for once it looks like Avery and Kazie are totally in sync."

"I think you mean in shock," Isabel replied. "Romance shock!"

The crowd quieted down as Mr. Madden got ready to make an announcement. "If there's one thing we've learned today, it's that life is short. That's why we are going to get married right on the ship, this very week. That is, if Captain Bob will do us the honors, of course."

Captain Bob tipped his hat to the couple. "Aye! The best part about being a Captain is officiating at weddings on board! It'll be my honor."

Mr. Madden and Andie turned to find their daughters to discuss the happy news. But Avery and Kazie were nowhere to be seen.

Unofficially Sisters

"I thought you'd be here," Kazie murmured.

Avery was skipping small stones along the water's edge on the calm side of the beach.

Kazie picked up a smooth black stone and expertly skipped it along the surface of the water.

Avery watched, admiring Kazie's technique. "You're pretty good at that."

"Yeah, it's surfing that's the problem," Kazie replied.

Both girls smiled awkwardly and then were suddenly silent, as if remembering that they weren't supposed to like each other. The waves crashed against the beach, hurling a few pro surfers into land, and muffling the sounds from the crowd of people who surrounded Andie and Mr. Madden in the distance.

Kazie nodded toward the crowd. "Pretty weird, huh?"

"Did you know it was coming?" Avery challenged.

"No way!" Kazie exclaimed. "Did you?"

"Nope," Avery answered. "And I think it's totally not cool that he just sprung it on me."

"I know!" Kazie concurred. "I mean, hello? A little heads-up?"

"That bit about life is short—" Avery started to say.

Kazie finished the thought for her. "That was totally about my little stunt today and you know it."

"Although I guess my dad is kinda big on surprises," Avery said thoughtfully.

"Like what?" asked Kazie.

Avery whirled around. "Um, like you coming on this cruise?"

Kazie crossed her arms over her chest. "Yeah, but that's a totally awesome surprise."

"If you say so." Avery cracked a smile.

"I do."

Avery traced her initials in the sand with her big toe and then watched as the waves crept up on the shore and washed them away, along with her smile. "It's just, I don't know. Your mom is a nice person and all, but, this is just weird. I'm not sure if I like it."

"I know!" said Kazie. "The Snurfman totally rocks, but I'm used to things being, you know, just Mom and me."

Avery nodded. "I mean, what are my brothers gonna think? And my mom? They're all, like, a million miles away." She kicked the sand as hard as she could, sending a spray of tiny rocks into the surf.

"I've never even *met* your brothers," Kazie complained.

"They're cool," Avery assured her. But what she was thinking was a lot more complicated. *My brothers are totally awesome, but they're mine. Not yours. Except, maybe I wouldn't mind it if you came snowboarding with all of us. As long as Dad comes too, instead of skiing with Andie.*

Avery glanced over at Kazie and noticed she was rubbing her eyes really hard. Was she crying? "They have no idea!" Kazie spat. "Why'd the Snurfman have to ask? Why'd Mom say yes? It's like she didn't even *see* me standing there!"

"I know what you mean," Avery grumbled.

For a while, the two girls just stood there chucking rocks out into the water as the sun dipped closer to the distant waves.

Kazie finally broke the silence. "You know what's really weird?"

"What?" Avery asked.

"Finally, there's something we totally agree on," Kazie uttered with a note of exasperation.

Avery took one last look at the horizon. "C'mon, we better head back. We don't need any more rescues today."

CHAPTER
15
I Don't!

"There you are, snurfette!" Avery's dad slid into the bus seat next to her. "I've been looking for you! Man, ask someone to marry you in public and you're a sudden celebrity." He grinned, but Avery didn't grin back. She was staring across the crowded bus to where Andie had just sat down with Kazie.

"Look, I know this seems all totally spur of the moment, Ave. But I really did mean to talk to you about it. Then that wave . . . almost losing Andie . . . I love her, Ave."

Avery nodded slightly. "Uh-huh."

Her dad put an arm around her shoulders. "Want to talk about it?"

Avery met Kazie's eyes and shook her head. Kazie's steely look cut through both their parent's apologies, and Avery knew Kazie felt the same way she did. *No way am I ready to talk yet!*

Masking the Problem

"I've always dreamed of attending a masquerade!" Maeve gushed, twirling around in the fourth dress she'd tried on since returning to the BSG's cabin from the beach. "Where are we supposed to get our masks?"

Katani reached into a drawer and took out little packages of tissue paper. "Isabel and I have a surprise for all of you!" she announced, and began to unwrap the opera masks that she and Isabel had made especially for the trip. Even though all the girls had read the itinerary carefully, only Katani had thought to check all the possible dinner themes and pack for each. The masks Isabel had helped make were covered with brightly colored satin and embellished with rhinestones, silk flowers, or feathers.

Avery watched the whole scene from her seat on the sofa. She hadn't said more than two words at once to any of her friends since her dad's surprise engagement on the beach. Charlotte and Isabel were worried about her, but didn't really know what to say.

"Is there a pink one?" Maeve asked expectantly. She loved pink!

"Hold on!" Katani cautioned, "I haven't found that one yet!" She carefully unfolded the tissue paper off of the last mask—pink satin dotted with fuchsia rhinestones—and handed it to Maeve. "There you go, one pink-tabulous masquerade ball masterpiece!"

Maeve held the mask up to her face and looked through

the eyeholes. She batted her lashes dramatically. "You guys really are miracle workers! These are amazing!"

Isabel blushed. "Thanks, Katani and I worked awfully hard on them." She pulled her long dark hair in a ponytail and tried on her mask, which was green satin, accented with dark blue feathers.

Charlotte held her mask—lavender with black satin trim—up to her face and said in her best French accent, *"Bonjour, mes amies!"*

"Bonjour!" Franco called from on top of Charlotte's suitcase. It was his new favorite perch.

Isabel laughed, keeping an eye on Avery. "You should teach him French, Char!"

Avery smiled a little, so that was good.

Maeve sat down at the edge of her bed. "I'd like to get married in Paris," she sighed dreamily. "Although on a cruise ship in Hawaii is a close second. Can you believe your dad is engaged, Avery?"

"Ummm," Avery said. Charlotte and Isabel shared a look.

"We don't have to talk about it, Ave. If you don't want," Isabel offered.

Avery shrugged, "It's okay," and strode through the chaos of clothes and masks and shoes to hide in the bathroom for a minute. She knew there would be plenty of wedding talk at dinner, but she was hoping to avoid it for as long as she could.

"What do you think Andie's going to wear?" Maeve whispered once Avery was safely out of earshot. "You don't pack a wedding dress on a cruise. Or do you?"

"*You* probably would," Katani joked.

Avery sighed and looked in the bathroom mirror, holding her mask up in front of her face. It was blue with little dolphins painted on it. *Maybe no one will recognize me*, she hoped.

"I just realized what we have to do!" Maeve exclaimed, loud enough so Avery could hear. "We have to plan the wedding!"

Avery heard Charlotte laugh. "No, we don't."

"Katani will obviously help with the dress," Maeve said, more quietly this time. "Isabel, you'll do the invites, since you're our resident artist. Our writer—Charlotte, naturally—will find a poem. I'll pick the music and . . . what else?"

"Franco!" Franco blurted out.

Maeve huffed. "No, Franco, no parrots at the wedding. Now I know I'm forgetting one more thing . . . oh! The flower girl! That will be Avery, of course." Maeve danced around to the bathroom door and tapped on it. "Avery, come out please? What's wrong?"

"I'm NOT coming out of this bathroom until you stop talking about *weddings*!" Avery shouted.

"I didn't mean to forget her!" Maeve whispered, looking worried.

"I don't think she's upset that you forgot her," Katani said. "Did you ever think for a second that maybe Avery doesn't want to play wedding?"

"But weddings are so much fun!" Maeve insisted. Actually, she'd only been to one wedding, her Aunt Lisa's, and she had been too young to remember much of it. But Maeve had spent more than her share of time flipping through bridal magazines in the supermarket and dreaming up ideas for her own future wedding someday.

Charlotte put down her mask and sat next to Maeve on the bed. "But it's her dad. So it probably isn't fun to her. She's still in shock."

"I'm so clueless," Maeve whispered, suddenly embarrassed that she'd gotten so carried away. It was just so hard to keep in her excitement!

"I'm sure it's okay. Just give her some time," Charlotte assured her.

Maeve put her head in her hands. "I am such a bad friend."

Isabel ran over to hug her. "You just didn't think."

"Avery, you okay in there?" Katani tapped on the door.

The knob turned and Avery poked her head out. "No more wedding talk?"

"No more! I *promise*." Maeve looked stricken.

"Flower girl!" Franco cried.

Maeve whirled on the parrot. "Franco, be quiet!"

Franco hissed back.

"FRANCO!" Maeve yelled, "You are the meanest, most nasty parrot EVER!"

"No! No! No!" Franco stopped suddenly when Isabel wagged her finger at him.

"Franco, apologize!" Isabel scolded him.

Franco turned back to Maeve and bowed his head. "Bad Franco."

The stern look on Maeve's face melted. "Okay, Franco, even I can't stay mad at you." She picked the last piece of pineapple off the plate and handed it to him. "Truce?"

"Ha-ha-ha!" Franco cawed, then delicately took the piece of fruit from her hand. "Pineapple!"

A knock came at the door. Everyone turned toward the door, then back to Franco. *What to do?* The knock came again.

"Who's there?" Franco asked.

"It's Jake Madden," came the reply from the other side of the door.

Isabel quickly took charge, gently removing Franco from Charlotte's suitcase.

"Franco, you're going to sit on another perch for just a couple of minutes, but you're going to have to be quiet. Okay?" She placed him on the rod that extended across the closet and then gently shut the door.

"Not in the middle of all my clothes again!" Katani hissed.

"We have no choice!" Isabel mouthed back.

"Night-night!" Franco squawked quietly as Isabel swung the closet shut. She turned around, keeping her back pressed against the door, and nodded to Avery to let her Dad in.

The door swung open, and a tall figure in a black shirt with a freaky green, wart-covered face strode across the room and plopped down on the couch!

"Ahhhhhh!" Isabel screamed, hearing Franco join in from the other side of the closet door.

Avery ripped off the monster mask and Mr. Madden grinned.

"Got you!" He took in the girls' elegant opera masks. "I guess that's what they meant by masks?" He lounged back on the sofa and tapped his fingers together nervously. "Nice place you got here, girls . . ."

Charlotte could sense that Mr. Madden wanted to talk to his daughter. Maybe she could convince him to talk to her somewhere *other* than the room with the parrot? "Marisol's just about to take us to dinner," Charlotte said. "But you and Avery could go ahead now."

"I'm not that hungry yet," Mr. Madden remarked just as Marisol stepped in from the next room.

"Was that a scream I heard?" Marisol tried to hide her surprise at seeing Mr. Madden there with a giggle and a quick compliment. "I love your masks!"

"Thanks!" Katani said louder than necessary as Marisol pulled Isabel into the hall. "Franco?"

Isabel shrugged helplessly.

"I think Ave and I should just hang out here for a little while," Mr. Madden continued. "We haven't had much, y'know, time together, huh Ave?"

"Uhhh," Avery stammered. She'd kind of gotten some thoughts together after the bus ride, and she really wanted to talk to her dad, but not in the room where they were trying to hide Franco! There's no way her dad wouldn't figure it all out, and then they'd all be in huge trouble.

"So you all just go on ahead. You must be hungry!"

Avery's dad waved the girls out the door.

"Come as soon as you can, Ave!" Maeve called back.

Charlotte looked at the closet, then at Avery, and then back at the closet meaningfully.

"I will *take care*," Avery said, nodding that she knew what Charlotte meant. Then the door of the cabin shut and it was just Avery, her dad, and . . . *nobody else. No hidden parrots, stowaways, or future stepsisters.*

Mr. Madden sat down on the sofa and looked out their porthole. The sun was just beginning to set behind the clouds, and the window offered a front-row seat to a spectacular sunset.

"That's a pretty fancy mask you got there," he said.

Avery glanced toward the closet. How long would Franco stay quiet? "Thanks. Katani and Isabel made it."

"Shoulda asked them to make me one!" Avery's dad held up the green rubber thing. "This isn't exactly cruise ship material," he joked.

"Hey, it's not what you wear—"

Mr. Madden finished Avery's sentence. "It's how you tear. Exactly."

He paused for a moment, looked out the porthole and then back at his daughter. "Ave, I know you're probably still in shock from this afternoon. I did have a whole plan to rap with you about it before popping the question. It's just that things got . . . *gnarly.* I just want to make sure you're okay with all of this."

Avery snorted. *Okay? Am I okay?* Her dad had gone from surprising her by showing up with Andie and

Kazie on the cruise to springing a brand new family on her. How could she explain the difference between "my dad's girlfriend's annoying daughter, Crazie Kazie" to "my stepsister, Crazie Kazie." She wasn't even close to okay!

A rustling sound came from the closet. *Franco!*

"What's that?" asked Mr. Madden.

Avery coughed. "What? Oh, that's nothing."

Franco moved around in the closet again. It sounded like he was rubbing his beak against the closet door. Avery panicked!

"Listen, you're right, it is a shock. And it'll take some getting used to, but I'll get used to it. Pinky swear." She took her dad by the hand and led him to the cabin door. "And I'm starving, but I have to go to the bathroom quick . . . meet you in the hall in a few?"

Her dad hugged her, and gave her a thumbs-up. "I knew you'd be on board. I'll just, uh, wait here!"

Avery shut the door behind him before he could wonder why he had to wait in the hallway and breathed a huge sigh of relief. She retrieved Franco from the closet and carried him into Mr. Ramsey's room to his actual cage. "Sorry we had to do that, Franco. That was close!"

Franco nodded, and hopped on his perch. He peered at Avery with his beady black eyes.

"Sad?" Franco asked.

Avery scratched the feathers on the bird's head. "Oh, Franco, if you only knew."

Freaking Out

The Masquerade Dinner swung into full gear! Mysterious music played through the loudspeakers while masked waiters set down plates loaded with salad, roast chicken, fish, and rice in front of the girls.

Isabel's eyes grew wide. "I can't believe I'm saying this, but I'm actually sick of eating."

"Speak for yourself!" Charlotte exclaimed in her French accent. "I think *zees poulet* is *merveilleux*!" And she popped a piece of chicken in her mouth.

"Did you see they posted the order for the karaoke contest tomorrow?" Maeve said between bites. "We need to think about practicing, pronto."

Katani leaned over to Maeve. "Speaking of practicing—"

Maeve saw how nervous Katani looked. "You're freaking out?"

"Who's freaking out?" Avery said with a mouthful of rice. The food was definitely helping her sorta kinda forget about the wedding for a little while. She'd at least managed to convince her dad to sit at his and Andie's table for the evening and let the BSG have some time together.

Katani glanced to the table where Kara-Lee sat with her parents. Kazie was sitting with them, too. Katani was singing with the Kgirls, sure, but these girls at this table were her friends. She should just tell them. "The Kgirls don't know I can't sing."

Avery burst out laughing, then coughed, choking on her rice. She took a sip of water and caught her breath. "How could they not know?"

"Because I didn't tell them!" Katani cried.

"Why not?" Isabel asked.

"I just didn't. And now I'm going to go up there and everyone's going to laugh at me!" Katani wiped her mouth and folded her napkin back up carefully. "I'm toast."

Isabel and Charlotte shared a look. They didn't like the fact that Katani wouldn't be performing with the rest of the BSG, but they also didn't want her to look bad.

"Hang on," Maeve said "what about the whole backup vocals thing we practiced? You don't feel comfortable doing that?"

Katani shook her head. "You don't understand how good these girls can sing! It's gonna fall flat."

"There's only one option, then," Charlotte concluded. "You have to tell them."

"But what if they kick me out of the Kgirls?" Katani asked, totally not feeling like herself. Since when was the Kgirl afraid to speak her mind? *Maybe since there started being three Kgirls . . .* , she realized.

The table looked at her, silent. Avery was the first to speak. "If they're really your friends, they'll understand," she said quietly. "But if you're really their friend, you'll tell them."

Katani nodded. "You're right." She sighed. But knowing what the right thing was and actually doing it? Totally different!

Under the Stars

After dinner everyone except Mr. Madden and Andie, who had wedding plans to discuss, gathered on the top deck to listen to Vivianne Grace, the onboard astronomer, lecture on the stars' role in naval navigation.

It was a perfect evening for stargazing—the air had turned chilly and the sky was clear. Stars twinkled in the night sky like lit candles on a birthday cake. The girls sat on adjoining lounge chairs, huddled under blankets.

"Let's start," said Miss Grace, "by identifying some of the major constellations in the night sky . . ."

Charlotte listened to Vivi, transfixed. Her landlady, Miss Pierce, was an astronomer and she let Charlotte and her friends use her brass telescope in the tower room to observe the stars and the planets. Charlotte wondered what it would be like to sail across the sea using only the stars as a guide! *Maybe Nick Montoya would come with me.* Charlotte smiled to herself, remembering his cute brown eyes.

Maeve, on the other hand, had a different star in her sights: Chad. He had come to the lecture with his parents and Will. She had already imagined Chizzam as her leading man. They could do a whole series of movies together, like William Powell and Myrna Loy! Or Bogie and Bacall! *And in the grand finale, we'll surf off into the sunset!* She could see the headlines now! "Surf Bunny and Chizzam rock the Blue Crush!"

She suddenly realized that Chad was staring at her. "Did you say something?" she whispered.

He laughed quietly, which made his blue eyes light up even more. "You're totally not listening!"

"I am," Maeve insisted. "I just didn't hear you!"

Chad laughed again. "Did not!"

"Did too!"

"Did not!" Chad said again, and then burst out laughing. Everyone in the room turned to stare.

Maeve flushed red. "Chad! Keep it down!"

Chad hung his head. "Sorry," he said, and gave her a puppy dog look.

Riley would never act this immature . . . , Maeve realized as the lecture ended to thunderous applause and everyone gathered their things, getting ready to head back to their cabins for the evening.

"I was going to check on my dad before I headed back to the room," Charlotte told Marisol. "Is it too late?"

"Not at all," Marisol said gently. "I'll go with you. Anyone else coming?"

"I think I'm going to pack it in," Katani said. She had plenty to think about, like how she was going to break the news to Kazie and Kara-Lee that she couldn't sing!

"Me too," said Maeve and Isabel, yawning.

"Avery? Do you want to come?" Charlotte asked.

Avery shook her head. "I think I'm done too." It had been the longest day, ever, and Avery wanted it over as soon as possible.

Postcards Home

Dear Sam,

I'm going to a wedding! No, not mine! ☺ Avery's dad

and his girlfriend are getting married. Isn't that the most romantic thing ever? I'll see you soon!

XOXO,
Maeve

Dear Nick,

My father always says there's a story in everything. I think this trip has a whole novel in it! Tonight we watched the stars from the top deck—I've never seen so much of the sky at once before! I can't wait to tell you all about everything, but I'm running out of room on this postcard. I hope you're having a fun vacation, too.

See you soon,
Charlotte

Dear Candace,

I did something super dumb. I still haven't told my new friends I can't sing, and the karaoke contest is tomorrow! I know, you're laughing. Why did I let them think I could sing? Clearly I have been away from you too long—you always remind me that being yourself is the most important thing. If only it wasn't so difficult! Miss you tons!

TTYL,
Katani

Dear Elena Maria,
  Avery's dad is getting married tomorrow! Can you believe it?
                    Adios, Isabel

Dear Scott,
  Turn your phone on! I tried to call and I know you won't get this stupid postcard for like a week, but anyway, Dad is getting married. NOT A JOKE.

                    Later,
                    Ave

16

Practice Doesn't Always Make Perfect

The ship's horn sounded three short blasts, waking the girls up. Charlotte stretched and peered out of the porthole. "We're in Maui!" she said excitedly.

Isabel yawned. "We are? It still feels like we're on a ship."

Avery threw a pillow at her. "Up and at 'em, Izzy! I don't want to miss *one second* of beach time."

Katani was already dressed and brushing her hair. She made it a practice to get up before everyone so she'd always have enough time to get ready. Yes, she was tired, but these were the kind of sacrifices the future CEO of Kgirl Enterprises would have to make, so she'd better get used to it!

Avery slid off the top bunk and managed to kick Maeve's arm, which had been hanging off the side of her bed. Maeve made a sound like *mmmrrgff* and turned over.

"Maeve! Get up!" Avery whispered in her ear. "It's beach day!" She still didn't move. "And karaoke day!"

That got Maeve's attention. She opened her eyes and smiled sleepily. "Time to rise and sing!"

"Isn't it rise and *shine*?" Katani took one last look in the mirror before settling down to wait for her friends to get ready. She wished everyone would stop talking about karaoke and singing!

"Did you have a chance to talk to Kazie and Kara-Lee yet?" Charlotte asked as if reading Katani's mind.

Katani shook her head. *Why bother?* she thought. *Because they're going to find out the truth on their own soon enough.*

Two hours and a bumpy bus ride later, the BSG found themselves on the most gorgeous stretch of beach any of them had ever seen. The sun glinted off the sea and white sand shaded by swaying palm trees stretched as far as they could see in each direction.

"You girls sound *maravilloso*!" Marisol exclaimed after the BSG's first karaoke run-through. "I'm going to sit over here and read. Just let me know if you need anything."

Marisol was chaperoning them today, because Mr. Madden and Andie still had to write their vows and pick out a cake. They had asked Avery at breakfast if she wanted to help them, but she just shook her head and said, "Maybe later." Kazie also opted to go to the beach, tagging along with Kara-Lee's family.

"We'd better practice those harmonies," Maeve pronounced. "We're sounding flat." The BSG had a lot of work to do if they were going to take on the Kgirls in karaoke!

Avery stared longingly out at the water. The sky was blue, peppered with fluffy white clouds and the waves lapped gently at the warm sand under their feet. For the first time since her Dad's marriage proposal, Avery was feeling pretty okay. Like she could forget about everything under the surface of that bright blue green water. But here they were—practicing karaoke!

"I think we sound fine," Avery complained.

"Which is why it's good you're not in charge of our performance," Maeve lectured. "Because when I said we were flat, I meant *you* were flat."

"No! Not . . . flat! " Avery groaned and fell over in mock horror.

"If it makes you feel any better, I can't tell either." Charlotte laughed and helped Avery up. It was good to see Avery being her old silly self.

"Well, Maeve's right," Isabel added. "Let's try just a few more times through . . . we'll have it down, Ave."

"Then beach time?" Avery asked hopefully.

"Then beach time," Maeve promised. "Now from the top!"

As Maeve counted them in, Charlotte glanced over to the picnic benches where Katani was practicing with the Kgirls. *Has she told them yet?* she wondered.

Kicked Out?

Katani spent most of her morning sitting around a picnic table discussing dance moves and karaoke outfits with

Kara-Lee and Kazie. Anything to keep from revealing her embarrassing secret. But she knew she was stalling, and Kazie was growing impatient.

"None of this is gonna matter if we can't rock out our parts."

"Kazie's right," Kara-Lee said. "Let's run it through once and then we can go back and figure out which parts we need to work on."

Katani took a deep breath. "There's just one thing."

Kara-Lee and Kazie looked at Katani expectantly. Katani froze, suddenly not knowing what to say. Whether she told them the truth now or they found it out themselves, she was going to ruin everything.

"What's up, Katani?" Kara-Lee asked.

Katani swallowed and shrugged as Kazie jumped up from the bench and cheered, "Let's rock this thing!" But the only rock Katani wanted was a rock to crawl under!

Kara-Lee began to sing the first lines of the Nik and Sam song. Her voice was like her accent, thick and sweet. As she reached the crescendo, her voice swelled and as she finished on a high note, she nodded toward Kazie.

Kazie was just as good a singer as Kara-Lee, only her voice was different—lower, more soulful. Suddenly Katani realized they were looking at her. *It's my verse!*

Katani opened her mouth, trying to remember everything Maeve had taught her. *Just breathe and let the song flow.* Closing her eyes, she belted out her verse, giving it everything she had.

*"Even though I know it's true
The way you feel about me,
The way I feel 'bout you,
Only three hours —
Three hours till you."*

Katani finished and opened one of her eyes. Kara-Lee and Kazie were staring at her, horrified.

"Um, was that a joke?" Kara-Lee asked gently.

"If it was, sing it for real this time," Kazie continued. "The karaoke contest is tonight!"

Katani swallowed hard, trying hard not to cry, and looked up at her friends. "I have something to tell you."

Kara-Lee and Kazie stared back at her. She took another deep breath and shut her eyes. "I can't sing."

"WHAT?" Kara-Lee and Kazie screamed in unison.

"I can't sing. I can't carry a tune. That? What you just heard? That's my singing voice. That's how I sing."

Kazie groaned and slapped the top of the picnic table with her palms. "You're joking. Please tell me you're joking."

Kara-Lee blinked once, then twice. "Why did you wait so long to tell us?"

Katani felt terrible. She had sabotaged their chances of winning the contest! "I don't know. It's just that . . . I just don't know."

"Well, now we can't win," Kazie pointed out bluntly.

Katani swallowed the lump in her throat. "I didn't tell you 'cause I thought you might kick me out of the Kgirls."

She looked from Kara-Lee to Kazie. Neither girl said a word. Katani felt more than embarrassed. She was guilty, ashamed, and regretful, too. *I'm kicked out!*

I Got You, Babe

"Maeve, I can sing this song backward and forward and in five different languages. Can we please go swimming now?" Avery groaned.

"We still need to practice our dance moves," Maeve insisted. She spotted Chad and Will digging trenches in the sand just down the beach and started formulating a plan. "A change of scenery will make you feel better. Why don't we move down there?" She pointed down where Chad and Will were now jumping in and out of the surf as it filled up their trench.

"Maeve, I think the only one benefiting from that change in scenery is you," Charlotte jested as the group picked up their backpacks, towels, and extra clothing to move down the beach.

Avery watched as Chad and Will abandoned their sand moat and started trying to bodysurf. "That looks like fun," she said wistfully.

"Just imagine how fun it'll be when we win tonight!" Maeve reminded everyone. She caught Chad waving at her and she waved back. *Good, he knows I'm here. Now time to wow him with my singing voice!* "From the top!"

Maeve started to sing the first verse and turned to see if Chad was listening. But of course he was trying to dunk Will in the water! *Boys!* She was so annoyed, she forgot the next line and the rest of the BSG stopped singing along with her.

"Okay, one more time . . . ," Maeve instructed.

That's when they heard it. A girl's voice. She was singing the new Nik and Sam song in a way that was both sweet and strong. Maeve craned her neck to see where the voice was coming from.

It was Kara-Lee! *We've got to make our act even better!* Maeve thought. She pointed over to where the Kgirls stood. "Kara-Lee is good. Really good. And so is Kazie. So we have to be, like, better than our absolute best to beat them!"

"Kazie can sing?" Avery was astonished. Was there anything the girl couldn't do? Other than surf, obviously. Although Avery had no doubt she could learn to surf like a pro if she tried.

"I'll practice as long as it takes," Avery announced, suddenly serious. There was no way she was going to let Kazie beat her!

Isabel leaned over to Charlotte. "I don't see why we can't all work together."

"That's a really good idea," Charlotte replied. "Tell everyone."

"Tell everyone what?" Maeve demanded.

Isabel cleared her throat. "I just thought maybe it would be a better idea to have everyone work together. Y'know, combine groups."

Maeve and Avery looked at each other. *Combine groups?*

Avery shook her head. "No way, no how, am I working with Kazie." Just looking over in Kazie's direction made Avery remember her dad and Andie, and the stupid wedding that was one stupid day after today.

"But Katani's over there, and she's our friend too," Charlotte reminded her. "We could help her out and we wouldn't have to compete with Kazie and Kara-Lee. It would be . . . nicer."

"Yeah, but Katani's over there," Avery said, "with her new club, the Kgirls. Not with us." Avery crossed her arms in front of her chest.

Charlotte and Isabel shared a look. This was going to be so much harder than they thought.

Kgirls Need Some Khelp

Katani wasn't kicked out of the Kgirl club, but all three of the girls were worried that they might have to drop out of the competition altogether.

"It's no use," Kara-Lee complained. "We sound terrible." She sighed and slumped down on the picnic bench.

Katani felt horrible. This was all her fault! "I'm so, so sorry. You girls are fabulous! *I'm* the one who's terrible. Can't I just be the producer? Or the costumer?"

"It said on the sheet, 'you sign up, you sing!'" Kazie reminded them.

"Maybe if we just go through it one more time?" Kara-Lee said weakly.

"Trust me, I've been through this before with the BSG,

I don't get any better," Katani told her. "Singing is just not my thing."

"We'll make it your thing!" Kazie shouted. "Ready? Repeat after me: do-re-mi!"

BSG to the Rescue

"Okay," Maeve relented, "I agree with Isabel and Charlotte. I vote we ask the Kgirls to join us."

Everyone turned to Avery, who stared back at them, hands on her hips. "I don't see why we should let them. They need us more than we need them."

"Katani's your friend," Charlotte reminded her again. "Let's do this for her!"

"Katani's *Kazie's* friend," Avery muttered, crossing her arms.

"Avery! Being friendly is one of the things the BSG are all about," an exasperated Isabel replied.

"But she chose them over us!" Avery yelled, not even sure what she was yelling about. She didn't hate Katani, or even Kazie, not really! Everything was just so jumbled up. *This is all Dad's fault!*

Maeve sat down in the sand next to Avery and put her arm around her friend's shoulders. "Ave, she didn't choose anyone over us. She just met new friends. She's allowed."

Charlotte sat down on the other side of Avery. "We're the ones who forced her to choose. If Katani had been hanging out with anyone else and Kara-Lee, it would have been no big deal, right?"

Charlotte felt bad. Poor Avery thought she was going

on an awesome vacation with her friends and ended up smack dab in the middle of a huge family drama. But Avery was responsible for some of that drama, too.

"Ave," Charlotte said gently, "this isn't about Katani. It's about you and Kazie and this whole competition thing you've got going."

"You've always been competitive, and we like that about you," Isabel continued. "But the stuff between you and Kazie isn't good. She almost got hurt yesterday."

"I know," Avery whispered hoarsely. "We talked after . . . and . . ."

"What?" Maeve asked.

"Shhh, give her time!" Charlotte hissed.

Avery knew in her heart that her friends were right. But if she admitted they were she would have to deal with everything—with Kazie, her new stepsister. With her dad and her new stepmom. She didn't know if she was ready to do that. It was a lot to take in, especially all at once.

But then she thought about Kazie paddling out to the break, where she was completely outclassed by the waves. While Kazie had escaped unharmed, she could have been seriously injured. Andie, too. Avery shivered. That would have been the worst thing in the world. Everything else, she'd figure out a way to deal with.

"Well, Kazie and I are cool, I think," Avery finally admitted. "I hope. Maybe it *would* be a chill idea to try singing together."

"Group hug!" chorused Isabel, Charlotte, and Maeve as they grabbed a struggling Avery.

All Together Now!

Maeve, Charlotte, Isabel, and Avery made their way across the sand toward the Kgirls' picnic table.

"We were thinking—" Maeve began.

"Can't you see we're *practicing*?" a red-faced Kazie interrupted. Poor Katani looked ready to crawl away and hide.

Maeve took a deep breath and ignored Kazie. "Kara-Lee, the BSG would like to know if the Kgirls would like to join up and perform as a single group for the karaoke contest?"

"That's a *wonderful* idea!" Kara-Lee sounded relieved, and Katani was so happy she gave Maeve a gigantic hug!

"But . . . ," Kazie countered, looking sideways at Avery, who shrugged and rolled her eyes.

Katani gushed, "See, I told you! These guys are the best!"

"I guess it's okay . . ." a defeated Kazie muttered as the girls gathered around the picnic benches and Maeve called the meeting to order. "The first thing we've got to decide on is what to sing."

"There need to be enough parts for everyone," Kara-Lee reminded them.

"But not all of the parts have to be sung," Katani added.

When everyone was done laughing, Avery stood up.

"What about that new Janey G song?" she asked.

"BFF? I love that song!" Kara-Lee declared.

"I know some dance moves that'll totally work!" Maeve jumped up and started rocking out, motioning for Kara-Lee to join her.

Kara-Lee mimicked Maeve's choreography. "I like it!"

As Kara-Lee went over the dance routine with everyone, Katani pulled Maeve aside.

"We still haven't solved my singing problem," she whispered.

"That's because you're not going to sing," Maeve replied.

"But the rules say everyone has to sing!" Katani worried.

"I know," said Maeve. "That's why you're going to rap!"

"Rap? Me?"

Maeve dragged Katani over to the rest of the girls, who were still rehearsing. Maeve smiled. *It's like a Hollywood happy ending!* she thought. But they hadn't reached the end yet. There was still a karaoke contest and a wedding to get through! And if she wanted to win, she'd better get back to work.

Avery took a break and grabbed a lemonade from one of the coolers the ship's tour guides had brought for the guests.

"Toss me one?" Kazie stood behind Avery with her hand out.

Avery tossed her a lemonade and sat down with her back to a palm tree. Kazie sat next to her.

"For once in my life, I think I totally don't care about a contest," Kazie admitted.

Avery snorted and took a sip of her drink. "Y'know what? Me neither."

The two girls sat in silence, watching everyone else practice. The sun was starting to go down on Lahaina.

"It's weird to think that I'll have a stepmom and a stepsister by tomorrow," Avery confessed. She couldn't believe she was telling Kazie, but who else would really understand? She'd sat with her cell phone the night before staring at her mom's and her brother Scott's phone numbers, and then when she finally got up the nerve and dialed Scott, his phone was off. What if they didn't even know yet? She didn't want to be the one to break the news!

"You think it's weird?" Kazie interrupted her thoughts. "It's been just my mom and me for ages. Suddenly I have a stepdad, a stepsister, and two stepbrothers!" Kazie picked up a handful of sand and let it drain through her fingers. "I'm not saying it's bad, it's just—"

"Weird. I know." Avery couldn't imagine going from having almost no family to having a family. Her brothers and her mom had always been around, and while her dad lived in Colorado, they visited each other as often as they could. And they always talked over e-mail or IM. Sometimes their schedules were crazy, but they always tried to work it out.

Sort of like this trip, she thought, and suddenly felt a rock in the pit of her stomach. She had been so upset about her dad showing up with Andie and Kazie that she hadn't stopped to think about what her dad must have felt. Sure, she had felt left out a lot of the time, but she realized that she hadn't even tried to meet him halfway.

"I just can't believe it's happening," Kazie blurted out.

"But it is." Avery still didn't know how she felt about Andie and her dad getting married. But it was kind of nice to know that she wasn't the only one who felt that way. *I need to call Mom and Scott,* Avery realized suddenly. *ASAP.* Too bad she'd left her cell phone back in the room.

"C'mon," Avery said, standing up and wiping the sand off of her shorts. "If Drill Sergeant Maeve finds out how long we've been gone, we'll be in big trouble."

"And they say we're competitive!" Kazie exclaimed.

"I think we've got it down," Maeve said as they joined the group. "Now we only need a name! I was thinking 'the BSG with the Kgirls!'"

"It's a little wordy," Kara-Lee responded. "What about 'The Kgirls with the BSG?'"

"That's got the same number of words," Charlotte told her.

"It does?" Kara-Lee said, pretending not to know.

Everyone laughed, but Maeve clapped to keep their attention. "Focus! We need something that rolls off the tongue! Doesn't our resident writer have any ideas?"

Charlotte shook her head. "Nothing comes to mind."

"Hang on a second." Isabel held up a hand.

Everyone turned toward her and waited.

"I have an idea," she said with a sly smile.

17

Karaoke!

"Dad?" Charlotte knocked on the glass window in the infirmary. Marisol stood behind her, holding out a mask.

"Whaaa—?" Mr. Ramsey rolled over and opened his eyes. "Sweetheart!"

"Dad, are you feeling better yet?" Charlotte rushed into the room, but from the sheen of sweat on her dad's forehead, she knew he was still sick.

"The fever's almost gone. Dr. Steve says he'll let me out once it breaks."

"Really?" Charlotte shifted from one foot to the other. "Do you think . . . it might break before seven o'clock?"

The karaoke dinner started at seven. The rest of the BSG and the Kgirls were still running around like crazy trying to get ready in time, but Charlotte had to squeeze in a quick visit to her dad. Just to let him know.

But now that she saw how sick he still looked, she didn't want to make him feel bad.

"What's at seven?" Mr. Ramsey asked.

"Just a pirate-themed dinner and karaoke," Charlotte said with a shrug. "But it's okay. You just need to get better."

"Marisol's taking good care of you?"

Charlotte turned and smiled at their chaperone. "She's the best!"

Going for Pirate Gold

In the center of the vast dining hall, Captain Bob stood decked out in his pirate best: a ruffled white shirt, black pants, and an eye-patch. On his shoulder sat a stuffed parrot.

"Why am I not surprised that it's a pirate theme night?" Katani asked as the BSG made their way through tables decorated with fake parrots and small treasure chests filled with chocolates covered in gold foil.

Isabel stared at Captain Bob's fake parrot. If he only knew!

"Ye got a problem wit' pirates?" Captain Bob sauntered over to their table.

"Not a bit!" said Maeve, giggling.

"Good," he responded. "Cause if it's complainin' I hear, I'll have ye thrown in the brig!"

"Aye-aye, Captain!" Avery said, saluting. "So what's your parrot's name?"

"I call 'im Squawk," he responded.

"That's better than Franco," Maeve blurted out. She slapped her hands over her mouth and looked at Charlotte and Isabel apologetically.

Captain Bob peered at them over his eye patch. "I think Franco would be a fine name for a bird." He winked at Isabel. "Now if you'll excuse me, I have some more piratin' to do at the other tables." Captain Bob bid them farewell, and everyone breathed a sigh of relief.

"Sorry," Maeve apologized. "I don't know what I was thinking. It just came out!"

"We just need to keep him a secret just one more day," Isabel reminded her. "Tomorrow we take him to the bird sanctuary."

"That'll be a relief to have him safe and sound," Katani breathed. She was tired of that bird messing up the inside of her closet! And it was getting a tad annoying when Franco woke them up with random squawks in the middle of the night.

"Yeah. I guess," Isabel replied. She wanted Franco to be safe, but she hated the idea that she would never see him again.

Avery squeezed her hand. "I know how you feel. This is almost like when we thought we'd have to give up Marty! That was the worst."

"He'll be safe and cared for by people who know what they're doing, and that's the important thing," Charlotte consoled her.

"Hey, is your dad going to make it tonight?" Isabel asked, changing the subject.

Charlotte shrugged. "He still didn't look great. But Dr. Steve says he'll be out maybe by tomorrow morning, and definitely by tomorrow afternoon."

"Maybe they'll make a recording of the contest, and we can buy one for your dad!" Maeve suggested.

"Hey, everyone, it's starting!" Katani pointed to the middle of the dining room, where Captain Bob stood with a microphone.

Kara-Lee and Kazie joined them at the table, and everyone scooted over to make room. "Are y'all ready?" Kara-Lee asked.

"Totally psyched," Kazie replied.

The lights in the dining room dimmed, and Captain Bob stepped into the spotlight. "Evenin' all. I'd like to welcome you all to Aloha Cruise Line's Pirate Treasure Feast and Karaoke Extravaganza!"

The room erupted in applause. The captain waited for the clamor to die down, then continued. "We've got a heck of a show for you tonight, but let's first give it up for our favorite onboard astronomer, Vivianne Grace, who will be working the music!"

Miss Grace waved from behind a laptop computer, which was hooked up to the speakers and connected by a long wire to the microphone.

Captain Bob pulled a stack of note cards from his pocket and began to read. "Tonight we're starting off with a cute couple who are going to make it all official on board tomorrow—with the help of Captain Bob, that is. Let's give it up for Andie and Jake!"

Everyone clapped as Mr. Madden took the mic from Captain Bob. He was dressed in khakis with a blue shirt and a black tie with red Jolly Rogers pirate flags printed on it. He turned to Andie. "I'd like to dedicate this song to my bride-to-be."

Andie blushed. "Thanks, darling!"

Maeve turned to Isabel. "Isn't that the most romantic thing ever?"

Avery rolled her eyes. "Maeve, you think everything is the most romantic thing ever!" She held up the butter dish. "Butter! Isn't it romantic?"

Kazie snorted with laughter, and Maeve threw her napkin at her. "You'd think you two would be enjoying this, since those are *your* parents."

Kazie shuddered. "Don't remind me!"

Avery laughed. "Exactly. Could they be any more corny?"

As Mr. Madden and Andie crooned together, ". . . to the one I loooove!" Kazie made ridiculous faces as Avery stared at the butter dish like it was her long lost soul mate.

It was all Maeve could do to keep her straight face focused on the happy couple! Mr. Madden and Andie stared into each other's eyes as they took their bows and left the makeshift stage, handing the microphone back to Captain Bob on the way out.

"That was Jake and Andie!" Captain Bob cheered. "Let's give 'em a big round of applause!"

As the servers brought out plates of salad followed by spaghetti and meatballs, a trio of elderly ladies took the stage. Then a group of little kids with their mom, another two couples, and a group of college boys dressed in hilarious pirate-like business suits entered the stage one after another.

"How can we possibly follow *them*?" Katani wondered, admiring the college boys' sophisticated yet silly costumes.

None of the BSG or the Kgirls had even touched their spaghetti.

"Next up, we have"—Captain Bob peered at his note cards under the spotlight—"Me! Singin' the classic sea shanty, 'The Pirate Song.'"

Katani groaned. "Does this ever end?"

Maeve swatted her. "I appreciate that he's staying in character. It's a lot of work."

"Think of it this way," Kara-Lee whispered, "it'll make us stand out even more!"

Katani wrung her hands nervously. With Maeve's help, she was ready to perform, but she didn't know how much she wanted to stand out!

"Shhh!" cautioned Charlotte. "We're next!"

The music slowed to a stop and Captain Bob bowed, even giving his fake parrot Squawk his own curtain call. The girls crept up to the side of the stage.

"Everyone ready?" Maeve asked.

"And do you have your shirts?" Isabel added.

Everyone nodded. "The shirts are amazing, Izzy," Charlotte confided.

"I'm so glad I had time to make them this afternoon!" Isabel whispered as her eyes sparkled.

Captain Bob caught his breath and used his eye-patch

to mop up a bead of sweat on his forehead. "Our last act," he said into the microphone, "well, our last act hails from all over. I seen 'em practicing on the beach, and these girls 'ave some talent. Performing Janey G's song 'BFF,' let's give it up for PARROT TALK!"

The girls burst into the spotlight. They were wearing denim skirts and T-shirts hand-drawn by Isabel. Each t-shirt had a different parrot on the front—scarlet macaws, blue-and-gold macaws, amazon parrots and, on Isabel's shirt, an African Grey that was the spitting image of Franco.

Charlotte pointed to Miss Grace, who nodded and with a click of her mouse, Janey G's song filled the dining room. Avery sat off to the side and kept the beat on a drum made out of an overturned bucket, while Charlotte, the backup singer, stood next to her. Maeve sang in the mic.

> *"You've been there for me,*
> *I'll be there for you.*
> *Whatever we need—*
> *It's what BFFs do"*

Charlotte and Avery joined Maeve for the chorus.

> *"Best Friends—*
> *Best Friends Forever*
> *BFF!*
> *Best Friends—*
> *Best Friends Forever"*

Maeve danced over to Kara-Lee and Kazie and handed them the mic. Kazie and Kara-Lee held the microphone between them and began to sing.

> *"Sometimes we argue—*
> *We don't always agree.*
> *But we're BFF's!*
> *And we'll always be!"*

The crowd clapped along to the beat of Avery's drum. The girls gathered around the mic.

> *"Best Friends—*
> *Best Friends Forever*
> *BFF!*
> *Best Friends—*
> *Best Friends Forever"*

"Did you know they were up to this?" Andie asked Mr. Madden.

"Not a clue!" he responded.

Kara-Lee danced over to Katani and handed her the microphone. Katani took it, and swallowed the lump in her throat. She looked at Maeve, who winked at her. Katani took a deep breath, and began to rap into the mic.

> *"Hangin' together—*
> *Best Friends Forever!*

Don't matter whether,
We're all together!

"Near or far away,
no matter what they say!
Best friends today,
and that's how we'll stay!"

The crowd loved it, jumping to their feet to clap along with Katani. She couldn't believe it! They were cheering her!

"I say best friends, you say forever!" Katani rapped, her voice strong and sure. Maybe she couldn't sing, but she sure could talk with the beat! "BEST FRIENDS!"

"FOREVER!" yelled the crowd.

"BEST FRIENDS!"

"FOREVER!" the crowd chanted back.

Katani handed the mic back to Maeve, and the girls gathered around to sing the final chorus.

"Best Friends—
Best Friends Forever
BFF!
Best Friends—
Best Friends Forever!"

The girls struck a final pose . . . the speakers went silent . . . and the crowd exploded.

"We did it!" screamed Maeve. "Take your bows, Parrots!"

Each of the girls bowed, but the applause grew even louder. Captain Bob took the microphone from Maeve. "I'd say from the sound of it that we have a winner! Ladies and gents, may I present to you Aloha Cruise Lines Karaoke Contest Winner! PARROT TALK!"

Marisol stepped out from backstage with official Aloha Cruise Lines T-shirts and baseball caps for each of the girls!

Kazie took her cap and put it on right away. So did Avery. "That's the style!" The soon-to-be-sisters congratulated each other.

As the lights came up in the dining room, Andie and Mr. Madden rushed up.

"You were amazing!" declared Andie, hugging Avery and Kazie.

Mr. Madden high-fived everyone. "You girls rocked it out!"

"We're not bad," Kazie admitted.

"What do you mean? We're totally *bad*!" Avery cheered. *Yesterday we were worried about losing to the Kgirls,* thought Avery, *and today we won with them.*

"You know what's awesome?" Kazie said. "This time we both got to win."

She held her hand up and Avery high-fived her. "Crazy," replied Avery.

"Excuse me," barked a woman in a stylish Hawaiian skirt and huge sunglasses as she made her way through the crowd.

"Who's that?" Avery whispered to Kazie, who only shrugged.

"Allow me to introduce myself." The woman held out a hand adorned with several glittering rings and long fuschia fingernails. "Yvonne Marshall. Music producer."

Avery just stared in surprise, so Katani shook her hand. "Pleased to meet you."

"You girls were simply *a-mazing* up there. And you know, I'm always looking for talent!" As if by magic, the hand suddenly held a glittery, purple business card. Katani took it, stunned.

"Call me." Yvonne winked, and disappeared into the crowd.

Maeve was the first to recover. "OMG! That was sooo totally, like, wow!" And she started hugging everyone in sight. She couldn't believe that they had pulled a performance together in less than a day. *Now a famous producer has discovered us, and we're headed for stardom!*

Then, out of nowhere, she felt someone flip off her new cap. It was Chad!

He smiled and gave her a surfer salute before handing back the cap. "That was gnarly!" he said. "Like, totally incredibly cool! I can't believe how good you are!"

Maeve blushed. She was used to receiving compliments like this, but not from boys she liked!

"Thanks! I take a lot of dancing and singing classes. My vocal coach says that I've got the best voice in seventh grade!" She couldn't help but brag a tiny bit. She wanted Chad to be impressed!

His eyes grew wide. "Really? I totally thought you were in sixth," he confessed.

Sixth grade? Now she was confused. "No, I'm in seventh. Like you."

He shook his head. "I'm in fifth."

Maeve's jaw dropped. "But . . ." Her voice trailed off.

"I'm just tall for my age," he explained. "I get that a lot."

Maeve couldn't believe it. Chad was a fifth grader? That meant he was practically her little brother's age. How could that be? Her leading man was, in fact . . . just a kid!

"Maeve, are you okay?" Chad asked, concerned.

Maeve remembered that when she first met Chad, there was something about him that reminded her of her little brother. Now she knew why! "Earth to Maeve," Chad said, interrupting her thoughts.

What have I been thinking? All that time in the sun must have made her a little dizzy. Riley back home was her true crush! Chad was more like another little brother.

Maeve smiled at Chad. "I'm perfect! You'll have to meet my little brother Sam some time, though. Let's go find some ice cream!"

"Now you're making sense!" Chad exclaimed.

The Real Parrot Talk

"I'm just too jazzed to go back up to my cabin," Kara-Lee chirped as the girls gathered their belongings from the dinner table. "Do all y'all want to do anything?"

"Sure!" replied Charlotte. Avery and Isabel both gave her a look. "But we have to stop by our cabin first," Isabel protested.

She was thinking about feeding Franco, but Avery had to get back to the cabin and call her mom. There hadn't been a single free second amidst all the karaoke preparations to grab her phone and make the call.

"We can meet you somewhere," Kazie offered.

Isabel looked to Charlotte and Katani, who both nodded. "Can you keep a secret?" she asked Kazie and Kara-Lee.

"Yes," said Kara-Lee.

"Totally!" said Kazie.

"Want to know why we called the group 'Parrot Talk'?" Isabel whispered.

"I thought it was because of Captain Bob's wacky costumes?" Kara-Lee guessed.

Izzy grinned. "Nope, we have a real parrot. Hiding in our cabin."

"No WAY!" Kazie yelled, and then covered her mouth. "No way!" she said more quietly.

"Way," said Avery, thinking that the more people there were in the room, the less anyone would notice if she took off with her cell phone. "So zip it and let's motor!"

18

The Bird is Out of the Bag!

I can *not* believe you guys have been hiding a parrot in your room!" said Kazie as she shook her head back and forth. "That is way beyond awesome."

Everyone stood in the hallway outside their cabin door while Charlotte fumbled for her room key.

"Remember to keep it down," Isabel instructed them, "so you don't startle Franco."

Charlotte finally located the key card in her book bag and held it up for everyone to see. *"Voilà!"* She slid it through the lock and opened the door.

"DAD?" Charlotte cried out.

Mr. Ramsey and Captain Bob were sitting in their room . . . *with Franco!*

"Girls . . . ," Mr. Ramsey started to say.

"HOLA!" Franco squawked from his favorite perch.

"A parrot! However did a parrot get in here?!" Maeve exclaimed in mock horror.

"An Academy Award–worthy performance, Maeve, but we need the truth." Mr. Ramsey countered.

Charlotte bit her lip, unable to meet her father's eye. *The doctor said he wouldn't be better until tomorrow!* As much as Charlotte was glad to see him back to normal, she really hoped they'd get a chance to explain. *He'll understand. . . .* "We weren't really lying—" She nodded to Kazie and Kara-Lee that they could leave now if they wanted, but the two girls stood their ground.

"But you broke the ship's rules." Mr. Ramsey sighed.

"I'm sorry," Charlotte whispered as her dad continued sternly. "About an hour ago, Dr. Steve gave me a clean bill of health. Imagine how excited I was to come back to my room and surprise you guys! But when I got here, I found . . . this, this *bird* . . ."

"FRANCO!" Franco squawked again.

". . . *Franco* perched on the TV."

"He doesn't like to stay in his cage," a morose Katani muttered.

"Yeah, and he's super friendly," Avery offered. "And smart."

"And not ours." Mr. Ramsey raised his eyebrows for emphasis.

"This is where I come in," Captain Bob explained. He was still dressed in full pirate gear, but he must have left his accent behind at the karaoke contest. He stared each girl in the eyes. "Mr. Ramsey was *pretty* sure that he didn't check in with a bird."

"He's an African Grey," Isabel declared, stepping forward. "And he's mine." She felt parrot-sized butterflies flapping all over inside her stomach as she spoke, but there was no way she would let Marisol lose her job! She was just too sweet, and she'd only been trying to do the right thing and find a safe home for Franco.

"I may have been sick and feverish for the last few days." Mr. Ramsey crossed his arms. "But I'm sure I'd remember you bringing a parrot."

"She found him on the deck." Avery improvised as Maeve nodded along. "He was, uh, injured."

Captain Bob inspected Franco, who was thankfully being quiet. They didn't need to get in more trouble than they already were! "Hmmm. He looks fine to me."

"That's because Izzy's taking totally good care of him," Kazie added.

Avery snuck a look at Kazie. *She's covering for us?*

"It was the darndest thing!" Kara-Lee jumped in. "We were all on the deck, just enjoying a bit of sunshine when this poor, dear . . ."

"Franco," Isabel supplied, filling in the blank.

"Franco," said Kara-Lee, flashing her most brilliant smile, "just up and crashed right into the deck!"

Katani nodded. "We didn't want to bother you, Mr. Ramsey, since you were in the infirmary."

Mr. Ramsey looked skeptical. "So you just decided to keep—"

"Franco," Charlotte finished. She hated lying to her father, but she couldn't imagine letting Marisol down. Not after how patient she'd been with them for the past few days, making sure they got to all their activities on time and had everything they needed. Besides, Marisol wasn't hiding Franco for herself, she'd made a promise to her aunt Consuela, and Charlotte and her friends were going to help Marisol keep it! "We just didn't—"

"You really didn't think, Charlotte," Mr. Ramsey admonished gently.

Isabel couldn't let Charlotte take the blame. "Mr. Ramsey, please don't be angry at Charlotte. It's my fault."

Maeve watched the whole scene unfold. For once, she could have done without the drama. After all, it was just a parrot. Nobody was hurt or anything. "Mr. Ramsey, that's not true. It's my fault. If you're going to punish Charlotte and Isabel, you need to punish me, too."

Katani raised her hand. "Me too."

Avery nodded. "And me."

Kazie threw her arm around Kara-Lee. "And we were totally in on it from the beginning."

Captain Bob had a funny look on his face. Instead of talking to the girls, he looked right at Franco. "You crashed on the deck, did you?"

"Franco sorry!" he squawked.

"You know you're not native to Hawaii, hmm? So . . . did you fly here all the way from Africa, or stop by some friendly pet shop on the way?"

The girls gulped and looked at each other. Obviously, the captain had seen through their story.

"Africa!" Franco flapped up and over to the captain's shoulder. "Captain Smelly!" Avery tried her hardest to hold in a laugh, but it came out her nose in a snort. The captain gave the bird on his shoulder a stern pirate look.

Mr. Ramsey sighed. "The bird says he flew here from Africa. Maybe I should go back to bed for another few days—" A knock at the door interrupted his thought.

"Girls, it's Marisol!"

"Kiss kiss Marisol!" Franco cried out.

Captain Bob walked over to the door with the parrot on his shoulder. He looked so much like a pirate with Franco there that Isabel had to wonder, *Will he make Marisol walk the plank?* The girls watched nervously as Captain Bob opened the door to the cabin.

"I'd say Franco's doing A-okay," Captain Bob said in his most un-pirate-like voice. "As for you, I wouldn't mind an explanation."

Marisol's smile fell from her face as she realized her boss was standing in front of her—with Franco on his shoulder! Her lip began to tremble. "I can explain."

Captain Bob stood aside so she could come in the room, and shut the door behind her as she sunk down onto the hard wooden chair at the desk, right across from the sofa where Mr. Ramsey sat. The girls huddled around their bunks, none of them sitting down. Charlotte held Isabel's hand.

Marisol told everyone the story about how she had

dropped out of school to take care of her aunt. "Franco was everything to Consuela," Marisol explained, fighting back tears. "I promised I'd find him a home, and I tried. I just needed one more day."

"One more day?" Captain Bob asked.

"I—we were going to bring him to the Maui Animal Rescue and Sanctuary," Marisol explained. "They're expecting him. I know it's wrong, but I couldn't afford to send him any other way, and I thought, well, I just wanted him to be safe and happy."

Charlotte knew exactly how Marisol felt. She had gone through the same thing when she had lied to her father and hidden Marty in the Tower. The look of disappointment on her father's face when he found out was almost too much to bear. Thankfully, Miss Pierce, their landlord, had let them keep Marty. She worried that Marisol wouldn't be so lucky!

"But it's not Marisol's fault Franco's here!" Isabel cried out suddenly. "It was my idea. I love birds, and I just wanted to keep him company . . ."

Mr. Ramsey turned to the captain. "Captain Bob, I would like to apologize on behalf of the girls. I don't know what kind of restitution—"

Captain Bob waved him off. "Sometimes out at sea, a big wave comes at you that you weren't expecting. Do you get angry and try to stop it with your bare hands? No. Do you freeze in fear and let it crash into your ship? No. You just have to stay calm to deal with things. Franco's here, so we'd better deal with it. He's made it thus far, so I don't see the harm in having him one more day."

"*¿Verdad?* Really?" asked Marisol.

"Really," replied Captain Bob.

The girls cheered and Franco flapped his wings from his perch on Captain Bob's shoulder.

"You'll get to keep your promise!" Charlotte exclaimed, rushing over to Marisol to give her a hug.

Marisol blinked back tears. "I couldn't have done it without you. Without all of you!" As she stood up from her chair at the desk, a stack of papers fluttered to the ground.

"What's this?" Mr. Ramsey asked, picking up one after another. "Tuesday morning, 8:05 a.m., five fruit smoothies. Tuesday evening, eight fruit smoothies, Wednesday another five smoothies . . . how many room service bills *are* there?!"

"The pineapple garnish," Charlotte explained through clenched teeth.

"Franco—" Avery started.

"Love pineapple! Ha-ha-ha!" the bird finished.

"What he said." Avery thrust her thumb at the bird.

Captain Bob grabbed one of the fallen papers. "So that's what you hooligans were up to that night on the deck . . . collecting pineapple! You know, I *can* tell the difference between a bird and a ventriloquist." He winked meaningfully.

"You knew the whole time?" Isabel wondered out loud.

"And you didn't say anything?" Kazie challenged. She may not have known about Franco until ten minutes ago, but both Kazie and Kara-Lee were just as invested in his fate now as any of the girls.

The captain shrugged. "I knew the bird would come out of the bag sooner or later."

Mr. Ramsey was still shuffling through receipts, his eyes wide. "Ten to twelve smoothies a day? Do you girls realize how expensive that is? You're trying to send me back to the infirmary, aren't you?" He collapsed on the couch.

Captain Bob placed a hand on Mr. Ramsey's shoulder. "I'd say there were extenuating circumstances. I'll see what I can do."

Mr. Ramsey breathed a sigh of relief. "I don't think the magazine would be pleased at all."

"We're so, so, sorry, Captain Bob!" Maeve held her hands to her chest in her most serious apology stance.

"And thank you for being so understanding," Isabel added.

Captain Bob waved them off. "You girls are pretty resourceful," he commented, "and those are the sorts of sailors you want on a ship."

"Captain?" Franco asked, rubbing the top of his head into the captain's bristly beard.

"Yes, Franco?" he responded.

"Captain Smelly!"

The girls collapsed in a fit of giggles. Even Captain Bob shook with laughter. He placed Franco back on top of the TV and wagged his finger at him. "Remember yer a guest of this Captain!" Captain Bob had returned to his pirate persona. "Speakin' o' which, I got to be gettin' back to sailin' this ship. Marisol and I will see you all for the trip ter the animal sanctuary on the morrow."

"I'll just get my things out of Mr. Ramsey's room." Marisol grabbed her two small suitcases, then turned to the girls. "You helped me fulfill my aunt's last wish, and I will never forget that." She hugged Isabel and Charlotte and followed Captain Bob out the cabin door.

"Captain Bob told me about your karaoke victory!" Mr. Ramsey smiled at the girls, and Charlotte knew everything was forgiven. "I wish I could have been there."

"Miss Grace said she would make a CD for you." Charlotte hugged her dad. "You look pretty wiped."

"I am. If you need me, I'll be in my stateroom. Finally!"

"You girls were amazing," Kara-Lee marveled once Charlotte's dad closed the door. "The way you covered for Marisol!"

Kazie high-fived Isabel. "You totally threw yourself on the grenade. That was gnarly."

"That's what friends do." Avery shrugged.

"Then I'm glad all y'all are my friends!" Kara-Lee put one arm around Avery and another around Katani.

"Totally," agreed Kazie, "but we gotta motor. Can I pet the bird first?"

Avery retrieved Franco from his perch. "Just let him get used to you for a second," she suggested.

Kazie leaned down and smiled. "Who's a pretty bird? Hi there! I'm Kazie."

"Bonita!" Franco squawked, letting her scratch his neck feathers.

"We should go," Kara-Lee apologized. "My momma never got to see me after our karaoke victory!"

"'K, coming!" Kazie gave Franco the surfer salute, and he lifted one foot in response, cocking his head to the side quizzically.

"Gnarly, dude!" Kazie exclaimed as she backed out the door.

Mom Knows Best

The moonlight poured in through the porthole, casting long shadows across the cabin walls. Everyone was fast asleep in their beds.

Everyone except Avery.

She still hadn't talked to her mom or Scott, and now it had to be too late at night.

Avery never had problems sleeping. The second her head hit the pillow, she was off to dreamland. She thought it was because she was always out running around, playing soccer or basketball, or just being active. But when Charlotte turned off the lights, Avery knew she was going to spend a long night staring at the ceiling above her bunk. *Dad's getting married in two days.* Two days! No matter how many times she pushed the thought away or covered it up, it kept bobbing back up to the top. Like a beach ball in the ocean.

Just last week she had been looking forward to a Hawaiian cruise with her friends and now she was here in her bunk, wondering what it was going to be like having a stepmother and a stepsister.

Avery listened to the waves lapping against the side of the ship and realized that her mom wouldn't care what time it was. She climbed down from her top bunk, careful not to wake Maeve, who was sleeping below her.

The floor creaked as Avery crept over to the desk to grab her cell phone out of her backpack. She brought it into the small cabin bathroom and shut the door. Sitting cross-legged on the cold tile floor, she dialed the familiar number.

Her mom answered sleepily on the third ring. "Hello?"

"Mom, it's Avery."

Avery's mom bolted awake. "Are you okay?"

"Yes. I mean, no. I don't know." Avery blinked back tears. Now that she was talking to her, Avery couldn't figure out what to say.

"Avery, honey, I'm here," her mom soothed. "Just talk to me."

Her voice sounded so far away through the receiver. "It's just—it's Dad." Suddenly Avery found her voice, and everything she had been holding back for days came pouring out. "I mean, first he just shows up to surprise me. But showing up with Kazie? And Andie? That's not exactly a great surprise, y'know?"

"I know, Ave," her mom said. "Your dad can be a little clueless sometimes . . . but he didn't mean to be insensitive."

"He thinks Kazie and I are going to be all BFFs, and he spends all of his time with Andie when he said he'd go surfing with me. That's what we do together! And then—" Avery's voice trailed off.

"And then what?" her mom asked after a few moments.

"And then—" Fat teardrops began to slide down her cheeks. Avery took a deep breath. "And then . . . he's getting married, Mom."

There was silence on the other side of the line.

"I know, Ave."

Avery was shocked. "You do?"

Her mom began to laugh. *What is so funny?*

"I do, Ave. At least, I knew he was thinking about it. "

"Well, he's gone from thinking to doing because he asked her right on the beach. Without saying anything to me first!" Avery wiped her wet cheek with her shirt-sleeve.

"Ave, I promise you that your dad didn't do this to make you feel bad."

"But it does," Avery whispered into the phone.

"I know, honey. It's a lot to get used to. But he loves you. And your brothers."

"It just feels like I'm being replaced," Avery confessed.

"I understand. But just because he's marrying someone else doesn't mean that there's not room for you. The great thing about love is that there's plenty for everybody. You don't run out."

"I guess," Avery managed to say.

"When I had your brothers, I kept thinking I couldn't possibly love anyone more. And then when I found out that we were finally going to adopt a perfect baby girl, well, Avery, my heart just grew."

"But he hasn't had any time for me this whole *week*!" Avery sniffed. Her tears were slowing, but the lump in her throat wouldn't go away.

"He's just . . . wrapped up in the moment, honey. You know how you get all worked up before a soccer game?"

"In the zone. Yeah."

"Well, he's in the zone on this one. I promise you that he doesn't realize how upset you are. If he did, you'd be talking to him right now."

"I guess." Avery sighed.

"No guessing, it's true, Ave. And tomorrow, you've got to talk to him about this. It's okay that you're hurting, and it's okay that you're upset with him. But it's not okay if you don't tell him and give him a chance to explain his side of things."

"I hate when you're right."

"That's what moms are for. I'll always be there for you, even at five a.m."

Avery giggled, loopy with tears and tiredness. "It's five a.m.?"

"Well, not for you. There's a five-hour time difference between Hawaii and Boston! But don't worry about it. The important thing is; you're okay?"

Avery thought a moment. "I'm not okay. But I'm better."

She then realized she had only been thinking about herself. "Mom, what about you?"

"What about me?" her mom asked, confused.

"Are you . . ." Avery searched for the words. "Are you sad that dad's getting remarried?"

Avery's mom was silent for a second, then said, "Oh, honey, I'm not sad exactly. I'm happy for your dad."

"Really?"

"Really. Your dad and I, well, we just didn't work together. We loved each other, but that was a long time ago. We found out that we wanted different things. But I have great affection for your dad and consider him one of my dearest friends, and I'm glad that he's got another chance for happiness. Friends want that for each other."

"I guess that makes sense," Avery admitted.

"Besides," her mom continued, "your father gave me the very best gift that anyone could give me."

"What's that?" she asked.

"You. And your brothers." She paused while Avery took this all in. "I love you, Ave. And so does your dad. So talk to him tomorrow. Promise?"

"I promise," said Avery. They said their good-byes and she hung up the phone, smiling to herself in the dark bathroom, remembering the BSG's seventh amendment to the Tower rules.

When in doubt, phone home!

19

Questions Without Answers

When Avery woke up, the sun was just peeking out over the horizon. After trying for nearly an hour to go back to sleep, she took the phone into the bathroom again and tried to call Scott. No answer. She left a rambling message, then stared at the phone for a full ten minutes before finally calling her dad.

"Can we take a walk before everyone gets up?" she asked.

"Sure thing, Aloha Jedi," her dad said, and five minutes later he was at their cabin door. Avery left a note for Mr. Ramsey and walked with her dad up to the top deck of the ship.

They strolled together beside the railing, watching the seagulls dive as the cruise ship maneuvered into Kahului Bay on the north shore of Maui.

"Killer idea, Ave!" her dad exclaimed. "Check out the early morning surfers!" He pointed toward the waves crashing on a distant beach, where surfers littered the landscape about twenty yards out. "Bet you wish you could be out there!"

Avery shielded her eyes against the sun and stared out over the ocean. It was another perfect day. The waves crashed against the white beach while the sunlight streaked through the palm trees, casting frond-shaped shadows on the far away sand.

"Actually, Dad, for the first time since this cruise started, I think I'd rather be right here where I am."

"Really? What's up?" her dad asked, confused.

Avery took a deep breath. "Ever since you surprised me that first day, with Andie and Kazie, I feel like . . . I don't know, things just haven't been like they used to. It's kinda weird."

"Like you're a skier who woke up on a snowboard?" he joked.

"Or like a snowboarder who thinks she can surf," Avery retorted.

Mr. Madden stopped and turned to Avery. "I think we should rap about that."

She swallowed hard. A lecture was coming.

"Ave, why did you let Kazie go so far out?" he asked. "That's totally unlike you. You're usually Captain Safety."

"I told her to go back!" Avery shouted. "I did! But you know Kazie! She just wouldn't listen!"

"Yeah, I do know Kazie," he said, "but so do you."

Avery looked away. No matter how much she proclaimed her innocence, she knew that he was right.

"Which means deep down, my little Surf Betty," her

dad continued, "you knew she was going to follow you out there. So you should have—"

"Okay, I should have turned back, and I didn't," Avery admitted. "I know I messed up big time. She could have gotten really hurt. But why are you acting like this is all my fault, Dad?" Avery sniffed.

Mr. Madden turned toward the water and shielded his eyes from the sun's reflection off the waves. They watched as one of the surfers glided into the curl of the wave, cutting back and forth across the frothy water, riding it all the way to the beach.

"Dad," Avery finally said in almost a whisper, "you really *don't* get it."

Mr. Madden turned back to Avery, confused. "Tell me, Avery. What don't I get?"

Avery panicked. She had gone over this moment in her mind, playing and replaying what she was going to say. But now that she had a chance to tell her dad how she really felt, her emotions were whirling and her mind was blank!

"Ave?"

Avery blurted out the first thing that popped into her head. "It's just that, well, you're getting *married*. Scott and Tim . . . they aren't here . . . Do they even know? Are they going to miss it? That just feels, so—"

He interrupted her. "No worries, snurfette, we're covered!" He laughed. "Of course they know. In fact, Scott and Tim are going to meet us in Honolulu tomorrow. See? Nothing to worry about. Your dad has it all covered! We're cool, right?" He held up his hand for a high-five, but Avery looked away.

"That's not all," she mumbled. "I guess I just . . . I wish you had, umm, asked me first and . . ."

To her surprise, her dad didn't say anything. His face was suddenly grim as he nodded and waited for Avery to let it all out.

"Dad, I don't even really know Andie! I only met her one time before this, and I don't need another mom!" Avery felt the words tumbling out of her mouth randomly, like the seagulls wheeling in the sky.

"Are you going away on a honeymoon? And can I keep my room in Telluride? What about your shop?" Avery paced back and forth by the railing as she spoke, tearing apart a napkin she'd found in her pocket and tossing the pieces overboard.

"Where will Kazie sleep? Will she come with you every time you visit Boston? What is she, anyway, my half-sister or stepsister or what?"

Mr. Madden stopped Avery mid-pace and enveloped her in a big hug. "Avery, you're my number one snurfette and you always will be, got that? I'm so, so, sorry you've been worrying so much about this. Sometimes I don't think before I act, y'know? That's what your mom always told me. *Look before you leap, Jake!* But I guess that's just not how I am. I go with the flow . . . y'know, ride the waves.

"I should've thought to talk to you again. That's what your mom said when I called to tell her about all this and plan Tim and Scott's travel. She said, *make sure Ave's okay.*

❃ 255 ❃

But I thought we were cool after that talk in your room the other night. I guess I was wrong, huh?"

Avery nodded against her Dad's ATS shirt.

"Lots of stuff is gonna change," he continued, "and I don't even know the answers to all those questions! This is new territory for all of us. Think of it like cutting new powder on an uncharted mountain slope. We'll break ourselves a trail, one day at a time."

"Yeah?" Avery sniffed.

"Definitely. If you can take on gnarly slopes and monster waves, kiddo, you can take on this. Andie is a wonderful woman, and while she'll never take the place of Mom in your life, I hope one day she can be your friend. That would mean a lot to me." Avery's dad paused for a minute, one hand on the railing, the other on his daughter's shoulder. "Is there anything I can do that would make this all easier on you?"

"Don't give Kazie any more of my stuff! She can keep that cap, though. And *don't* let Andie cook when we come for Thanksgiving." Jake snorted so hard at that comment that he had to let go of Avery and recompose himself. "And maybe when you come to Boston to visit," Avery finished, "could you come just by yourself sometimes?"

"I think I can promise all that." Her dad nodded and smiled. "No problemo!"

Sad Good-byes

Marisol balanced Franco's cage on her lap. For once, he wasn't trying to pick the lock and get out. Everyone was crammed into a van driven by Captain Bob. They were barreling toward the Maui Animal Rescue and Sanctuary in Haiku, Maui.

"We're just about an hour out. Everyone okay back there?" Captain Bob asked.

"I think we've got some sad campers here, but fine," Mr. Ramsey replied. He turned to Marisol. "You sure they're expecting us?"

"I've been e-mailing with them for weeks," Marisol said. "They've got a little room set up for Franco when he arrives, then over time they'll slowly introduce him to other birds he'll share a habitat with."

"No! No! Franco love Izzy!" Franco squawked.

Isabel blinked back tears and scratched his head through the bars of his cage. "Izzy loves Franco, too. But this will be good for you, Franco. I promise." She looked to Marisol for confirmation.

Marisol nodded. "It's a wonderful place. He'll be well taken care of."

Isabel took a deep breath. *I will not cry. I will not cry*, she repeated to herself over and over. But how could she keep calm when she had to give away the smartest, silliest, most wonderful bird in the whole world?

Charlotte squeezed Isabel's hand. "It'll be okay."

"I'm sure they can keep you updated on his progress, Izzy," Katani said, trying to console her friend.

"I bet they'll e-mail you pictures!" Maeve exclaimed.

"Or maybe there's a parrotcam!" Avery added.

Isabel nodded, unable to speak. She knew this was the

best thing for Franco. She did! But right now she felt worse than she could ever have imagined.

"Kiss kiss Izzy!" Franco squawked.

Isabel watched as the scenery outside went from shops and hotels to a sprawl of green fields dotted with palm trees. Mist still clung to the ground, like clouds that had lost their way.

"Y'know, parrots can fall in love," Captain Bob said, interrupting her thoughts. Katani and Charlotte laughed, but Captain Bob continued. "No, it's true. I've had my share of feathered friends. That's probably why you had such a hard time finding this one a home, Marisol."

"Because he was in love with my aunt?" Marisol wondered. "I guess that makes sense."

"And now he's in love with Isabel there," Captain Bob concluded.

"Franco love Izzy!" Franco repeated from his cage.

Everyone laughed, easing the tension in the van. Marisol shifted the cage in her lap so she could turn toward Isabel. "Isabel, I just had a crazy idea. Why don't you keep Franco? *¿Qué te parece?* What do you think?"

"My aunt won't let me have a parrot," Isabel replied sadly. "Besides, how would I even get him home?"

Marisol thought for a moment. "You're right. I'm sorry."

Captain Bob pulled the van over to the side of the road and slowed to a stop. He turned to face the backseat. "Y'know, I have a reunion coming up."

"Excuse me, Captain Bob, but our friend is having an

emotional moment. Your social schedule isn't exactly our priority right now," Maeve lectured.

Captain Bob laughed. "Yes, but I am a graduate of the Massachusetts Maritime Academy. Which means that I could fly Franco out to Boston in my personal plane."

"You have a personal plane?" Her dad sounded a tiny bit jealous, Charlotte thought!

"I'm a captain of many ships, both of land and air!" He replied with a flourish of his hand.

"Izzy, you have to keep Franco!" Avery begged.

"I know that the Animal Sanctuary would take great care of Franco, but he'd much rather be with you, Isabel. What do you say?" asked Marisol.

"Boston!" Franco decided.

Isabel was in shock. "But, I can't. My aunt would never let me."

"Isabel, you have to at least ask!" Charlotte suggested.

"Don't take no for an answer," Katani advised.

Maeve turned to her. "Izzy, you know that I have not been Franco's number one fan. But it's destiny! And you can't argue with destiny!" She dug her cell phone out of her purse and thrust it at Isabel. "Call. Now."

Isabel looked around at all of the expectant faces, and then at Franco. "Okay, I'll call." She dialed her Aunt Lourdes' number. By the fourth ring, she figured she was off the hook. No one would answer, and she'd have a few more minutes to figure out what to do. But then someone picked up.

"Hello?"

"Aunt Lourdes, it's Isabel."

"¡Dios mío! Is everything okay? I was taking your mom to the doctor. Just a check up, but we're running late—"

"I'm fine, but slow down a second. I need to ask you something."

"Keep it short, amorcita, we have to—"

"Can I have a parrot?" Isabel blurted out.

"What?" her aunt asked.

Now she had Aunt Lourdes's attention. Isabel took her time explaining Franco's story, Marisol's promise, and the bird who sat in his cage with his head cocked, as if waiting for the answer.

"So, what do you say? We already have a way to get him home and—"

"Isabel," her aunt said gently, "you cannot have a parrot."

Isabel felt the sting of tears at the back of her eyes and slumped in her seat. Maeve grabbed her hand and squeezed. Isabel heard another voice through the phone. It was her mom talking to her aunt in the background. "Lourdes! Lourdes! I had a parakeet when I was little."

Isabel covered the receiver. "My mom is trying to talk her into it," she whispered.

Everyone silently cheered and Isabel put her ear back to the phone.

"But this is different" her aunt argued. "This is a parrot. Un papagayo!"

"And I always wanted a parrot," her mother added.

Isabel heard her aunt sigh, and then her mother got on the phone.

"What's his name?"

"Franco, Mama," Isabel replied. "Can I keep him? I promise to clean his cage and play with him every day and buy all his food . . ."

"Franco Martinez," Mama mused, "that's got a good ring to it. Okay, Lourdes agrees. Franco can come live with us. But Isabel Alicia Martinez, you must be completely responsible for him!"

"I will, I promise." Isabel shut the phone off and screamed, "She said yes!" Charlotte, Maeve, Avery and Katani leaned in to hug her. Isabel couldn't believe it! "Franco, you're coming home with me!"

"I'd better turn this van around," said Captain Bob. He made a U-turn and pointed the van back in the direction of the dock.

"I guess this means I haven't seen the last of you, Franco," Maeve sighed.

"Love Izzy!" Franco squawked. "Maeve smelly. Ha-ha-ha!"

Happy Good-byes!

Charlotte and Isabel sat in one of the ship's many gorgeous lounges with Mr. Ramsey and Franco's cage. Marisol had gone to call the sanctuary to let them know that Franco had found a loving home, and Captain Bob went to talk to the crew about where to keep Franco safely for the last day of the cruise.

"I can't keep breaking regulations to let you keep him in your room," Captain Bob had said. "But we'll take good care of him, and before you know it, he'll be back in Boston with you."

Isabel knelt down at the side of Franco's cage. "I'm going to see you in just a couple of weeks, Franco. Don't forget me."

"Franco love Izzy!" Franco said for the zillionth time since they'd set out in the van that morning.

Charlotte laughed. "I don't think there's any danger of *that* happening."

Just then, Captain Bob returned with two young men in Aloha Cruise uniforms. When they picked up the cage, Isabel pet Franco on the head one last time . . . for now!

"Captain Bob, I don't know what to say." Isabel felt close to tears again. "Thank you."

Captain Bob waved one hand. "Don't say a thing. I've always had a soft spot for these squawkboxes, so I'm happy that I get to be deliverin' one to a happy home."

"Captain Smelly!" Franco squawked as the young men carried the cage away from Isabel.

"We'll have to work on that one!" Captain Bob wagged his finger at the parrot as they made their way back to the crew quarters. Isabel waved, and before she knew it, she was crying. But this time, they were tears of joy.

CHAPTER

20

I Now Pronounce You . . .

Avery craned her neck, trying to see over the crowd of people who were milling around the dock below. She and Maeve were waiting for Avery's brothers, Tim and Scott, who would be arriving any second for the wedding. Avery was anxious and excited and nervous . . . all at the same time!

"I don't see why we can't wait for them down there," Avery complained.

"Because you might miss them in the crowd," Maeve reminded her.

"Are you calling me short?" Avery asked. "Wait! I think I see them!" She pointed to two red baseball caps weaving through the crowd.

"How can you tell?" asked Maeve.

"I just know," Avery replied.

Maeve squinted at the two figures on the dock. "They're wearing Red Sox caps."

Avery giggled. "Like I said, I just know!"

"Okay, since you're in good hands," Maeve said, "I'm going to go get ready. See you in a few!"

Avery nodded and turned back to see Scott and Tim making their way up the gangplank. She waved and ran over, nearly knocking them down in a bear hug.

"You guys! I'm so glad you're here! You have no idea how totally weird this is!" she cried.

"Like bizarro land, eh, Ave?" asked Tim.

"And I'm sure you've been a perfect angel, not getting into any trouble, right?" inquired Scott.

Avery swatted him. "Hey, I've been dealing with this solo. Alone. *Mano-a-mano.*"

"Sorry I missed your calls," Scott gave her another hug. "But we're here now, and you've got my undivided attention, Ave!"

Tim checked his watch. "But not for too long. Because we're supposed to be on the deck for the wedding ceremony in like, forty-five minutes."

"I can't believe your flight was delayed!" Avery groaned. "What if you'd missed it?"

"Dad would've pushed the wedding back if he had to." Scott grinned. "So, forty-five minutes. Plenty of time to talk!" Scott picked Avery up and carried her to a plain white bench on the front deck. "Oof, have you gained weight this week?"

Avery giggled. She'd missed her brothers! "Yep, wait till you taste the food on this ship!" She patted her tummy.

"Nice!" Tim slapped her a high-five. "So, little sis, you okay?"

Avery shrugged. "I've been better. Things are gonna be way different, huh?"

Scott shrugged. "Yeah, but we'll get through it together, 'k?"

"Okay." Avery perked up suddenly. "You guys haven't met Kazie yet, have you?"

"Nope, not yet." Tim shrugged. "Why?"

"Man, you guys are in for it! She's even crazier than *me!*"

"Is that even possible?" Scott joked.

Avery jumped up and crossed her arms. "Also, you know Andie is like the worst cook in the world, right?"

"I'd heard some stories from Dad . . . ," Tim said. "Something about a tuna casserole?" Avery nodded and fake-gagged.

"There has to be something good about Andie and Kazie, though, right, Ave?" Scott insisted, suddenly serious. "Like it or not, they're gonna be family now."

Avery sat down on the bench again. "Yeah . . . I guess."

"And most important of all," Scott continued, "Dad's been, like, super chill and happy since he and Andie started dating. It's weird they're getting married so quick, but I think it's cool."

"You do?" Avery asked.

Scott nodded. "He was getting lonely by himself all the time."

"Yeah, it's cool," Tim said as he fake-noogied Avery. "Especially since we get a surprise trip to Hawaii in the bargain!"

She hugged her brothers again. *I wonder if they have any idea how glad I am they're here!* she thought.

Officially Family

White streamers wound around the railings of the upper deck, which had been reserved for the wedding ceremony. Marisol, in her official staff uniform, was in charge of letting in the guests. Charlotte, Isabel and Mr. Ramsey were the first to arrive, followed by Maeve, Katani, and Kara-Lee.

"Everyone looks so pretty!" Marisol exclaimed.

"That's because we travel with our soon-to-be world famous stylist, Katani," Maeve replied, twirling around in her pale pink skirt and silvery top.

"Are Avery and Kazie here yet?" Katani asked. She wore a red dress with orange fabric Hawaiian flowers pinned artfully at her shoulders and waist.

Marisol glanced at Mr. Madden, who looked nervous as he fidgeted with the cuffs of his dark blue suit. "Kazie's helping her mom get ready. And it looks like Avery's right behind you guys."

Avery bounded in with Scott and Tim, who had changed into matching dark blue suits with Hawaiian print ties. "I'm here and I brought back-up." She introduced Scott and Tim to Marisol and Kara-Lee. "So what now?"

Tim laughed. "We watch Dad get married! Scott and I hafta stand up there . . . we're the best men."

"You mean the best bozos!" Avery gave Tim a shove.

Andie had asked Avery if she wanted to be a bridesmaid, but she said she'd rather just watch. Kazie was going to be the maid of honor, though.

"I helped Kazie pick out a dress at that Bananas boutique!" Katani whispered as the BSG all sat down together with Mr. Ramsey on the groom's side. "She looks *sooo* gorgeous in it!"

Captain Bob, wearing his white captain's uniform, took his place at the bow of the ship next to Avery's father. A steward dressed in a ship's uniform entered, carrying a violin. He tucked it under his chin and began to play.

Captain Bob cleared his throat. "Will everyone please rise?"

Avery stood up, but her legs felt like jelly. She turned to see Kazie walking down the aisle ahead of her mom. Kazie wore a yellow mini dress and had matching ribbons laced in her hair. The beaming bride looked stunning in a simple white sundress with silver sandals. She carried a bouquet of tropical flowers, and a single hibiscus was tucked behind her ear.

Avery had never seen Andie smile like that, like she couldn't stop smiling even if she wanted to. When she turned back to her dad, she realized he was smiling the exact same way. He couldn't take his eyes off Andie. It was like there was a magnet pulling them together!

Kazie stepped off to the side, across from Scott and Tim. Just as the violinist ended his song on a long, high note, Andie took her place next to Mr. Madden, and Avery realized her dad had never looked happier. Not ever. Not even after executing a perfect 360 surfing, or tearing up a black diamond on the slopes of Colorado.

Avery felt someone tug at her sleeve.

It was Charlotte. "You can sit now," she whispered.

Avery slid down into her seat. She had seen plenty of weddings, at least on TV, thanks to Maeve and those romantic comedies she forced everyone to watch at sleepovers, but Avery had never been to an actual ceremony. She wondered for a moment what her parents' wedding had been like. She pictured her mom smiling like Andie, and for some reason it made her feel better. *I'm going to go up to Andie after and tell her how pretty she looks,* Avery promised herself.

"Do you, Jake Madden, take Andie Walker to be your lawfully wedded wife?"

Mr. Madden smiled even wider. He nodded. "You bet I do."

Maeve dabbed at her tear-filled eyes with a hanky. *One day*—she sighed—*someone will look at me that way!*

Captain Bob turned to Andie. "And do you, Andie Walker, take Jake Madden to be your lawfully wedded husband."

Tears spilled down her cheeks. "I do . . . I really do."

What would it be like if Dad got married again? Charlotte wondered. She snuck a peek at him from the corner of her eye to discover he was looking right back her! Was he wondering the same thing? *Whoa!* Charlotte wasn't quite ready to think about that. One wedding at a time!

"Then by the power vested in me, I now pronounce you, husband and wife!"

And stepsisters, thought Avery, glancing up at Kazie, who looked to be in shock. *Sort of like me*, Avery thought.

"You may kiss the bride!" Captain Bob exclaimed.

Mr. Madden took Andie in his arms and dipped her for a kiss. The guests broke out in applause.

"I present to you, Mr. and Mrs. Madden-Walker!" cried Captain Bob.

Everyone rushed around the couple. Scott and Tim high-fived their dad and Mr. Madden twirled Avery around. Charlotte snapped pictures of the chaos. These were going on the last page of her travel journal! The rest of it was completely full.

Just then, Avery noticed Kazie sitting off by herself on the bride's side of the deck next to Kara-Lee's empty seat.

She turned to Katani. "I think you should go hang with Kazie."

"Are you sure?" Katani asked, shocked.

"Yeah," Avery decided, "I'm sure. Grab Kara-Lee too. It can be the Kgirls' last party."

Katani excused herself and Avery watched Kazie's face light up when Katani and Kara-Lee sat down next to her.

After a staff photographer had taken at least a hundred photos of the happy couple, Andie motioned for all of the girls to gather around. "Since you were all a part of this day, I wanted you to have something to remember it by." She took apart her wedding bouquet and gave a flower to each of the girls. She saved the biggest and brightest hibiscus for Kazie. Her daughter's cheeks looked a little shiny, but she was smiling.

Maeve clutched her flower to her chest and sighed.

"I don't think any of us could ever forget it." Katani tucked her orange flower in her hair. It matched her dress perfectly!

Isabel and Charlotte nodded, but they noticed that when Andie turned back to Mr. Madden, she left her flowers on her chair.

Scott picked one up and waved it under Avery's nose. "Aren't you supposed to, I don't know, dry this and hang it on your mirror or something?"

Avery shook her head back and forth. "Do I really look like that sort of girl?"

"I'm going to dry mine, and then hang it above my mirror!" Maeve exclaimed.

"Me too!" replied Kara-Lee as she took a sniff of her pink orchid.

Scott laughed and looked over at his sister, who definitely wasn't laughing. He guided her to a quieter part of the deck. "What's up?"

"What's up?" Avery couldn't believe he was taking this so well. "Um, Dad just got married, Scott."

Scott shrugged. "To an über-cool lady who's a ski bum and free spirit just like him. We just talked about this a little while ago, right?"

"Yeah, but I can't stop thinking about it. Now he's got this new family. Now when we visit, it's not going to be just us and Dad," Avery protested.

"You're totally right," said Scott. "But now when we leave, we're not leaving Dad alone."

Avery paused. "I never thought of it that way. But, Kazie—"

"Is like you, Ave," he insisted.

"She is not!" Avery retorted.

Scott shook his head and laughed. "You have tons in common, but stubborn is at the top of the list." He put his arm around her shoulder. "But Ave, there's only one you. Kazie's not going to replace you, just like Andie's not going to replace Mom. They're just making our family bigger. And more fun."

"That's what Mom said," Avery admitted.

"Are things gonna change? Well, yeah. They are. But it's going to change for the better, Ave. Trust me."

"For the better?" Avery wanted to know.

"Yeah. I won't have you tagging after me when I go 'boarding. I can pawn you off on Kazie now," he replied.

Avery elbowed him. "If we were in Telluride, that would have bought you a fistful of snow down your coat."

"Then you can owe me one. C'mon, we're missing out on all the action."

Everyone gathered around the newlyweds at the railing of the deck to watch the sun as it made its descent down the horizon. The sky burned from orange to red.

Maeve cleared her throat. "I think we need to thank Mr. Ramsey for a trip that we're never going to forget in our entire lifetimes!"

"Even if we wanted to," Avery joked. She made her way over to where Katani stood with Kara-Lee and Kazie.

"I haven't had a chance to congratulate you," said Avery.

"For what?" asked Kazie.

"For getting me as your sister," Avery replied.

Kazie snorted. "Good one. Shake."

Kazie held her hand out for the secret handshake that Kazie and her friends used back in Telluride, but then pulled back her hand.

Typical Kazie, Avery thought. *I tried, but—*

"Y'know what?" Kazie said, interrupting Avery's thoughts. "We should come up with our own handshake. A stepsister thing. What do you think?"

Avery was stunned. *Does Kazie actually want to be my friend?*

"Earth to Short Sta—I mean, Aloha Jedi! Are you there?" Kazie said, waving her hands in front of Avery's face.

"A sister handshake is an awesome idea," Avery exclaimed.

"Everyone, if I could have your attention!" Captain Bob bellowed from the railing.

"I hope everything's okay?" Isabel murmured to no one in particular, worried that maybe Franco wouldn't be able to come home with her after all!

Captain Bob peered through a set of binoculars. "Everything's just great. Look to eleven o'clock, about two hundred yards out, and it'll get even better."

A pod of humpback whales sailed through the water, cascading through the waves. Isabel burst with joyous laughter. "Whales!" she shouted.

"Humpback whales," Captain Bob said. "Amazing creatures. Never forget where they come from, never forget where they've been. The bonds of friendship and loyalty run strong through their pod."

The Beacon Street Girls crowded around the railing to watch the gentle giants glide through the water.

They knew exactly what it felt like to know your friends and family would always be there, through thick and thin, sickness and health, everyday life and life-changing adventure.

Epilogue
Two Weeks Later . . .

Is that the doorbell?" Isabel asked, wringing her hands.
"It was just a car horn, *mi hija*," her mom said sooth-
ingly.

"Relax, Isabel! You're beginning to make me nervous,"
her aunt warned.

Isabel stopped pacing, but she couldn't relax! She
hadn't been able to sleep a wink last night!

Ding-dong! Isabel jumped and almost fell over the
couch.

"Now that's the doorbell," her aunt said. "You two sit,
I'll get it." Aunt Lourdes got up and strode purposefully
to the door.

Isabel could hear her aunt greeting Captain Bob in
the hallway. Seconds later, he appeared in the living room
with Franco's cage, which was covered by a tarp.

"I wanted it to be a surprise!" Captain Bob whispered. He waved Isabel over. "You should do the honors."

Isabel nodded excitedly. She couldn't believe Captain Bob was in her house. With Franco! She looked at her mom, who nodded. Her Aunt Lourdes, however, didn't look entirely convinced.

Isabel crept over to the cage and quietly lifted off the cover. Franco stretched out his wings and cocked his head to one side. Isabel slid open the latch on his cage. Franco stepped onto her outstretched arm.

"Kiss Franco!" the bird demanded as he rubbed his beak against Izzy's chin.

Franco was home!

Ready! Set! Hawaii!

BOOK EXTRAS

 Endangered!

 Trivialicious Trivia

 Word Nerd

 Surf Lingo

 Book Club Buzz

Endangered!

Hi! Avery here. Did you know that Hawaii has more endangered species per square mile than anywhere else on earth? Totally crazy! If you're as concerned as me, read on to learn more about a few of these disappearing critters and plants.

Hawaiian Goose (nene)—*Branta sandvicensis*

We got lucky and saw one of these black and white striped geese on Kaua'i! Aside from the honor of being Hawaii's state bird, the nene is super cool because it had to adapt to life on lava flows, so it developed claws on its webbed feet! There are about eight hundred wild nenes and counting . . . the Hawaiian goose is making a comeback.

Kauai Cave Wolf Spider (*Pe'e Pe'e Maka 'Ole*)—*Adelocosa anops*

This creepy crawly isn't your ordinary spider. Rather than spinning a web, it hunts by chasing down prey and attacking! Even weirder, it doesn't have any eyes, and gets around by sensing chemicals on the ground. There are only three known caves on Kauai where these spiders still live.

Hawaiian Monk Seal (*'Ilio-holo-i-ka-uaua*)—*Monachus schauinslandi*

That long Hawaiian name means "dog that runs in rough waters." Adults can grow up to seven feet long and weigh as much as six hundred pounds! They love to eat crustaceans, fish, lobsters, octopuses, and eels (ewww!). Only about one thousand of these seals are left in the wild. Too bad the BSG didn't get to see any on our trip!

Oahu Tree Snails—*Achatinella*

Once upon a time, there were more than forty different kinds of these tiny snails. Now, there are only seven or eight species left, and some exist only in captivity! These inch-long critters spend their entire lives crawling around on the leaves of native Oahu trees and shrubs, chowing down on fungus.

Hawaiian Stilt (*Ae'o*)—*Himantopus mexicanus knudseni*

This black and white shore bird plays a cool trick: It will pretend to have a broken wing to lure attackers away from its nest! Stilts live on most of the Hawaiian islands in marshy areas. They're in trouble because people like to drain wetlands to build houses or shopping malls.

Silversword (*Ahinahina*)—*Argyroxiphium sandwicense*

Isn't silversword the coolest name ever? This plant is basically a ball of spiky, silver leaves that grows on the slopes of the Haleakala and Mauna Kea volcanoes. When it blooms, a head of maroon flowers sticks out like a thumbs-up. Don't walk too close or you'll crush its roots!

Save Endangered Species!

To find out more, visit www.EarthsEndangered.com. And if you want to get even more involved, talk to your teachers about starting an endangered species club at your school!

Ready! Set! Hawaii! trivialicious trivia

1. What is so cool about the ship's pool?
   A. It has three waterslides.
   B. The swim-up juice bar
   C. You can see the ocean from the pool.
   D. All of the above

2. What's wrong with Mr. Ramsey for most of the cruise?
   A. He has the flu.
   B. He's seasick.
   C. He's allergic to parrots.
   D. He has an unknown disease.

3. Where do Isabel and Charlotte first find Franco?
   A. On the top deck
   B. In the Atrium
   C. In Marisol's cabin
   D. In the jungle

4. What is Hawaii's state flower?
   A. Yellow hibiscus
   B. Royal poinciana
   C. Bird of paradise
   D. Orchid

5. Which Hawaiian island do the BSG go biking on?
   A. Kauai
   B. Lahaina
   C. Maui
   D. Hilo

6. How do you say "beginner" in surf lingo?
   A. Landshark
   B. Surf Betty
   C. Gidget
   D. Snurfette

7. What is the name of the onboard shopping boutique Katani loves?
   A. Gifts of the Isles
   B. Bananas
   C. Tropical Treasures
   D. Hula Hoops

8. What song wins the Karaoke contest?
   A. "All My Love" by the Royal Brothers
   B. "Three Hours Till You" by Nik and Sam
   C. "BFFs" by Janey G
   D. "The Pirate Song" (traditional sea shanty)

9. What kind of bird is Franco?
   A. Cockatoo
   B. Parakeet
   C. African Grey
   D. Scarlet macaw

10. What amazing sight do all the wedding guests admire after the ceremony?
   A. A pod of Humpback whales
   B. Fireworks off the bow of the ship
   C. Jumping dolphins
   D. A flock of doves taking flight

ANSWERS: 1. D. All of the above 2. A. He has the flu 3. C. In Marisol's cabin 4. A. Yellow hibiscus 5. D. Hilo 6. A. Landshark 7. B. Bananas 8. C. "BFFs" by Janey G 9. C. African Grey 10. A. A pod of Humpback whales

Book Club Buzz

10 QUESTIONS FOR YOU AND YOUR FRIENDS TO CHAT ABOUT

1. What is the coolest place you've ever gone on vacation? What would you pack for a tropical fantasy cruise? List the top-ten things you'd love to do on a trip to Hawaii!

2. Avery is blown away when her dad shows up on the cruise! What do you think made this surprise totally coolio, and what made it more of an uncomfortable shock? Do you think her dad should have told her about his plan?

3. Katani tries to follow the saying "make new friends, but keep the old," but sometimes that isn't easy to do! How can Katani be a Kgirl and BSG at the same time? Think

about a time you felt like you had to choose between two groups of friends. How did it make you feel?

4. Why did Marisol bring Franco on the cruise? Do you think it was a good idea, even though she could lose her job? When is it okay to break the rules?

5. Maeve tells Avery, "The only person who can ruin a beautiful day for you is your-self." What do you think of this quote? What could Avery have done differently to have more fun on the cruise? Why do you think she is so upset with Katani, Kazie, and her dad?

6. Mr. Ramsey is delighted that Charlotte and Isabel take over working on his article when he gets sick. How do you help your parents? Think of some things you could do this week without being asked that would make your parents really proud of you.

7. Animals are not always easy to take care of! Think of three problems Franco causes in this book. If you have a pet, how do you help take care of him or her? What's the smartest or silliest thing your pet can do?

8. Why doesn't Katani tell the Kgirls she can't sing? Have you ever been afraid to admit you didn't know how to do something? Katani talks to both Andie and the BSG about her problem. What advice do they give her?

9. Andie and Kazie both have to be rescued while surfing. Have you ever had an accident that really scared you or your family? Do you know what to do if an accident happens?

10. Avery and Kazie can't stand each other at the beginning of the cruise. What do you think they are really competing for? Do you think they would get along better if their parents weren't dating? What changes about Avery and Kazie's relationship when their parents decide to get married?

Word Nerd

BSG Words

fantabulous (p. 9) adjective—*fantastic and fabulous combined!*

coolio (p. 29) adjective—*cool*

snurfette (p. 29) noun—*Mr. Madden's nickname for Avery; an awesome girl boarder*

wicked (p. 31) adjective—*awesome; really cool*

mega-awesome (p. 40) adjective—*very awesome*

obv (p. 66) adverb—*obviously*

surftastic (p. 177) adjective—*a fantastic surfing move*

chillax (p. 179) verb—*chill and relax combined*

pink-tabulous (p. 193) adjective—*pink and fabulous*

squawkboxes (p. 258) noun—*parrots*

bizarro land (p. 260) noun—*weird situation*

über-cool (p. 266) adjective—*very cool*

Other Cool Words

dejectedly (p. 4) adverb—*sadly; without hope*

discerning (p. 18) adjective—*showing insight and understanding*

feral (p. 24) adjective—*wild; no longer tame*

parquet (p. 25) noun—*a section of floor*

scurvy (p. 55) noun—*a disease (once common to sailors) resulting from a lack of vitamin C*

simultaneously (p. 63) adverb—*at the same time*

placard (p. 63) noun—*a small sign*

itinerary (p. 79) noun—*schedule*

gait (p. 106) noun—*way of walking or moving*

competence (p. 117) noun—*one's level of ability to do something*

mesmerized (p. 117) verb—*fascinated*

haphazard (p. 120) adjective—*lacking order or plan*

surreptitiously (p. 129) adverb—*secretly*

dormant (p. 149) noun—*not active; sleeping*

monolithic (p. 149) adjective—*large; like a statue*

quandary (p. 164) noun—*a puzzling decision or situation*

embellished (p. 193) verb—*decorated; added to*

Spanish Words and Phrases

fabuloso (p. 1)—*fabulous*

qué terrible (p. 24)—*how terrible*

¿está usted de Mexico? (p. 54)—*Are you from Mexico?*

mi familia (p. 54)—*my family*

un papagayo (p. 69)—*a parrot*

hola (p. 81)—*hello*

bonito/a (p. 69)—*pretty*

¡oye! (p. 70)—*oh, no!*

lo siento (p. 70)—*I'm sorry*

ay, qué tonto (p. 70)—*oh, I'm a fool*

loco (p. 76)—*crazy*

escapista (p. 76)—*escape artist*

telenovelas (p. 124)—*soap operas*

muy furioso (p. 79)—*very furious*

¿qué piensas? (p. 80)—*What do you think?*

chaperón terrible (p. 81)—*terrible chaperone*

hasta (p. 81)—*good-bye*

numero uno (p. 87)—*number one*

¿qué paso? (p. 131)—*What happened?*

dame un beso (p. 283)—*give me a kiss*

maravilloso (p. 208)—*wonderful*

verdad (p. 240)—*true*

¿qué te parece? (p. 254)—*What do you think?*

dios mío (p. 256)—*my god!*

amorcita (p. 256)—*little love; darling*

mano-a-mano (p. 260)—*hand to hand*

mi hija (p. 270)—*my daughter*

French Words and Phrases

Bon voyage! (p. 7)—*Have a good trip!*

ma cherie (p. 57)—*my dear*
au revoir (p. 57)—*good-bye*
bonjour, mes amies (p. 194)—*hello, my friends*
poulet (p. 201)—*chicken*
merveilleux (p. 201)—*marvelous*

Surf Lingo

shreddy (p. 31) adjective—*surf or snowboard code for "ready"*
cowabunga! (p. 40) exclamation—*shout it out when you're really happy*
hang ten (p. 41) verb—*a move where you get all ten toes on the nose of your board*
sick (p. 45) adjective—*anything awesome in the surfing universe*
gnarly (p. 86) adjective—*a vintage word for "cool"*
carve up (p. 87) verb—*to surf with skill*
landshark (p. 170) noun—*someone who can't surf but pretends to know how*
rip up (p. 173) verb—*do some awesome surfing*
Surf Betty (p. 249) noun—*a good-looking, skilled female surfer*
Beach Bunny (p. 284) noun—*a girl who goes to the beach to watch the surfers*
roundhouse (p. 284) noun—*a turn executed while surfing*
360 (p. 177) noun—*a spinning move on the face of a wave where you swing around in a full circle*
random stander (p. 178)—*inexperienced or uncommited surfer*
righteous (p. 179) adjective—*totally cool*
big kahuna (p. 178) noun—*the best surfer on the beach*
truckin' (p. 178) verb—*moving quickly*

gidget (p. 179) noun—*a young or small girl who's really an awesome surfer*

banzai (p. 180) exclamation—*shout this as you execute a rippin' move*

Share the Next

BEACON STREET GIRLS

Adventure

Sweet Thirteen

Ooh la la! When Sophie comes to visit from Paris, French-mania sweeps through AAJH. Is Charlotte's fashionable friend too cool for her? Meanwhile, there's serious trouble with Maeve's thirteenth birthday bash—can the BSG and Sophie save the day?

Check out the Beacon Street Girls at
BeaconStreetGirls.com
Aladdin M!X

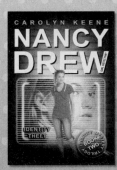
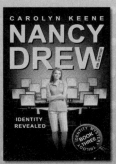
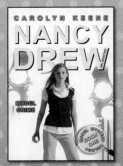
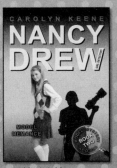
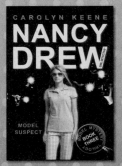

Real life. Real you.

Don't miss any of these terrific Aladdin Mix books.

The Secret Identity of
Devon Delaney

Devon Delaney Should
Totally Know Better

Trading Faces

Portia's Exclusive and
Confidential Rules
on True Friendship

City Secrets

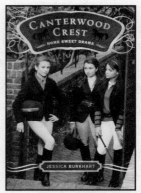

Home Sweet Drama

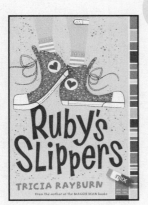

Ruby's Slippers

Nice and Mean

Things Are Gonna Get Ugly

Front Page Face-Off

Do you love the color pink?
All things sparkly? Mani/pedis?

These books are for you!

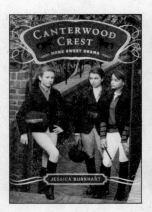

From Aladdin
Published by Simon & Schuster